LITTLE BLACK LIES

GILLIAN JACKSON

BLOODHOUND
BOOKS

www.bloodhoundbooks.com

Print ISBN: 978-1-917449-9-77

PROLOGUE

1998

The delivery room was suffocating as the walls seemed to close in on the girl, a girl who was too young to be giving birth, let alone to twins. 'I can't! Leave me alone, go away,' she cried out.

Karen, the firm but compassionate midwife gently wiped the girl's brow with a cool cloth, offering reassurance. 'These babies will be born whether you're ready or not. You can do this, sweetheart. Come on, at the next contraction, push as hard as you can.' Moving to the business end, the midwife continued her support. 'I can see the head. One big push and you'll have your baby.'

'I don't want a baby!' the girl exclaimed.

'Push!' Karen silently reserved judgment and encouraged the young mother. This wasn't the first time she had attended an unwanted delivery, and sadly, it happened all too often. Nevertheless, she preferred not to judge, knowing that each person's circumstances were complex and unique. 'Good girl, come on, push,' she urged.

As the baby's head was delivered, a smile spread across

Karen's face. Even though this mother did not want her babies, Karen knew there were many childless couples eagerly waiting for a new baby to love and cherish. The miracle of birth never failed to astound her, and she hoped these babies would find a loving home.

'It's a boy!' Karen announced as the baby slipped into her waiting hands. She passed the crying child to her colleague to clean and check while she attended to the mother. 'Do you want to see him?' She smiled at the sullen girl.

'No. I've told you. I don't want to see them, ever!'

Karen glanced at the beautiful baby boy, a picture of health, and nodded to her colleague, who would take the baby to the nursery after the usual checks had been made.

Ten minutes later Karen announced the second baby was also a boy. Her voice cracked as she asked her colleague to fetch the paediatrician – the baby was tiny, and his colour wasn't good. He was slight, a fragile bundle swaddled in hospital blankets, his breaths shallow and erratic. The girl in the bed showed no concern for her second child, who was swiftly removed from the delivery room and into an incubator.

The paediatrician was examining the newborn within ten minutes of his birth. The two-pound baby lay in the incubator, struggling to breathe. The midwife stood close, ready to help in any way she could. 'He's the second of twins,' Karen informed the doctor.

The paediatrician nodded, 'Ah, selective foetal growth restriction. He needs oxygen – a nasal CPAP, please, nurse.'

Within minutes, two tiny prongs were placed in the baby's nostrils, which started gently pushing oxygen into his lungs. Karen felt relief as the doctor smiled. 'He'll live although he has an abnormal heart rhythm as well as breathing difficulties. I think this little chap will be in ICU for several weeks. We'll test for jaundice, too, but judging from his colour, it seems likely. How's the mother taking it?'

'She doesn't want to see the babies. They're both going for adoption.'

'I see. Well, it may be some time before baby number two will be ready to go into foster care and on to adoption, but I suppose social services will be made aware of the situation.'

'Yes, doctor, the first twin is due to be collected by foster carers tomorrow. The mother's determined to have no involvement with them.'

The next day, the healthy six-pound baby boy was given the go-ahead to leave the hospital with experienced foster carers, while his brother was transferred to a specialised children's hospital sixty miles away.

Jane, a new social worker, accompanied the foster parents to the hospital to collect the healthy twin. Although aware her charge had a sibling, in her eagerness to showcase her new skills and competence, Jane forgot to inform her colleagues that the baby was a twin and failed to include this important detail in the paperwork.

When she eventually realised her omission, four weeks later, the baby was already settling with his new parents. Jane decided not to admit to her error – saving face was more important to her, and she convinced herself that no one would be any the wiser. After all, the second twin was the responsibility of another local authority now and may not even live. And so, the twins were separated just days after entering the world. The healthy baby boy began his life with a new family, loved and cherished. The second twin, hooked to machines that beeped and whirred, fought for each breath in the sterile silence of the specialist hospital sixty miles away.

After two months of excellent care, the second boy gained

weight, his lung function improved, and his abnormal heart rhythm resolved. He was soon adopted and started life several miles away from his brother, each unaware of the existence of the other.

ONE

The sudden chime of the doorbell jolted Samantha Freeman from sleep. She lay on the sofa, her broken leg elevated on a mound of pillows, her body cocooned in a cosy duvet. From the kitchen, her mother called out that she would answer the door – as if Sam could do so herself. She just longed to sink back into the comforting embrace of sleep to temporarily escape the throbbing pain in her leg.

Yet it wasn't only the pain of her injuries which troubled her but the constant and very tangible agony of grief since the death of her fiancé, Ravi, only a week previously. It was an all-consuming pain, solid and heavy, which threatened to suffocate Samantha with every breath she took. Would it ever ease? Sleep was the only respite, yet from the sound of voices in the hall, this was no longer an option.

Brenda Freeman poked her head around the door of the lounge, peering at her daughter with a concerned expression. 'Are you up to receiving visitors? It's Ravi's parents.'

Sam pulled herself up to sit and ran her fingers through her unwashed hair. Her appearance had been the last thing on her mind since returning home from the hospital, but she didn't want her visitors to see her in such a state.

'Yes, of course.' Sam cleared her throat, trying to compose herself.

As ever, Divya, Ravi's mother was dressed immaculately. Her dark hair, with perhaps a touch of grey starting to show, was smoothed into a sleek knot, but her perfect makeup couldn't conceal the sadness in her features. Arjun, her husband, followed her into the room, appearing stooped and so much older than when Sam and Ravi had seen him on that last fateful day. Was it only a week ago? None of them could have predicted that their joyful goodbyes would be permanent, at least as far as Ravi was concerned.

How cruel life could be to bring such joy and delight into her life only to snatch it away before there was time to truly appreciate it.

'Samantha!' Divya gushed, kneeling beside her and enfolding her into a warm embrace, prompting tears from both women. Pulling away moments later, Ravi's mother looked into Sam's eyes, eyes which reflected her own sorrow. 'I'm so sorry we haven't been before... we should have come to the hospital...'

'No, please don't apologise. I didn't expect you... you wouldn't be up to visiting.' The women were suddenly lost for words.

'How are you, Sam?' Arjun stepped forward and, taking her hand, squeezed it gently.

'I'll heal, thank you.' She sniffed back more tears. It was hardly appropriate to share her true feelings and rail at the unfairness of life. Ravi's parents were suffering, too.

'Tea, anyone?' Brenda disappeared into the kitchen without waiting for an answer while Divya and Arjun sat down.

'When did you come home?' Divya asked.

Samantha groaned inwardly. Was the visit going to consist

of awkward small talk? As she answered, Sam was aware of the clock ticking rhythmically on the mantle. Was it usually so loud? Brenda reappeared with a tray of tea and biscuits and fussed over serving their visitors, who accepted the tea gratefully and declined the biscuits. Sam sipped her tea and tried to think of something to say.

'Divya, we have to tell her,' Arjun said, breaking the silence and gently touching his wife's arm. Sam couldn't interpret the sadness in the look they exchanged.

'Tell me what?' Nothing could be as bad as losing Ravi. Why do they look so nervous?

'You tell her, Arjun.' Divya dabbed at her eyes with a cotton handkerchief.

'Samantha, after the accident, decisions needed to be made, which the doctors asked us to consider. If you'd been conscious, we'd have consulted you...' Arjun shuffled uncomfortably on the chair and swallowed hard. He ran his finger around the inside of his collar before continuing. 'They asked about organ donation. Ravi was still alive when he arrived at the hospital, and as he died there, there was a chance his organs could be harvested, but they needed an immediate decision.'

Sam groaned. This was totally unexpected; it was not something she and Ravi had ever discussed, but the thought of his body being carved up sickened her. Her face betrayed her shock and unable to speak she shook her head.

'I'm sorry, Sam, we had to act quickly to make a decision before it was too late.' Arjun's brow creased.

'No, no... I understand. It's just... I didn't even know if Hinduism allowed organ donations...'

'Oh yes, Vedas, our Hindu scriptures, teach that whatever sustains life is acceptable as Dharma – that is, righteous living. The doctors were able to use Ravi's heart to give someone else a chance of life.'

The words hit Sam hard, and she could only nod while trying to push the disturbing images from her mind. *They had taken out Ravi's heart, and it was still beating in someone else's chest!* Processing this shocking information and accepting the harsh reality would take time.

'I'm sure you made the right decision, and I'm sorry I couldn't help.'

During the week following the accident which took Ravi from her, Sam had been too consumed by grief to consider practical matters. However, Arjun and Divya had lost their son and were grieving as well. As next of kin, the burden of bureaucracy associated with death fell upon them. Allowing Ravi's heart to be harvested for transplant must have been a difficult decision.

'We understand and would have consulted you if possible. It looks as if... Ravi's body will be released after the inquest on Friday. Then there'll be the funeral to consider...' Tears pricked Divya's eyes. Arjun took over the conversation.

'We've started the arrangements, but if you wish to be involved, we're happy to work with you.'

'That's so kind, but whatever you feel is appropriate will be okay with me.'

'Thank you, Sam. There'll be other things to sort out in time.' Arjun leaned forward in his chair. 'Before you visited us at Christmas, Ravi drew up a will which he signed and lodged with our family solicitor. I know you probably don't want to hear this now, but Ravi was keen to ensure you'd be taken care of if anything happened to him. The solicitor is also the executor of the will, and he'll look into all the formalities, probate, and such, so I can't tell you any details yet. It could take several weeks, but we'll keep you informed.'

Sam could no longer hold her tears and covered her face with her hands. The thought of Ravi thinking of her and ensuring she would be looked after was almost more than she could bear. Her Ravi – such a sensitive man, full of life and fun – was her rock. How could such a vital, strong man be dead?

Brenda moved to comfort her daughter as Arjun and Divya stood to go. 'We'll go and maybe ring you tomorrow when you've had time to think if you'd like to include anything in the funeral.' Divya squeezed Sam's shoulder as the couple quietly let themselves out.

'It's so like Ravi to think of you in his will...' Brenda spoke almost to herself.

'I don't care about the will, Mum! They took his heart; they took Ravi's heart!' The room blurred as Sam sobbed bitterly on her mother's shoulder.

TWO

Samantha's leg remained in a cast for six weeks, itchy, hot and uncomfortable. Her boss, DCI Aiden Kent, made it clear that she was not to return to work until the cast was removed, an order Sam came to appreciate. Yet the physical healing wasn't the problem – the pain of losing Ravi was still raw and cut far deeper.

During her recovery, Sam was obliged to use a wheelchair when leaving the house, although such occasions were few as her preference was to remain at home, locked away from the world with its ugly realities, the world which had robbed her of Ravi. Her attendance, however, was required at the inquest, an emotional experience endured with the support of her parents and Jenny Newcombe, her friend and colleague.

On the morning of the inquest, the weather was dark and damp, perfectly matching Samantha's gloomy mood. She chose a black jersey dress, pulled it over her slim figure, and brushed her short, dark hair into place. Although she rarely wore make-up, she applied a little foundation to give her pale elfin features some colour.

Jenny picked her up in her car, easily lifting Sam's petite

frame to transfer her from the wheelchair to the passenger seat, which was pushed as far back as it would go. They travelled the short journey to the coroner's court, parking as close as possible. Then Jenny pushed Sam to where her parents waited outside and greeted their daughter solemnly.

Sam and Jenny had attended the coroner's court many times before in the course of their work, but this time, it was personal. Sam knew that after the day's experience, she would have greater empathy for the grieving relatives with whom they regularly came into contact.

The proceedings were remarkably and thankfully quick, with the expected verdict of accidental death recorded. Arjun and Divya sat gravely upright, Divya dabbing at her eyes and leaning heavily on her husband. Afterwards, Ravi's parents waited in the foyer to speak with Sam. Divya's eyes were red, and the couple appeared to have aged considerably, the cruel effects of grief. Divya hugged Samantha; the women had always liked each other, but the loss of Ravi created a genuine bond of affection between them.

'How are you doing?' Sam was the first to speak.

'Coping. And you?'

'The same.' Sam smiled sadly.

'Did you get the copy of the funeral arrangements we posted and the order of service?' Arjun asked. 'If you wish to change anything, there's still time.'

'Yes, thank you. It all looks good. I'm sorry for not being much help...'

'You don't have to apologise. If you think of anything you'd like to add or alter, just ring.' An embarrassing silence was broken as Ravi's brother appeared behind his parents. Sam gasped, struck again at how much like Ravi he was – an older, shorter version. Her heart ached at the sight of him, and tears stung her eyes as they said their goodbyes. The next time they would meet would be at Ravi's funeral.

Sam, her parents and Jenny returned to the house she had shared with Ravi. Entering the front door was a bittersweet experience. Perhaps this was why she was reluctant to go out other than when necessary – coming home was painful. Her parents entered the kitchen, leaving Sam and Jenny alone to talk.

'How are things at work?' It was the first time Sam had shown an interest in work, and Jenny's smile confirmed her opinion that it was a good sign.

'Remarkably quiet, actually. We keep busy with the odd burglary, the usual druggies and the local yobs. Why? Are you missing us?'

'I can't honestly answer that one, Jen. I think I'll be glad to get back if only to give me something to do, you know, to take my mind off Ravi, but at the moment, I haven't the energy.'

'There's another three or four weeks until the cast comes off, right? You might feel differently by then – and the office isn't the same without you. Oh, Paul's got a date for his sergeant's exam. It's next week, Friday, I think.'

'Tell him to revise. He's a lazy sod but quite capable if he puts his mind to it.'

'Yes, Layla's working out a revision programme. She'll keep his nose to the grindstone.'

Samantha smiled. It would be good to get back – after Ravi, work was her second love and immersing herself in her role as detective inspector would offer a degree of respite from her grief – but not yet – there was a funeral to endure first.

By mutual agreement, Samantha planned to join the funeral party when they arrived at the crematorium. Ravi would begin his final journey at his parent's home, where close friends and family would view the open casket. Hindu funeral chants and prayers would be performed, and 'pinda' (rice balls) would be placed close to his body. Arjun and Divya made it clear that Samantha would be welcome, an offer she appreciated, but with no desire to participate in their rituals, she decided to meet them at the crematorium to say her goodbyes there.

It was as bad as expected. Another dark morning with rain lashing Sam's bedroom window, waking her far too early. Wishing it was possible to stay cocooned in her warm bed, she gave way to the ever-present tears leaking from her tightly closed eyes. But hiding from the world wasn't an option, so pulling herself together, Sam forced herself out of bed to face the day. Her parents would arrive soon to help her get ready and accompany her to the crematorium. Sam hated relying on others for help, but that morning, she needed their support, physically and emotionally.

By the time they left, the rain had ceased, but the sky remained dark and heavy, with a bitter wind gusting the clouds across the sky. The recently built crematorium was packed, and the glass-walled ante-room was crammed with more mourners, standing where they couldn't find seats. Sam wasn't surprised. Ravi had worked as a DI at Aykley Heads in Durham and was a popular figure among his colleagues.

Many of her colleagues from New Middridge station and numerous friends and relatives were there. For once, she was glad of her wheelchair; had she been standing, she'd surely have ended up in a crumpled heap on the floor.

Sam's father pushed her chair beside Divya, who reached out for her hand, gripping it tightly. Ravi's family wept openly, and Sam could hardly lift her eyes to look at them as she struggled to maintain her composure. The celebrant spoke of Ravi's life, words which passed over her head, white noise on the periphery of her jumbled thoughts.

When the curtain finally closed on the casket, Sam

experienced a hollow sensation, a deep ache which she knew would remain with her always. The heavy curtain was a symbol of a permanent divide between them. To never see Ravi again, never feel his comforting arms around her, his gentle kiss on her lips – could she bear it?

When she stepped outside, the cold January air helped to revive her. Sam went through the motions of accepting condolences and talking to her and Ravi's friends and colleagues. They didn't need to tell her what a great man he had been or how much he'd be missed, but she listened and nodded appropriately until she could finally escape. As the cold air chilled her to the bone, Sam yearned for the impossible – to feel Ravi's presence beside her. Or better still, to find him waiting at home, reassuring her that the last few weeks had all been a terrifying nightmare. But Sam was deluding herself – Ravi was gone. The love of her life was dead.

The following four weeks dragged. There were appointments to attend, letters to write and a brave face to practise for the world to see. Finally, the plaster cast was removed, and Sam had one more weekend until her return to work. Religiously, she performed the exercises the physio had given her, determined to regain her previous good shape so that 'light duties' wouldn't be suggested.

Eventually, on a Monday morning in late February, DI Samantha Freeman stood outside New Middridge Police Station and inhaled several deep breaths of cold air to calm the pounding sensation in her chest.

THREE

Valerie Turner relished having a day to herself. It was Saturday and the weather was typically damp and gloomy so she was happy to mooch around the house. Her husband, Geoff, was playing golf with his mates while their daughters, Anna and Lizzie, were shopping together.

It was unusual for the girls to spend time together; they generally spent Saturdays with their respective best friends. Val hoped this was a sign of them growing up at last. Anna was sixteen, and Lizzie was fourteen. Was there a chance their constant bickering was finally coming to an end? Were they maturing enough to become friends? Hell, she hoped so; sometimes, their attitude drove her crazy.

Making a second mug of coffee from the shiny new machine Geoff had purchased for her Christmas present, Val carried the latte into the lounge, tucked her legs beneath her on the sofa, and switched on daytime television. A feeling of decadence crept over her – she hadn't yet showered or dressed, and the beds were unmade, but Saturday was heavenly – her day without clamouring teenagers or a brooding husband under her feet. Wearing her favourite silk pyjamas and her comfy old dressing gown, Val decided the housework would keep; she was entitled to some 'me' time, and it was only 9.30am, early for a weekend.

Sipping the caramel latte, Val channel-hopped and then, finding nothing to capture her interest, turned the television off. The silence was soothing, a balm to her soul. Pulling a throw over her legs and snuggling further down on the sofa, she smiled at the thought of how good her life was – and the secret knowledge that it would soon become even better. Val was a woman with plans and much to look forward to in the very near future.

Yet her life hadn't always run smoothly: there'd been plenty of bumps along the way, although nothing Val hadn't been able to handle. Geoff was generally easy-going – okay, for *easy-going*, read *boring* – but as she was the main breadwinner, he toed the line even though he was not always happy about it. Valerie knew how to handle Geoff. But a smile crept over her face at the thought of not having to do so for much longer.

Val was proud of her achievements at work. For someone who'd started a career with very few qualifications, she succeeded in holding down a challenging and time-consuming job as an office manager in an expanding solicitor's practice. The work was demanding, and keeping the office running smoothly often felt like spinning plates. However, her drive and determination paid off, and she was rightfully proud of her success. It made days off like today feel more special and enjoyable.

Valerie's childhood was best forgotten, and she worked hard to block those days from her mind. Yes, there were regrets and mistakes that couldn't be undone, but didn't everyone have misgivings about events in their past?

Closing her eyes, the peace and warmth of the room made

her drowsy, and with no one else to consider today, she might allow herself the luxury of an extra hour or two's sleep.

An image of Ben appeared behind her eyelids – handsome, gregarious Ben whose sudden and unexpected entry into her life had come perilously close to wrecking the family unit. Yet, ultimately, Val won Geoff over. Her husband knew better than to cross her. Ben had been her secret, but not anymore.

Maybe another of my secrets is about to come knocking at my door. Val knew this was entirely possible, yet the idea left her untroubled.

With her eyes closed and a smile on her lips as she drifted off to sleep, the sound of the back door rattling startled Valerie. Lifting her head to listen, she shouted, 'Is that you, Geoff?' Her mood rapidly changed as she wondered which of her family had returned home unexpectedly. Had the girls fallen out again? *I knew that truce was too good to be true.* Or was Geoff's golf cancelled for some reason? *Whoever it is, they are not welcome.* Val cherished her 'me' time jealously.

'Geoff? She raised her voice, but the only reply was the sound of something breaking. Rising from the comfort of the sofa to investigate, Val's heart rate increased.

Pausing to listen for other noises, all remained silent, but Val was spooked. *Crazy woman,* she chided herself while looking around for her mobile phone, just in case. *Hell, it's upstairs by the bedside.*

Feeling somewhat pathetic, Val grabbed one of the silver candlesticks Geoff's parents had bought them for a wedding present. *This is stupid, melodramatic.* But her heart refused to stop racing as she took a few tentative steps towards the kitchen.

Valerie Turner wasn't to know she had just savoured the last caramel latte she would ever taste.

FOUR

I n the draughty corridors of New Middridge police station, nothing had changed, yet to Samantha, walking slowly to her office, everything had.

The lack of speed had nothing to do with her leg. It was more a reluctance to see her colleagues and feel their sympathetic eyes turn towards her, to listen to their condolences, which would need to be acknowledged with good grace; and she would have to find words of thanks when in her heart she felt anything but thankful.

'Hey, boss, good to see you!' Paul Roper was the first to notice her entrance. 'We've missed you.' Sam smiled her thanks, grateful his little speech stopped short of condolences – he and his girlfriend Layla had sent a card. It was sufficient.

As others turned to acknowledge her presence, she relaxed. Jenny was swiftly by her side, a smile barely concealing her concerned expression.

Sam raised a hand in the general direction of her team. 'Thank you all for your support and good wishes. I'm pleased to be back, and I'm here to work. So, Jen, what's happening?' Stepping into her designated corner cubicle of the office, followed by Jenny, Sam imagined a collective sigh of relief. Why were the bereaved always an embarrassment?

'Are you okay?' her DS asked.

'I will be if you treat me normally and not like a piece of porcelain! Sorry, Jen, it's good to be back; moping around at home doesn't suit me, and I know exactly what Ravi would have said about it. Don't worry. I'll tell you if things get a bit much – and thanks for everything you've done, you've been a brick.'

Jenny visibly relaxed. 'Okay, blow the dust off your computer and I'll get you up to speed, shall I?'

Sam spent the next hour being updated on what had occurred in her absence as Jenny talked her through each case, its progress or lack of progress.

'I thought you said our local criminals had been quiet while I was off. You didn't mention this one, did you?' Samantha stared at the file of an armed robbery in a local post office.

'Ah, well, DCI Kent took charge of this and gave strict instructions you weren't to be troubled, so I had no choice. There was nothing you could do and I think the DCI enjoyed coming down from his ivory tower. It gave him a chance to get to know the team on a more personal level, and it kept them on their toes. Your mum said she'd make sure you didn't see it in the papers or on the news.'

'Ah hah.' Sam's nose moved closer to the screen. She'd hardly possessed enough energy to watch television and didn't get a local paper so it had gone completely under her radar. 'Why am I not surprised that you and my mum have been colluding?' After skimming the details, she asked, 'How's the man who was injured?'

'It was just a flesh wound. He was kept in the hospital overnight and managed to give us a good description of the two suspects. We've also had a tip-off from an informant that they're from Leeds, and our colleagues there have assured us they're on their radar. Hopefully, an arrest is imminent.'

'Great, well done.'

'It's not cut and dried yet, but with assistance from Leeds, we should have them in custody this week.'

Samantha's first week back at work provided the much-needed distraction from thoughts of Ravi. Putting in longer hours than necessary became an avoidance tactic as going home to an empty house was anything but appealing. The extra hours ensured she was current on all cases, but Sam knew staying in the office forever wasn't an option. Life would go on whether she wanted it to or not.

Jenny did her best – suggesting getting a takeaway one evening and staying late at the office when her boss did – proving herself to be a true friend.

Sam volunteered to work overtime when the weekend arrived, but Aiden Kent wouldn't hear of it. He made a trip downstairs from his second-floor office to inquire how Sam was faring, wanting to ensure she was taking care of herself. 'You need to rest, Samantha. You're not 100 per cent yet, and I don't want you to burn out.'

Sam's protestations fell on deaf ears, so on Friday evening, she reluctantly went home to a house which evoked too many painful memories. Would those memories ever be welcomed as everyone said they would? Only time will tell.

Not for the first time, Samantha thought about Ravi's heart, wondering who the recipient could be and trying to come to terms with his parent's decision. It wasn't that she was opposed to the idea of transplanting organs; she'd heard so many stories of people who'd been given a second chance at life, and Sam had always intended to carry a donor card herself. But this was something she and Ravi hadn't discussed, and the thought of a part of him still being alive – his heart, of all things, beating in someone else's chest – was a difficult concept to process.

Knowing it was unwise, Sam googled information on transplant recipients, curious to know if donor organs could pass on the characteristics and experiences of their original owner. It was like picking at a scab – she wanted to know, yet was aware it wasn't a rational thing to dwell on. Discovering it was rare, it was scary to read that this was not an unheard-of phenomenon. Apparently, there's a process known as cellular memory, and some transplant recipients claim to experience altered personalities in keeping with the donor's characteristics. Sam disciplined herself to stop looking; it brought no comfort. But thoughts of Ravi's heart still beating disturbed her.

Three glasses of wine ensured Sam managed a few hours of sleep, shutting out all troubling thoughts and the very real dread of the long weekend stretching ahead without the distractions of work to maintain her equanimity.

———

Pulling back the curtains the following morning and rubbing the condensation from the window with her fist revealed a light covering of snow. An image of herself and Ravi laughing as they threw snowballs at each other last winter popped into her head, bringing back the familiar heaviness of grief pressing down upon her. Would she ever feel remotely happy again?

After a shower and forcing herself to eat a slice of toast, Sam stood in the kitchen and looked around, taking stock of her home and wondering how to fill the hours ahead. There was little cleaning to do. Her mother had left the house spotless before returning home, and the freezer was stocked with meals

GILLIAN JACKSON

and baking to last a month or more. Perhaps she'd visit her parents. They'd phoned every evening this week, checking up on her, their concern was evident and she loved them for their thoughtfulness.

Deciding to go after lunch, Sam settled in front of the fire with a book, reading although not absorbing the words. Poaching an egg for lunch, she ate it without enthusiasm, the single egg reminding her of her aloneness and making each mouthful hard to swallow. As she was about to call her mother, the phone rang, and Jenny's number appeared on the screen.

'We've got a suspicious death, boss. You don't need to come; we can handle it if you're not up to it?'

'Don't be ridiculous, I'm in on this one.' Sam simultaneously experienced excitement and shame. Excitement at the challenge of being involved in a potential murder case and shame that her first thoughts were not for the victim and their family but for herself and how much she wanted to be involved. 'Give me the address and I'll meet you there.'

FIVE

It felt good to be needed. Sam's team was capable, yet she was a vital part of it and they worked better as a whole. Wrapping up warmly and hurrying out to the car, Sam tapped the postcode Jenny had given her into the sat-nav. It was 1.45pm and her visit to her parents would have to wait for another day. The area she was heading to was in a pleasant part of the town, with neat semis and detached family homes in streets and cul-de-sacs with grass verges – a typical leafy suburb.

It wasn't so leafy on this damp February day, though, as Sam drove past bare gnarled branches to the address of the suspicious death. Grey skies hung heavily over number 22 Juniper Grove, and the almost freezing temperature was congruent with the scene she was about to encounter.

Three marked cars were parked in the street, two of them blocking the road, much to the disgust of some inconvenienced drivers. Sam manoeuvred her little Mini into a spot as near as possible, jumped out and headed towards the house. A few neighbours huddled in groups to watch what was going on, kept back by the inevitable crime scene tape. Sam shook her head and sighed. The door to the semi stood open, and an impossibly young uniformed officer lifted the tape to allow her to pass while his partner scribbled her name into the scene log.

Jenny was already there, suited and booted. After waiting for Sam to suit up, she led the way into the kitchen, where Rick Fielding, the pathologist, leaned over a woman's body. He lifted his head to greet Sam. 'Good to see you, DI Freeman, although the circumstances could be better.'

'Yes.' Sam nodded at Rick before glancing around the room, taking in the position of the body, the glaring head wound and the copious amount of blood on the floor. The stylish, modern kitchen with grey units, marble worktops and fitted appliances was marred by the gruesome act which had occurred there that morning.

Rick paused for Samantha to take in the scene before speaking again. 'Without the benefit of an autopsy, I'd guess the cause of death is our recurring enemy, the head wound. Blunt force trauma with a fairly smooth instrument.' Rick returned to his examination of the cadaver.

Keeping well away from the body, Sam moved around the perimeter of the room to where a CSI was taking fingerprints from the glazed kitchen door. Broken glass littered the floor, and the detectives were careful not to disturb anything that may offer a clue about the incident.

'The glass panel was smashed, and as the key was in the lock, it was easy for the assailant to effect an entry,' the CSI explained.

'Who found the body?' Sam turned to Jenny.

'Geoff Turner. The victim is his wife, Valerie, aged forty-four. He's in the lounge with Kim; unsurprisingly, he's not in a good way.

'We'll need to ask a few questions.'

'Yes, Kim's already explained the procedure. There are two

daughters as well who we'll need to get hold of, Anna and Lizzie, sixteen and fourteen, respectively.'

For the first time since Sam had received the call, the finality of this woman's death struck her. This wasn't just a case to distract her from her own problems; this was a dead woman, a man who had lost his wife and two girls who would never see their mother again.

Her eyes stung, and she blinked back the threatening tears as an image of Ravi's face swam into her mind. *This isn't about Ravi or me. It's about this family. I can't bring their mother back, but I do have a chance to help them.*

'You okay, boss?' Jenny scrutinised Sam's face, a frown on her own.

'Sure. Let's go and talk to the husband.'

Geoff Turner was a tall man who must once have been handsome but was now carrying too much weight, and his hair was thinning. He sat motionless on a teal velvet sofa, his face pale with red-rimmed eyes staring blankly out of the window; his hands were palms down beside him on the sofa.

DC Kim Thatcher jumped up when her boss entered and shrugged. Sam smiled at her and moved towards the stunned husband. Sitting beside him, she spoke gently to gain his attention.

'Mr Turner? My name's Samantha Freeman. Please accept my condolences on your loss. I'm the DI who'll be in charge of finding whoever did this to your wife. Are you up to answering a few questions?'

Geoff Turner turned to face Samantha and nodded, his face blank, body still slack with shock.

'Thank you. I know this must be difficult, but the sooner we learn the facts, the quicker we can progress the investigation. What time did you find your wife?'

'Umm, about 12.40pm. I came home early, and... and she

was there...' Geoff took a handkerchief from his pocket and blew his nose loudly. 'The girls, they'll need to know...'

'Do you know where they are?'

'Shopping. They left together at the same time I did, about 8.45am. Should I ring them?'

'It might be best to provide us with their numbers and one of our officers can call and arrange to bring them home. It's not the sort of news they should hear over the phone.' Sam turned to Jenny, who stepped forward as Geoff fumbled for his mobile to get the numbers. Jen took the phone from him and left the room to search his contacts and make the call.

While Sam waited for Jenny to return, she asked Geoff if there was someone she could call for him.

'Just the girls – but they shouldn't see their mother like this!' He stood up, clearly agitated at the thought of his daughters seeing their dead mother, but his legs failed him and he flopped back onto the sofa, running his fingers through his hair, an image of desolation.

'Is there a friend or family member whose house we can go to?'

'Er, yes, my parents. They'll have to be told, and we could go there. They live a couple of miles away on the new estate across town.'

'Okay, that's good. Can you give DC Thatcher their address and your contact numbers. She'll then arrange transport to your parents. Is there anyone else you'd like us to call for you? Your wife's parents, perhaps?'

'No. Val's parents are dead, and she has no siblings. Hell, this is bloody awful, I can't think straight...' Geoff sniffed and drew in a deep breath.

From the hall, Sam saw Jenny hurrying down the garden path and waited to hear if she'd managed to contact the daughters.

'I rang Anna's number – she's the elder sister. Without alarming her too much, I told her they were needed at home due to a family emergency. Naturally, she asked what it was, but I persuaded her to wait. They're somewhere near the Central Shopping Centre car park, so I told them to go to the main entrance where a car will bring them home. The car's on its way, they shouldn't be long.'

'Good work. Tell the uniforms outside to keep them out of the house when they arrive.'

Sam turned her attention back to Geoff. 'You said you returned home at 12.40pm. Can you tell me where you were until then?' Turner looked up, seemingly startled by her question. His hands trembled as he wiped tears from his face. 'I'm sorry to ask, but I want to put together a picture of your family's whereabouts this morning.'

'I went to play golf with my mates. I often go on a Saturday. Val likes – liked – the time to herself.'

'Do you know if your wife had any plans today? Either to go out or have friends at the house?'

'Not that she said. She wasn't dressed when I left. Val liked to take her time at the weekend and relax a bit, you know, after a busy week.'

'Where did she work?'

'The solicitors on Portland Street, Hammond, Birch and Fox. Val was their office manager. She'd worked her way up from a filing clerk… and… loved her job. Who the hell would do such a thing? She didn't deserve this.' Geoff took out his handkerchief and blew his nose again.

Kim took notes as he answered Sam's questions until a sudden noise from outside turned their attention to the window, where they saw Anna and Lizzie attempting to get past the cordon to their home.

SIX

'I want to see what's going on! Why won't anyone tell me?' Lizzie shouted as she struggled to get past two uniformed officers. Jenny hurried from inside their house and spoke softly to them as their father followed, stumbling towards them. The sight of his daughters prompted a fresh emotional outburst.

'Dad! What's happening?' Anna asked as Lizzie ran into her father's arms. Sam and Kim joined the little huddle outside the house until Sam suggested the three of them sit in the back of the car so Geoff Turner had some space to impart the worst possible news to his daughters. The officers stepped away from the car to allow them some privacy. Both girls could be heard sobbing, Lizzie more loudly than her sister, who seemed shocked and was visibly trembling.

While Valerie's daughters were learning of their mother's death, a woman came out of the house two doors down from the Turners'. She approached Sam and introduced herself. 'Hi. I'm Hayley Green, a friend of Geoff and Val. My husband Steve and I live at number 26. Can I ask what's happened and if there's anything I can do?'

'I'm sorry, Mrs Green. We can't discuss anything yet.' As

Sam spoke, Geoff and the girls exited the car, their faces streaked with tears. Lizzie ran into Hayley's arms, and the neighbour hugged the girl to her.

'Mum's dead!' Lizzie wailed. Hayley's face blanched and she squeezed the girl even closer.

'No! Oh, Lizzie, Anna, you poor girls!'

Sam turned to Geoff. 'Is she a close friend?'

'A good neighbour, she used to babysit for the girls. Look, can we go inside for some clothes and things and then get off to my parents?'

'Yes, of course.' Sam moved away to speak to Kim, asking her to return to the house and warn the CSI that the family was coming in and to ensure the kitchen door was closed so they wouldn't have to witness the spectacle of activity surrounding Valerie's body.

She then spoke to Hayley Green. 'Can I ask that you keep this information to yourself for now? We'll speak to the neighbours shortly, but speculation won't help our enquiries.'

'Yes, of course.' She turned to face Geoff. 'If there's anything I can do...'

'Thanks.' Geoff answered curtly, putting his arms around his daughters and steering them towards the house.

Extra personnel had arrived, swelling the buzz of activity. The machine of a murder investigation reminded Sam of the industry of ants – everyone busy with their own role to play, working in solemn and respectful silence, speaking only when necessary. With the kitchen door firmly closed, Kim and Jenny led the family upstairs to pack a few things to see them over the following days while Sam hovered downstairs.

Sam had been aware of Kim studying her at times, no doubt wondering how the scene playing out before them was affecting her, a trigger maybe? But witnessing the raw grief displayed by the family felt surreal to Samantha. Perhaps it was her professional persona taking over or a coping mechanism to block her feelings; she was uncertain. Yes, sympathy filled her for the distraught trio, yet her mind was moving forward, establishing the steps to follow to get the investigation off the ground.

The Turners gathered what they needed in less than ten minutes. As they returned downstairs, Lizzie spoke up, 'Dad. I want to see Mum.' The question was directed at her father, who looked at Samantha with pleading eyes.

'I'm sorry, Lizzie, but that's not possible at the moment. There'll be a chance to see her and say your goodbyes later.' Sam's negative answer prompted floods of tears from the girl, and even Geoff struggled to contain his emotions. Clearly, the family was too emotional to answer questions in depth, so Sam instructed Kim to take them to Geoff's parents. 'I'll come and see you tomorrow, Mr Turner, when I'm afraid I'll need to ask some more questions.'

Sam stood alone in the hallway, experiencing an inward struggle to rein in her emotions. She didn't return to view the body more closely as she would normally, only slightly concerned about what her team would think. The smell of death permeated the house. Sam held her breath as she hurried outside where the cold wind was welcome, cathartic as she filled her lungs with fresh, clean air. Everything was under control. It was time for her to leave.

SEVEN

Putting space between herself and the crime scene was a relief. The case was testing Samantha's resolve. Had she returned to work too quickly? Was it too soon after Ravi? There wasn't time for such soul searching – Sam climbed into her car – having insisted on being involved with the case, she would see it through. Jenny appeared at the Mini's window and tapped on the glass. 'I'll follow you back to the station. Everything's under control here.'

Kim Thatcher remained to accompany Geoff's family to his parent's home. Sam and Jenny returned to the station to set the cogs of the investigation in motion. Having already rung the team to commence background searches on the family, on entering the station, Sam was pleased to see Paul Roper leaning over his computer, staring intently at the screen.

'Anything jumping out at you, Paul?' She asked.

'Nothing, boss. Neither Geoff nor Valerie Turner have so much as a driving offence between them. Squeaky clean.'

'Okay, thanks.' Sam and Jenny hurried along to the largest room at their disposal to prepare it as the incident room. She set up the whiteboard and recorded basic details of their victim and the little information they knew for certain. The pathologist would confirm the time of death, but as Valerie Turner's family had seen her alive and well at 8.45am and her body was found at 12.40pm, it gave a reasonably tight window to commence working, and being Saturday, many of the neighbours would have been at home, with any luck someone may have seen something.

'Ask Tom, Paul and Layla to come in, will you, Jen?' Sam had followed her into the room. 'And any available PCs.'

When they were assembled, Sam presented a brief rundown of the murder. 'Valerie and Geoff Turner present as an ordinary family – Mum was having a quiet day at home, Dad was playing golf, and the teenage girls were out shopping. Initial impressions suggest a break-in through the kitchen door. It's a strange time to burgle a house, and although we'll need confirmation, nothing appears to have been taken.'

'They could have been scared off by Mrs Turner's presence,' Layla suggested.

'Yes, but why such a vicious attack? Most burglars would have turned to run. There's also no sign of a weapon unless the CSIs find something hidden, so the murderer probably took it away with him, which begs the question, did he also bring it? Was this a pre-meditated murder? Tom, I want you to grab a team of uniformed PCs and commence a house-to-house while events are still fresh in people's minds. Check for any CCTV and send anything recorded from 8am onwards to Paul and Layla to view. Jenny and I are going to take a trip to the solicitors where Valerie worked to ask some questions. We'll speak to the family first thing tomorrow; they were in no fit state to think clearly today.'

Jenny insisted on taking her car. The snow hadn't laid, and the roads were wet rather than icy. Portland Street wasn't far, but Sam used the few minutes to google the firm in preparation.

'Will the office be open today?' Jenny asked. 'I shouldn't think family law solicitors work weekends.'

'It's worth a shot, and we need to start somewhere. Valerie Turner had worked her way up from filing clerk to office manager, according to her husband. It says here there are three partners in the firm and five associate solicitors – there'll be clerks, secretaries and the like, so it's a good-sized firm.'

'Do you recognise any of the solicitors' names?'

'No, which isn't surprising, they don't practice criminal law.'

After a ten-minute journey, Jen manoeuvred into a parking spot on the street outside the offices and switched off the engine. Snow was again falling in large wet flakes as they exited the car. Hurrying into rather grand premises, it was a relief to find the front door open, and they entered a foyer with a security system to call for attention.

'Hello?' A female voice answered through the speaker. 'Can I help?'

Samantha introduced herself and Jen. 'We'd like to see a member of staff regarding Mrs Valerie Turner.' Two minutes later, a young woman pushed through the swing doors into the lobby. Her face was flushed.

'I'm sorry, there's only me in today. The solicitors don't generally work weekends.'

'And you are?' Sam enquired.

'Maddie. I'm Mr Birch's secretary. You can come through if I can help at all.'

Maddie spun around on recklessly high heels, and the detectives followed her through the glass doors into a large lobby. Blond wood panelling, a large reception desk and plush carpets hinted at a successful company. The secretary led them into a small office where her computer idled and papers were scattered across the desk. Gathering the papers into a pile, Maddie blushed. 'Excuse the mess. As I said, I'm the only one in today, using the peace and quiet to catch up a little, you know?'

'Sorry to disturb you, Maddie, we won't keep you long. I assume you know Mrs Turner?'

'Yes. She's been here forever – I think the place would fall to bits without her. Is something wrong?'

'I'm afraid Mrs Turner was killed at her home this morning. We're treating it as a suspicious death, and a full investigation is underway.'

Maddie's hand flew to her mouth. 'Oh, my goodness! I can't believe it... she was only here yesterday.'

'I'm sorry, it must be a shock, but do you think you could answer a few questions for us?' The girl nodded, her face pale and motioned for them to sit down before almost collapsing into her chair.

'Thank you. How long have you worked with Val?'

'Um, she was here when I started three years ago. Val trained me, I suppose. She knows everything about the firm, from how many paper clips to the partners' diaries. Gosh, they'll all be stunned. I can't believe it!' Maddie repeated.

'Did Valerie have any particular friends here?' Jenny asked.

Maddie chewed on her bottom lip as she thought about her answer. 'Not really. She was our boss, I suppose – the secretaries, that is – and Val wasn't one to socialise with her colleagues, but that's probably because she was a bit older than most of us. If truth be told, we were all a bit in awe of her. She could be a stickler for good practice, which, of course, was her job, but you certainly knew when you got on the wrong side of Val. She wasn't what you would call a warm personality.' Maddie's hand covered her mouth again. 'Sorry, I shouldn't really say that.'

'No, please speak freely. We need a true picture, nothing held back.' Sam smiled encouragingly. 'What about the partners and associate solicitors? Was she friendly with anyone in particular?'

'No, I don't think so. Mr Hammond is the senior partner, and Val was accountable to him, but we often joked it was the other way around. As I said, she was the glue that held the place together. We'll be lost without her. She's got two girls, hasn't she? Are they okay? It must be dreadful for them, I can't imagine...'

'It's been a tremendous shock, and naturally, they're grieving. Can you give me a contact number for Mr Hammond? We'll need to come back and speak to the other staff members at some point, but we'll leave you now to get on with your work. Thank you for your time.'

Maddie scribbled Mr Hammond's personal number on a business card which she passed to Jenny before showing the detectives out of the building.

Back in the car, Sam reached for her phone. 'I'd better inform Mr Hammond before Maddie does.' She tapped in the solicitor's number to impart the bad news about his office manager.

EIGHT

Alex Hammond thanked the detective for informing him and replaced the phone in its cradle. Although it was a cold day, he felt suddenly hot and ran his fingers under his collar.

'Who was that, Alex?' His wife, Elaine, stood with her hands on her hips and head tilted to one side. 'Not bad news, I hope?'

'I'm afraid it was. Our office manager has been murdered... this morning apparently. I can't believe it.' Alex moved to the drinks cabinet and poured himself a large whiskey. 'Want one?' His wife shook her head, and they both sat down.

'Have I met her?' Elaine asked.

'I'm not sure. Valerie Turner? Maybe you met at the Christmas party?'

'No doesn't ring a bell. Does she have a family?'

'Yes, two daughters, I believe, and her husband, Geoff. Hell, they'll be devastated. It'll cause problems at work too. Val was an excellent manager and ran a tight ship. She'll be difficult to replace.'

'Oh no, I hope you'll not use this as an excuse to get out of our holiday. It's already booked and I've been looking forward to it for ages. I need a break.'

'No, it shouldn't come to that. Don't worry.'

'Good. Now what shall we have for supper?' Elaine stood and left the room without waiting for a reply, and Alex swirled the amber liquid in his glass, staring intently at the prisms of light formed by the cut glass.

Life in New Middridge hadn't turned out to be as perfect as he'd hoped. The opportunity of a partnership had been too good to miss; he and Elaine were in agreement on that score, and as the role was senior partner, Elaine was enthused about the move. She'd probably had visions of being a version of the Lady of the Manor, chairing committees and presiding over charitable fundraisers. Still, it was clear to Alex that his wife wasn't as happy as they'd expected, and he had to admit the move had been a difficult one for him too.

For the first few months, Elaine was content with perfecting their home, a period detached residence, the grandest house they'd ever possessed. Joining the WI and other organisations seemed to satisfy her initially and if he was honest, he couldn't understand what had changed. But something had. Alex loved his wife; she'd given him two wonderful children, both grown up and independent. Could Elaine be missing them? But why had it taken so long for empty nest syndrome to kick in?

The couple's relationship wasn't passionate; it never really had been. He could barely remember what passion was like, but they rubbed along together well, content, he'd always thought – until lately. Alex would have described their marriage as a reasonable or even a pleasant union until these last few months. Could it be the move to New Middridge?

Alex's children were the best thing to have come from their marriage, a boy and a girl, both in their late twenties, children they were proud of. The family money Elaine inherited from her parents came a close second in the satisfaction aspect of his marriage. It was money which had bought him the senior partnership in Hammond, Birch and Fox, a move she appeared to want as much as him.

Being the senior partner's wife gave Elaine the status she'd always desired, yet her mood was in a downward spiral. No matter how hard he tried, he couldn't please his wife of thirty years, and the tense atmosphere at home was dragging him down, stirring a restless feeling inside, an itch which he couldn't scratch.

Alex wouldn't claim to have been the best husband in the world. He was only human, but he did his best. There'd been sticky patches over the years, but he'd hoped these were over and they could settle into their new life in peace,

The idea of a holiday had come out of the blue – Elaine's idea. Alex was happy to go along with it, yet she was right; with Valerie's death, things would be difficult at work, but Alex wouldn't dare to cancel. He was banking on this holiday to restore his wife's good mood and set their marriage on an even keel again.

Getting away would probably be a good thing for him too. The police were bound to be poking around at work investigating Val's murder, and Alex would much prefer a couple of weeks in Mauritius to being under scrutiny in the office.

NINE

Samantha Freeman rose early on Sunday morning. Sleep had again been fitful, but not only with thoughts of Ravi – the new case was affording a different focus. Forcing herself to eat a slice of toast and wash it down with two cups of coffee, Sam left the house, her mind racing to prioritise the many pressing tasks. It was a frosty morning, and after scraping her windscreen, she turned the heater on full and drove to the station.

Unsurprisingly, Sam was the first of the team to arrive. The quiet of the office in the early morning and the opportunity to mentally prepare for the day ahead were to be savoured. After checking her emails, the DI entered the incident room and, hands on hips, stared at the whiteboard displaying the facts they'd gathered.

Valerie Turner, 44, victim.

Geoff Turner, 45, victim's husband – absent from home, playing golf – TBC

Anna Turner, 16, victim's daughter – absent from home, shopping – TBC

Lizzie Turner, 14, victim's daughter – absent from home, shopping – TBC

Hayley Green, neighbour & friend

Steve Green, neighbour & friend

Donald Turner, Geoff's father

Mary Turner, Geoff's mother

Possible work colleagues – interviews TBA

It wasn't much to go on, Sam thought, but the morning would see formal witness statements being taken, house-to-house calls continued and information collated, and, with any luck, they'd find something useful on the neighbours' CCTV footage. And the autopsy was scheduled for Monday afternoon, when Rick may come up with a lead.

Although Sam enjoyed the tranquillity of being alone, she welcomed the arrival of her team, all of whom were early, despite it being Sunday, and keen to move the investigation forward. Jenny arrived with coffee and doughnuts from the deli across the road, and Sam surprised herself by eating one; the sugar rush would keep her going.

When all emails were checked, they assembled in the incident room to discuss any developments and divi out duties. Kim described the scene at Geoff Turner's parents' house; as expected, the Turners senior were shocked and upset at the news, and tears flowed freely. They lived only a couple of miles from their son, which was convenient for the family and the police.

'It's only a small retirement bungalow, so not ideal for a long stay. Geoff's sleeping on the couch and the girls are sharing the small spare bedroom. Anna and Lizzie were in bits, but Geoff and his parents are struggling themselves and unable to offer much comfort.'

DC Paul Roper reported that footage from four CCTV cameras had been made available, which he intended to view after the meeting. 'It's all from the front street, and as it appears entry was effected from the rear of the property, I don't hold out much hope.' The others nodded, similar thoughts having already occurred to most of them. It would probably be the same result from the house-to-house enquiries, reports which Layla and Tom Wilson were tasked with reviewing and following up where necessary.

'Right, you've all got plenty to do. Jen and I are off to visit the Turners to take more detailed statements. Kim, you can come too and interview the daughters before taking up the role of FLO. Paul, when you've finished with the CCTV, can you dig a little deeper into our principles' backgrounds? I want a report on the Turners' finances and phone logs from their providers. Keep me in the loop if anything of interest occurs, and thank you all for coming in on a Sunday.'

Samantha, Jenny, and Kim left the station and drove to Geoff's parents' home, about a twenty-minute drive.

'Any initial ideas, boss?' Kim's voice held a keen edge.

'It's early, and hopefully today will give us a break. As ever we start with the immediate family and work outwards, looking for motive. They may present as a happy, normal family, but we can't take first impressions for granted. What did you make of Geoff's parents, Kim?'

'They seem an ordinary retired couple. Mary has some

mobility issues, but they were keen to have their family stay. It's difficult to make judgements when emotions are running so high, but I'll keep my eyes and ears open today.'

Sam smiled. Kim was one of the most recent DCs on her team and was eager to learn. She'd made one or two rookie errors but was shaping up well and would almost certainly be an asset to the investigation.

They pulled up outside a neat little bungalow with a small front garden mainly planted with shrubs and covered with slate for easy maintenance. A wooden porch protected the front door. Two bay windows flanked the door, with Anna Turner watching from one of them. Mary Turner opened the door, leaning heavily on a walking stick and looking weary with dark circles accentuating her swollen eyes. Without a word, she stood back for the detectives to enter. Kim led the way into the lounge, where the rest of the family were gathered and made introductions.

'Apologies for the intrusion, but I'm sure you understand our need to move swiftly with the investigation.' Sam took in the blank faces watching her. Only Donald Turner nodded. 'What we'd like to do today is to take formal statements, details of everyone's movements yesterday, and some general questions pertaining to Valerie. Mrs Turner, is there a room we can use for individual questioning?'

'Well, the dining room, I suppose, or the conservatory.'

'That's brilliant, thank you.' As previously decided, Jenny and Samantha would question Geoff Turner while Kim would speak to Anna. The girl looked anxious.

'It's okay, Anna.' Kim reassured her. 'I just need a few details, and we can stop anytime it becomes too much for you.' The girl led the way to the conservatory, and her grandmother followed, fussing over putting a heater on to warm the icy room.

Geoff walked silently into the dining room, where he sat at the table opposite the detectives, a sad and weary air shrouding him.

TEN

'How are you feeling this morning?' Samantha opened the interview with Geoff. 'Did you manage any sleep?'

'Bloody awful, and no, I didn't sleep, and I don't know what else I can tell you. Shouldn't you be out there trying to catch the bastard who killed my Val?'

Jenny answered while taking out her notebook. 'We have a team looking at several CCTV images provided by your neighbours and another continuing with house-to-house enquiries. I know this is difficult, but we need information to determine why this happened, a motive, if you like, which will lead us to the perpetrator.'

Samantha smiled as she started with the soft questions, hopefully to relax Geoff before the more invasive questioning began. 'Perhaps you could tell us more about Val. How long were you married?'

'Twenty-one years. She was twenty when we met and we were married within a year. Val was so beautiful, yet there was a sadness in her which made me want to protect her.'

'Do you know why she was sad?'

'Val's parents died when she was eighteen, in some kind of

car accident, and with no siblings or other family, she was very much alone. She claimed I made her happy, and when the girls eventually came along, we had the family we longed for.'

'Were you living in New Middridge when you met?'

'No. We were both in Manchester. I worked for an engineering firm and Val had recently finished her accountancy training. We moved to New Middridge when I was offered a job here. Val took a few temping jobs until the girls were born, then stayed at home until they were at school when she landed the job at Hammond Birch and Fox.' Geoff paused and rubbed his eyes with his fists.

Sam was keen to move on, aware her next questions may be more trying for Geoff to answer. 'I'm afraid some of our questions will seem intrusive, but they are relevant, mostly to eliminate lines of enquiry that could otherwise waste our time. We need to build up a picture of everyone's whereabouts yesterday, everyone who is close to your wife, that is. You said you left to play golf. Can you tell us exactly what time you left, where you played and the names of those you were with?'

'I told you yesterday. I left at about 8.45am, and the girls left at the same time.' Geoff's face reddened, but he said no more.

'And where do you play golf?'

'Greenacres Golf Club. I've been a member there for about six years; it's near Barton Woods.'

'Yes, thank you, I know it. And the names and contact details of those you played with?'

'What the hell have they got to do with this? Is everyone a suspect?' Geoff frowned, his brows almost knitting together.

'We have to check everything – times, places, who was with whom. I know it's a pain but necessary, I'm afraid.'

Geoff hesitated, looking from Sam to Jenny, both women poised to hear his answer. 'I didn't actually play golf.' He spat the words out as if they tasted rotten in his mouth. 'I went to the club as arranged and waited for my mates in the car park, but they didn't turn up. They must have assumed we wouldn't be playing as the weather was bloody awful.'

'And, did you go into the clubhouse?'

'No. It was too early for a drink and I'd eaten breakfast before I left home.'

'Where did you go, Geoff? Because you told us you didn't return home until 12.40pm when you found your wife.' Samantha held the man's gaze, noting his reddening face and the way he squirmed in his seat.

'I drove around for a while, parked near the woods and went for a walk. Val values her days off work so I gave her some space. She deserved some time to herself. As do I, for that matter.'

'And did you see anyone on your walk?'

'No, the weather probably put people off, but I quite like the rain and was well wrapped up.'

'So, no one can confirm you were in Barton Woods?'

'You don't seriously think I killed my wife, do you? If I'd known she was going to be murdered, I'd have arranged an alibi!' Geoff's nostrils flared. 'It's ridiculous to suggest I had anything to do with it!'

'I'm not suggesting anything, Mr Turner, just trying to confirm your whereabouts.' Samantha looked at Jenny and gave a slight nod, the signal for her DS to take over the interview.

'Can you think of anyone who might wish to harm your wife, Mr Turner?'

'Hell no! Everyone loved Val. Surely it was a burglary which went wrong; it can't have been planned.'

'We have to consider every possibility, no matter how implausible it seems, so if a name comes to mind, anyone with whom Val had argued or someone who held a grudge perhaps, please let us know.' Geoff shook his head as Jenny continued.

'Have you been aware of anything unusual happening of late – someone hanging around, watching the house maybe?'

'Again, no. Look, we're just an ordinary family. Who would want to do this? Damn it, I don't even know why anyone would break in: we're not rich!'

'That's what we're trying to establish. Had Valerie mentioned anything strange occurring lately? Someone following her, or maybe a troubling incident at work?'

'No.'

'And had she seemed okay of late, or was there anything different about her attitude?'

'What do you mean?' Geoff scowled.

'Was she anxious or worried about something? Maybe a change in her behaviour?'

'No, nothing! Like I said she was looking forward to a day to herself – her *me time,* she called it.'

'And how was your relationship? Was everything all right between you and Valerie, or have there been any recent arguments or problems?' This question never went down well, but Jenny had to ask.

'You think I did it, don't you?' Geoff stood and turned angrily towards the door but was prevented from leaving as Kim entered.

'Boss, I need a quick word.' She looked apologetic.

'Please sit down again, Mr Turner. I'm going to have a word with my DC and ask your mother if she could make coffee. I think we could all do with some.' Samantha watched Geoff waver as he decided what to do. He took his seat and she followed her colleague into the hall. 'What is it, Kim?'

'Anna's just told me they have a half-brother, Ben. Apparently, Mrs Turner gave birth to him when she was a teenager and gave him up for adoption. He tracked her down last summer. Anna said her mum welcomed him into the family,

47

but her dad wasn't too pleased. I thought it odd that he wasn't mentioned yesterday. You'd think they'd want to let him know, wouldn't you?'

'Well done, Kim. See what else Anna can tell you and ask Mrs Turner for some coffee, please. I'll have another word with Geoff.'

ELEVEN

As Samantha returned to the room, Geoff glared at her but at least remained seated.

Sitting with her hands clasped and resting on the table, she spoke softly. 'Geoff, I'm sorry if our questions seem intrusive and personal. In a murder investigation, we need to gather as much information as possible to build an accurate picture of our victim, her family and all other contacts. Only then can we establish a motive and find the perpetrator. To gain this information, we have to ask questions which, I admit, are not always pleasant, and we rely on the honesty of those we speak to. Everything is relevant until it's ruled out. Details you may think unimportant may, further down the line, have significance.' Geoff stared blankly at her. 'So, what can you tell me about Ben.'

It was Jenny's turn to look blank as Geoff's face again flushed.

'He's nothing to do with me.'

'But he is Valerie's son, and therefore, we need to speak to him. Have you informed him of his mother's death?'

'No.'

A somewhat puzzled Jenny glanced curiously at her boss and then at Geoff. 'Can you give me Ben's surname and contact address, please?'

'Ben Chapman. He lives in Leeds. The number will be on Val's phone. I don't know his address.' Geoff was clearly uncomfortable with this change in the direction of questioning.

'Did you have regular contact with Ben?'

'I didn't, but Val did, and he came to the house sometimes. If you want honesty, I'll tell you. I don't like him. He turned up out of the blue – hell, I didn't even know she'd had a baby before we met – and I still haven't worked out exactly what he wanted from us.'

'Were you angry at Val for not telling you?' Samantha probed.

Geoff banged his fist on the table. 'And this is why I didn't tell you about him! You jump to conclusions. Do you think I'd kill her because of something which happened before we even met?'

'I don't know. Were you angry? Did it cause any arguments or bad feelings between you and Val?'

'I was more hurt than angry. She was only a kid when it happened, and we all make stupid mistakes. I felt hurt because Val hadn't told me – she hadn't trusted me enough to share it. I didn't think we had secrets.' Geoff sighed, suddenly appearing deflated. His head dropped and he stared at his lap.

'And what about the girls? How did they take the news of having a big brother?'

He looked up, his eyes moist. 'They were happy, quite excited, I suppose, and Ben knew how to play them all – presents and treats. He wormed his way into the family and all three were taken in by him.'

'But not you?'

'No.'

'Why was that, Geoff?'

'There was something false about him, as if he wanted something from Val, and I couldn't figure out what it was. I didn't– don't trust him.'

'Do you think he could have been after money?'

'Well, he'd be disappointed. We're certainly not loaded. Val's wage kept us comfortable, but I was laid off during lockdown for over eighteen months until things eased. Two teenage girls aren't cheap to keep, and for a while, things were tight, so there wasn't much spare cash if Ben had money in mind.'

'Did you and Val ever borrow money?'

'No. We tightened our belts while I was out of work, but Val earned a good wage. We were sensible and had no serious worries on that score.' Geoff rubbed his hands over his face and sighed. When Mary Turner appeared with a tray of coffee, Sam called a halt to the interview to give them all a break. Geoff took his coffee and returned to the lounge, and Kim, who'd finished questioning Anna, joined them in the dining room and closed the door behind her.

'Did you get anything else from Anna?' Jenny asked.

'She's terribly upset. I sensed there's been some recent friction between her and her mother, which is piling on the guilt now.'

'What teenager doesn't encounter friction with their parents? Did she say if it was anything specific?'

'I think it could be centred around Ben, but I'm not sure.'

Samantha finished her coffee and stood. 'Right. I think we need to have a chat with Mary and Donald. Kim, could you speak to Lizzie, please? If she wants someone with her, maybe ask Mary; and we'll start with Donald. If we can wrap up here ASAP, I'd like to pay a visit to Ben Chapman. Jenny, can you ring Paul and get him to find the number from Val's phone and an address, too, please.'

TWELVE

D S Jenny Newcombe took a call from Paul before they left the Turners' house and, as they climbed into the car, related what he'd discovered. 'Paul found Ben Chapman's contact number in Valerie's phone and called him to say we'd like to interview him regarding an ongoing investigation. He was curious but appeared not to have heard about his mother's death, so he's expecting us in about an hour.'

'Good. We should be able to make it. Has Paul sent the address?'

'Yes. It's in the Harehills district of Leeds. With a bit of luck, traffic should be quiet today. Paul also ran Chapman's name through the system, but he's not known to us, so there's nothing to work with.' Jenny entered the postcode into her satnav and switched on the engine. Normally, Sam would prefer to drive, but to placate her DS, she'd agreed to be driven since her return to work, ostensibly to give her leg more time to heal, although both women were aware that the accident which killed Ravi was still fresh in Samantha's mind.

The roads were quiet, and within the hour, they were driving down the steep row of pre-war terraced houses where

Ben Chapman lived. The red brick houses were small, two-bedroomed, Sam guessed, and mostly well-maintained. As they pulled up in front of number 14, the curtains fell back into place – someone had been watching for them to arrive.

A tall, handsome man opened the door. Samantha knew he was twenty-six, but he looked younger with a fresh, boyish face. Ben greeted them, his mouth twitching into a nervous smile. 'This is all very mysterious. I've never had a visit from the police before.'

'May we come in please, Mr Chapman?' Samantha asked. Ben stood aside to allow Sam and Jenny entry into a small lounge, tidy and furnished with old-fashioned but good-quality furniture. Colourful throws on the two small sofas where Sam and Jenny were invited to sit brightened the room, which smelled of furniture polish and had been recently vacuumed.

'Mr Chapman, I believe Valerie Turner is your mother?' Samantha wasted no time.

'That's right, why? Is everything okay?' A frown appeared on his brow,

'I'm afraid I have to tell you that Valerie died yesterday.'

'Dead, no! She can't be! How did it happen?' Ben's face paled.

'We're treating it as a suspicious death. Your mother appears to have been attacked while alone at her home. I'm so sorry for your loss, Mr Chapman, but if you're up to answering a few questions, it could help our investigation.'

Ben ran his hands through his hair and slumped back onto the sofa. 'Why didn't you let me know yesterday when it happened?'

'My apologies, but we've only become aware of your relationship with Valerie this morning.'

'Oh, I get it. Bloody Geoff forgot to mention me, did he? He never liked me, wouldn't give me the time of day, not like Val...'

Ben's face crumpled as he wiped a stray tear away with the back of his hand.

'I'm sure you can understand that the family are still struggling to come to terms with what's happened. I understand your relationship with Valerie only commenced recently?'

Ben sniffed, his face softening. 'Yes, we first met last summer. I always knew I was adopted but had never been interested in searching for my birth parents until my adoptive parents died. Mum went first, with cancer, and then Dad a few months later following a stroke.'

'I'm sorry to hear that.' Samantha sympathised, then paused to allow him to continue.

'I suppose being alone took its toll. I had too much time to think and eventually got in touch with social services to see if they could contact my birth parents with a view to meeting.' Ben paused and inhaled deeply before continuing.

'Like everything else, there's a process; they needed to write to Val first to see if she was willing to have contact – she was the only parent named on the original birth certificate. It was a couple of months before I heard anything, but she agreed to meet me – only the two of us initially. I suppose she needed to decide whether any kind of relationship with me was workable – it's quite a weird situation for both parties.

'Val told me her side of the story and how her parents had forced her to give me up for adoption. They were strict and old-fashioned and refused to put up with the shame of an illegitimate child in the family. Without their support, Val had no alternative but to stay with an aunt until after the birth and then give me up for adoption.

'She never saw them again, and they died in an accident a couple of years later. I asked more questions, difficult ones, and she did her best to answer them. We discovered we liked each other – we hit it off.' Ben's eyes filled with tears and he blew his nose, loudly. Jenny gave a reassuring nod and he continued.

'Val asked for time to prepare her family before we met again, which she did before inviting me to her home to meet them. It was weird for us all, but Geoff was clearly unhappy about my presence from the start and certainly didn't try to hide it. The girls were a little wary at first but soon came around, and I'd hoped we could build a relationship, which we did–'

'Why do you think Geoff was unhappy about you turning up?' Samantha wanted Ben's take on the reasons.

Ben shrugged. 'Maybe he was jealous of her having someone else in her life or even suspicious. He did get me alone one time and asked what I *really* wanted from Val. I found it quite offensive. I'd hoped he would see it from my point of view.'

'How did you answer his question?' Samantha looked directly at Ben as she spoke.

'Ahh, so you're suspicious too?' Ben shook his head. 'I told him the truth. I'd lost the only "family" I'd ever known and was curious about my origins. My intentions were motivated by nothing else. If you're looking at me as a suspect in Val's death, you're on the wrong track – I had nothing to gain from her dying and even more to lose.'

Sam nodded her understanding, then asked, 'Where do you work, Mr Chapman?'

'I'm between jobs at the moment. When my adoptive parents died, I took time off work to sort things out and was then made redundant. My parents left me this house, so I gave up my flat in the city and moved in here. I've been looking for work since then but haven't found anything suitable.'

'Did Valerie tell you who your natural father is?' Sam's change of topic to a more personal question startled Ben.

'Er, no. I asked, of course, and was told it had been a casual relationship. By the time she realised she was pregnant, they'd lost contact. Val couldn't even remember his full name. It appears I'm the product of a one-night stand.'

Samantha moved on. 'I have to ask you, Mr Chapman, where were you yesterday morning?'

Ben sighed. 'I was here... and yes, I was alone.'

'Did you have any telephone calls or visitors?'

'Not that I remember. My neighbours were at home. I could hear them, so perhaps they heard me.' He looked hopefully at the detectives.

'Thank you, Mr Chapman. We're sorry to have brought such bad news. We'll leave you in peace now.' Sam ended the interview.

It was mid-afternoon, and the two detectives hadn't eaten since breakfast. 'McDonald's okay? We passed one on the way in,' Jenny suggested. She took Samantha's noncommittal grunt as a yes.

THIRTEEN

With food in their stomachs, Samantha and Jenny travelled back to New Middridge to wrap up the day's work with a team catch-up. The sky was darkening, and rain was falling.

Jenny yawned. 'I hate February. It's the most miserable of months, dark, depressing with nothing to look forward to.' As soon as the words left her mouth, Jenny regretted them. What did she have to grumble about in comparison to her boss?

'Well, at least it's the shortest month, and it's nearly over.' Sam didn't appear to take offence. Jenny was constantly aware of Sam's loss and almost afraid to open her mouth and put her foot in it – something she could generally do without much effort. Working with Sam was like walking on glass. Having insisted on driving, Jen was concerned that even getting into a car may be a trigger for her and stir memories of the accident. Her boss hadn't argued too much about driving; perhaps her leg still troubled her. Jen was almost afraid to smile around her boss and knew their other team members felt the same. Yet Sam wasn't one to make a fuss and would probably prefer them to act normally, whatever normal was.

Samantha's mobile ringtone ended the short conversation, and Jen breathed a sigh of relief. The call was from Kim, and Sam switched to speaker so they could both listen.

'I've spoken again with the younger daughter, Lizzie. She didn't say much when her grandmother was with her earlier, but I asked some more questions when we were alone for a few minutes. She's still terribly upset and thinks that if she hadn't gone out, her mum wouldn't have been murdered – quite natural, I suppose. But she's lying about something.'

'Lying? How can you tell?' Sam asked.

'Because she crossed her fingers when I asked which shops she'd visited with Anna.'

'How do you figure she was lying from that?' Sam asked.

'You know – didn't you do it as a child? If you cross your fingers when you tell a lie, it doesn't count, so you haven't done anything wrong,' Kim explained. Sam looked puzzled.

'Yeah, I always did that too, but then I blushed and gave myself away,' Jenny added.

'Anyway, her gran came back into the room, and I couldn't continue our chat, yet I'm convinced she's lying about something. It might not be relevant, but then again, it might. I'm heading back to the office. I think the family need some time alone; they've seen enough of me today.'

'Okay, Kim. We're on our way back, too. ETA is about thirty minutes, so we'll see you then. Good work.' Sam closed her phone. 'Crossing fingers to nullify a lie? That's a new one on me.'

Jenny smiled as she manoeuvred onto the motorway. 'We all did it when I was a kid. Stupid, I know.'

It was 4.10pm when they arrived in New Middridge, where, in the incident room, a dozen people were still hard at work. Sam called them together, hoping to hear of new leads.

Paul and the PCs viewing the neighbour's CCTV, could offer zilch. They'd trawled through most of them – beginning with the nearest ones to the Turners' house – with absolutely nothing to report. There were still a few tapes to view from houses further along the street but it wasn't looking hopeful. The consensus was that the perpetrator had reached the house from the lane which ran behind the houses.

Layla had been busy digging into the Turners' financial records. 'It's apparent that Valerie was the main breadwinner but they don't appear to be in any financial difficulties. They used their credit cards more regularly when Geoff Turner was off work, but they're all paid off now. The bank and savings accounts are modest and show nothing out of the ordinary.'

Paul said, 'I'm still waiting on phone records from the provider, and I can't see anything unusual on our victim's phone unless she deleted something untoward.'

Jenny offered a brief report of their visit to Ben Chapman; and Kim shared her thoughts about her time with the family, including her opinion of Lizzie's lying.

Paul smirked. 'Crossing her fingers is hardly conclusive and not terribly scientific, is it? And I hardly think a fourteen-year-old girl is a likely suspect in her mother's murder.'

'Don't be sniffy, Paul,' said Sam. 'Everything's important at this early stage and we rule nothing out. Right, I think we'll call it a day. Thank you all for giving up your weekend, and I'll see you tomorrow.' She concluded the meeting, with Paul looking suitably chastised as they dispersed.

Samantha was the first out of the building. A lead cloak of weariness dragged her down, and she ached to get home, have a long soak in the bath, a couple of glasses of red wine with some dinner, and hopefully, collapse into a sound and dreamless sleep.

FOURTEEN

Her sleep was sound but, alas, not dreamless. More snow had fallen, blanketing the already icy road – a treacherous combination. Samantha was lulled by the vehicle's motion, a smile on her lips at the memory of their few days away. The raspy sound of an engine reached her ears before the lorry came into view, hurtling towards the car in which she and Ravi travelled.

Horror saturated her as she realised the trajectory of the lorry made a crash inevitable. The monstrous vehicle appeared completely out of control.

Sam was frozen, unable to breathe as panic constricted her chest – her instinct was to reach out to protect Ravi, but her body stiffened, refusing to move. It was as if she was a statue observing the oncoming tragedy yet helpless to stop it. Samantha knew that if she didn't do something, Ravi could die, and maybe she would too, but even her scream was silent, stifled before it could reach her lips.

Sam heard Ravi's laboured breath as he swung the steering wheel, but it was too late. When the impact came, the ice turned to fire. Grating metal pervaded Sam's ears while a burning sensation engulfed her body. Pain pierced her limbs; her lungs fought for oxygen. With her heart pounding and the pulsing of blood drumming loudly in her ears, she angled her head as best as she could to look at Ravi. His beautiful eyes were open but unseeing; his head lolled back on the seat. Sam longed to touch him, to shake him back to life, but she was trapped in a body which refused to obey her commands. Every movement brought an agonising pain from her legs to her head.

The burning sensation spread throughout her body until finally reaching her mouth. Samantha screamed and screamed as if she would never stop.

Still screaming when she awoke, it took Sam several seconds to realise it had all been a dream, albeit one concocted from the truth. Ravi was dead.

It wasn't the first dream in which she'd re-lived the crash in which he was killed, and it probably wouldn't be the last. Her imagination must be filling in the gaps as, in reality, she'd lost consciousness on impact and hadn't witnessed Ravi's death – he'd died later at the hospital and the shock of his death was imparted to her later there.

Flinging off the covers, Sam headed for the shower and stayed under the hot jets of water until she could breathe steadily again. Once dry and dressed Sam noted the time, 6.10am. It was early, but she was fearful to sleep again and needed something to take her mind off the dream.

Grabbing a pen and notepad, Sam concentrated her thoughts on Valerie Turner's murder. It was too early to leave for work but she was wired, eager to apply herself. Writing down the names of the immediate family, she intended to work outwards, and concentrate on motives and alibis. But she was painfully aware that there was little in the way of solid evidence to help their investigation.

Geoff Turner was the first name on Sam's list. Effectively,

the man had no alibi, and although he hadn't quite lied, he'd fudged his whereabouts until pressed for confirmation of his location.

Greenacres Golf Club is sure to have CCTV, Sam thought. She'd ask Layla to check it out.

'So, what about motive?' Sam spoke the words aloud. Clearly, Valerie was the main breadwinner and had been throughout lockdown when Geoff was out of work. Could he have resented this? Did they argue over money, and did Val call the shots in other aspects of their marriage? And then there was the adopted son turning up. It must have been a shock for Geoff, who, by his own admission, didn't like Ben Chapman. Would this prodigal son present a threat to him, competition for Val's affection, perhaps? But was any of this a strong enough motive to kill? Geoff *would* inherit the house, but it wasn't a mansion and, therefore, a weak motive.

Underlining the daughter's names next, Sam shifted her attention to them. They were unlikely suspects, but it was a strange world, and cases of violence among teenagers were sadly on the increase. And Kim was convinced Lizzie was lying – what was that all about? Sam decided to talk to both girls herself as soon as possible.

Ben Chapman was a strong candidate. He also didn't have an alibi. They may need to canvass his neighbours to see if anyone saw or heard him on Saturday morning. If that drew a blank, there was always CCTV to check for him leaving home, but that was some way down the line. A motive was lacking, too, unless Ben harboured ill feelings against Val for giving him up as a baby. It was a questionable stretch.

Valerie's colleagues were unlikely suspects. Initially, it would be prudent not to spend too much time looking into work colleagues – it was doubtful that the goings on at a provincial solicitor's office would provide sufficient motive for murder.

What about the neighbours? Hayley and Steve Green were friends, close in proximity if nothing else. They needed a more in-depth interview to ascertain how close the couples were and if there was a possible motive in their friendship. Compiling a list of other friends would have to be done. *Dig deeper, Sam, and wider!*

Checking her watch, Sam decided to leave for work. It was still early, but there was much to do. It was imperative to make progress, and hopefully soon.

The spectre of her nightmare was hard to shake off. Sam wondered if the dreams would ever cease or if they would haunt her forever. Friends assured her that one day, she'd be able to think and talk about Ravi with only happy memories, and when his image came to mind she would be able to smile at the recollection of their time together. She hoped they were right, and that the pain associated with thoughts of Ravi would diminish until she could remember him fondly and not dwell on how desperately she missed him. The unbearable longing for Ravi's arms around her was a very tangible sensation which, at times, made her want to scream.

Sam deliberately fixed her mind on her current case and picked up her early morning notes to take with her; they would form the basis of the team briefing and help her assign tasks for the day.

Locking the front door and turning away from the house, Sam noticed a clump of snowdrops poking their pristine bell-like heads through the cold damp earth. Having always loved the first signs of spring, she wondered why she'd not noticed them before. Perhaps her misery had clouded her vision as well as her mind.

As she drove to the station, she also noticed patches where crocuses had braved the cold to paint the verges at the side of the road with their vivid purple and yellow heads, reaching upwards, seeking the weak winter sunshine. How had she missed these, too?

Sam shook her head. Life went on, and although she was a long way from getting over losing Ravi, maybe it was time to look for the positives remaining in her life rather than dwell on the negatives.

FIFTEEN

Monday morning kicked off with a positive which all the team could celebrate. Paul and Layla arrived with beaming faces and proudly announced that Paul had passed his sergeant's exam.

Sam was the first to shake his hand and pull him into a warm hug. 'Congratulations DS Roper. You deserve it.'

Paul blushed and turned to accept the other congratulations coming his way.

Layla placed a huge box of doughnuts on the desk. 'Until we can get to the pub and celebrate properly.' She grinned, clearly delighted with her boyfriend.

Sam smiled, genuinely enjoying the buzz of excitement the news generated. Having feared the brain fog from lack of sleep would dull her senses, an encouraging start to the day went some way to cheer her up. When in the throes of an unpleasant murder case, good news was always welcome.

With the back-slapping over, Sam gathered her team and reminded them there was work to do. Her earlier notes provided focus as she outlined the objectives for them to follow and designated tasks before setting off to interview Hayley and Steve Green. She would save Lizzie Turner for later. The girl might still be sleeping; reality would dawn soon enough for her and there was no need to disturb her early.

Pulling up outside the Greens' house, Sam and Jenny noticed the CSI team two doors away at the Turners' home. It was day three of the investigation. The team should finish at the scene by evening, by tomorrow evening at the latest. Sam wondered whether Geoff Turner and his daughters would wish to return immediately.

Remembering how empty her home felt without Ravi caused a shudder – at least she was spared the disturbing image of his body in situ. Any reluctance by the Turners would be understandable.

Before leaving the station, Jenny had rung Hayley and Steve Green, and both agreed to be there.

Hayley opened the door, stepping aside to allow them entry. 'I've made coffee, or would you prefer tea?'

'Coffee will be fine, thank you.' Hayley appeared on edge; her doe-like eyes wide in anticipation as she bustled off toward the kitchen. Sam and Jenny entered the lounge and glanced around the room.

Steve Green sat in an armchair in the corner and nodded briefly to Samantha as she introduced herself and Jenny. He clearly didn't wish to talk until his wife returned to the room. The house was the same layout as that of the Turners, attractively decorated and furnished, with the smell of home baking and fresh coffee.

Samantha estimated the Greens to be similar in age to Geoff Turner, in their mid-forties or thereabouts. Steve, although seated, was clearly a tall man, like Geoff, but in better physical shape, with a full head of dark hair and a physique suggesting regular workouts. Hayley was a petite, attractive lady with blonde hair and wide blue eyes.

Hayley entered the room with a tray of coffee and biscuits. As she passed around the coffee, she asked, 'How are Geoff and the girls? We weren't sure if we should ring or if it might be too early...'

'It's a difficult time, but they might appreciate a call; you can only try.'

'Yes, I'll do that.' Hayley chewed her bottom lip and sat in the chair beside her husband.

'How long have you known the family?' Sam wanted to press on.

'Um, about ten years,' Steve answered without elaboration.

'They already lived here when we moved in, and being a similar age, we became friends,' Hayley offered.

'Would you describe your friendship as close?'

Steve looked to his wife to answer. Hayley hesitated, then said, 'Perhaps not so close now as we used to be.'

'In what way?'

'Well, when the girls were little, I often babysat for them – we don't have a family, and I was happy to help out; they're lovely girls. We did things together then, too – barbecues in the summer, out for meals together, that sort of thing and Val and I would have an occasional coffee together.'

'But not so much lately?'

'No. The girls no longer need a babysitter, and after Val's promotion at the solicitors, she became totally wrapped up in her work.'

'And what about you, Mr Green?'

'Yes, it's like Hayley said. We're still friends, but you know how it is, people move on, don't they?'

'Can I ask how you'd describe Valerie and Geoff's

relationship.' Sam glanced from one to the other, noticing the look which passed between them.

'It's difficult to say. Like any couple, they had their ups and downs, but generally, they got on okay.' Steve answered the question, and Sam looked at Hayley, waiting for her contribution to the discussion.

'Things were difficult when Geoff was laid off during lockdown. Val did say she hated having him at home and thought he should do more in the house, you know, with her out working. It wasn't serious, though. There were a few arguments, that's all.'

'Do you know of anything else which caused confrontation between them?' Sam picked up on another look between husband and wife before Steve answered.

'Geoff wasn't altogether happy about Val readily welcoming Ben into the home. He told me he felt over-ruled, as if he had no say in the matter, but Val was always the one to make the big decisions. Geoff's an easy-going bloke – anything for a quiet life – and I think he's accepted the lad now.'

'Have you met Ben Chapman?' Sam's question was directed at Hayley.

'Yes, a couple of times, although only briefly. Val was very proud of him, and he seemed like a nice young man.'

'And when was the last time you saw Val before Saturday?'

'I waved from the window on Friday evening when she arrived home from work, but we've hardly spoken properly for three or four weeks.' Hayley returned to chewing on her lip.

'And I haven't seen her for weeks – busy lives, you know?' Steve added.

'So, did you see her family leaving on Saturday morning?'

'No, sorry. I'd been on nights and came in at 8am, had some breakfast and went straight to bed.' He turned to his wife, waiting for her confirmation.

'Me neither, I'm afraid. I spent the morning catching up on the housework while Steve was in bed.'

'Well, thank you for your time and the coffee; we'll not keep you any longer, but if you do think of anything, please ring.' Sam handed Hayley her card and left the couple huddled together in their front doorway.

SIXTEEN

'What do you think of the Greens then?' They pulled away from the house, and Jenny asked the inevitable question before her boss could.

'There was nothing much to go on, although Hayley did seem quite anxious. I wondered if there was more to the cooling friendship with the Turners than they were letting on. It's quite a leap from being good friends and having coffee dates to hardly speaking for weeks.'

'Yes, I suppose, but life does get in the way. Maybe Val's friendship was offered only when she needed Hayley as a babysitter?'

'Could be. And they seemed to suggest that Val was the one to wear the trousers if that's not a sexist remark.' Sam rolled her eyes. 'Right, on to the Turner's senior. We'll see if Lizzie is any more forthcoming today.' As they travelled, Sam's phone rang.

'Hi, DS Roper.' Sam addressed Paul by his new title and imagined his face reddening.

'Um, hi... I've been onto the golf club, and the bad news is that the CCTV in the car park isn't working. They haven't bothered getting it fixed as they say they never have any trouble. Do you want me to go there and ask if anyone saw Geoff Turner on Saturday morning?'

'No, it's a bit of a long shot, and Geoff admits he didn't go into the clubhouse or see anyone. Try to trace his car through ANPR en route from the golf club to Barton Woods. There's bound to be a camera or two along there. We're on our way to see him and his daughters now. Thanks, Paul.'

Jenny grasped the gist of the conversation. 'Will you talk to him again this morning?'

'Yes, I'd like to speak to them all individually again, although I know they won't be happy about it. Perhaps Geoff's parents can offer more than when we spoke yesterday. I'd like to hear their version of their son's marriage and an opinion of their daughter-in-law. Now the shock's wearing off, they may be a little more forthcoming.'

Mary Turner opened the door, appearing calmer than before and greeting the detectives politely. 'Please come in. Geoff and Lizzie are around but Anna's still in bed. I'll tell her you're here.'

Donald Turner stood as they entered the lounge. Geoff remained seated and nodded. 'More questions?' he sounded resigned to the coming interrogation.

'I'm afraid so. Maybe we can have a chat and then talk to Lizzie?'

Donald tactfully left the room to find his wife, who'd vanished to the kitchen. When Sam and Jenny were alone with Geoff, he asked. 'Is there any news?'

'It's still early days, Geoff. The CSI should be finished with your house tomorrow, so if you want to go home, it should be okay.' Sam watched his reaction.

He turned to face the window, frowning. 'I'm not sure I can

face going back in there. And the girls... we'll have to talk about it.'

'That's perfectly understandable. I'm sure your parents won't hurry you into any decisions in that regard.'

'And is there any way you can stop the newspapers from speculating on the way Val died? Seeing their mother's picture splashed all over the pages is upsetting for the girls. Where do they get their pictures from anyway?'

'They often copy them from social media. Was Val on Facebook?'

'Yes, but she hardly used it.'

'That's probably where they copied the images from, or even off the girl's profiles. It might be a good thing to close her account down and ask the girls to avoid posting or looking at social media for now.' Jenny advised. 'We'll talk to our press officer about a release to try to halt the speculation, although there's very little we can tell early in the investigation.'

Sam moved the interview on to ask Geoff again about his whereabouts. 'We've been trying to corroborate your movements on Saturday. Unfortunately, the CCTV at the golf club, which might have confirmed your presence, isn't working. Is there anything else you can think of to help us with this?'

Geoff shook his head. 'I've told you everything I can.'

'It seems rather strange to take a walk in the woods in the rain when your plans fell through. Wouldn't you rather have gone home to the warmth and your wife?'

'Look, can't you stop your bloody prying! I'm sick of telling you the same thing – I preferred going for a walk to going home. Val liked her time alone and my presence wouldn't have been particularly welcome.' Tears filled the man's eyes. His admission presented another version of his relationship with his wife, one which wasn't quite so perfect.

'I'm sorry, Geoff. Please try to understand that we only ask what we need to. Your whereabouts will help us to eliminate you from the investigation. I know it's painful, but anything at all will be helpful.'

'There was a man walking his dog, a spaniel, I think, a fussy little thing. He had to stop it jumping up at me with its muddy paws.'

Sam smiled. 'That's great. It gives us something to work with. Can you remember the approximate time you met him?'

'I'd been walking for a while – it could have been about eleven or eleven thirty. We didn't talk much, but I like dogs. I've always wanted one but Val refused to have pets in the house.'

Sam nodded, pleased that Geoff was opening up a little more. After a few more questions, it seemed prudent to finish the interview and speak with Lizzie. 'Thanks for your help this morning, Geoff. Is Lizzie about? We'd like another word with her, please.'

Geoff left the room and called into the kitchen for his daughter. Lizzie entered the lounge with a tray of tea. 'Gran thought you might like this.' Placing the tray on the coffee table she sat down opposite Jenny.

'Thank you, that's very kind.' Jenny poured the tea while Sam turned to Lizzie. 'I need to ask you some questions which will help us in our enquiries, but first, how are you, Lizzie?'

'Don't know, really. I keep expecting Mum to walk in and tell us it's all been a mistake, but she's not going to, is she?'

'No, Lizzie. I'm so sorry. Did you and your mum get along well?'

'Yes, of course!' A defensive note crept into the girl's voice.

'I'm sure you did most of the time, but when I was your age, my mum and I were always arguing about something – make-up, boyfriends, what time to be in or when to go to bed.' Sam smiled at Lizzie, whose eyes were brimming with tears.

'I suppose we did argue sometimes. Mum was quite strict with us – me more than Anna because I'm the youngest.'

'Growing up can be hard. Parents don't always accept that we're old enough to do certain things and make our own decisions. Is that how it was with you?' Sam's question received only a nod and a slightly suspicious look. 'Lizzie, when you spoke to Kim yesterday, she had the feeling that you might not have been telling her everything about Saturday. If that's the case, it will make our job much harder. Maybe you've thought about what you said in your statement and remember things differently now. It happens, particularly when we're upset.'

Lizzie's tears flowed freely. She sniffed and picked at her fingernails in her lap. 'I wasn't with Anna when the police rang...' Taking a tissue from her sleeve, Lizzie blew her nose. 'I have a boyfriend, and Anna agreed to come to town with me and then leave us together. Mum would have gone crazy if she'd known...'

Sam nodded. 'Thank you for telling us. I know it wasn't easy. Where did you go with your boyfriend?'

'Costa Coffee, the one next to the post office. When Anna got the call to come home, she rang me and I ran to meet her – I feel awful for lying to Mum!'

'We all have regrets when someone dies, but your Mum loved you; that's the important thing to remember. Does your dad know you have a boyfriend?'

'No, but he won't mind. It was Mum who got angry when I wanted to see boys. I think Dad will be okay.'

'Then maybe it's time to talk to him about it?'

A tap on the door interrupted the interview and Mary stepped inside. 'I'm sorry but Anna doesn't feel well this morning. I think it's best if she stays in bed unless there's something important you want to see her about?'

'No, we can talk another day. We're about done here. Thank

you for the tea. Perhaps we can have a quick chat with you and your husband before we leave?'

'Oh, right, I'll just get Donald.'

'Can I go now?' Lizzie asked.

'Yes, and thank you for being honest with us, Lizzie, it really helps. Can you give Jenny the name of your boyfriend before you go?'

SEVENTEEN

The conversation in the car when leaving the Turners was a little more hopeful than on the way there. 'So, Kim was right about Lizzie lying. The poor girl must feel dreadful. Lying to her mum will be the last thing she remembers about her.' Jenny sighed.

'Yes, but it means we have to rethink the girls' whereabouts when their mother was killed.'

'I'll contact the boyfriend and confirm they were in Costa.'

'Good, but this means Anna has no alibi for Saturday morning either. She claimed to be with Lizzie, which we know isn't true, so where was she?'

'She must have been in or near town when I rang to ask her to come home, as the car picked them up within fifteen minutes of my call.'

'That was after 2pm. She'd been gone since 8.45am; time enough to go to town with Lizzie, jump on the bus to get home and kill her mother, then return to town to meet Lizzie as arranged.'

Jenny groaned. 'You don't seriously think Anna could have killed her mother, do you?'

'Maybe not intentionally, but we're now seeing a different side to Valerie Turner. Lizzie admitted there were arguments, and Val had a temper. What if Anna went home to talk to her mother about something? They argued, and Anna pushed Val, who hit her head on the worktop – remember, we haven't recovered a weapon – Anna then panicked and went back to town.' There were a few moments of silence. 'What do you think?' Sam pushed for an opinion.

'I can't see it. Or perhaps I don't want to see it. Why would she run away?'

'Oh, Jen. Don't you read detective novels – it's a classic scenario – Anna would have been frightened, thinking she'd be charged with murder. Once she's run and the lies start, it's too late to change your story, and you get deeper and deeper into it. If you remember, when the girls came home, it was Lizzie who appeared the most distressed and wanted to see her mother. Anna was quiet, almost too quiet perhaps?'

'Are you considering Anna as a viable suspect?'

'They're all viable suspects until proven otherwise. And what did you think about Mary and Donald's accounts of their son's marriage?'

'Yes, what a surprise. They'll not grieve too long, for sure. It sounds as if they didn't want Geoff to marry her in the first place. Do you think their attitude to her having had a baby and not telling Geoff could have influenced them? They seem to have decided that this secret baby confirms their suspicions that Val wasn't the woman for their son.'

'Yes, maybe Geoff listened to his parents more than his wife and it appears there were more holes in their marriage than we've been led to believe.'

'And what about Mary calling her *flighty*? Do you think she was suggesting Val was playing around?' Jenny steered into the station car park, switched off the engine and turned to Sam for an answer.

'Did she say flighty or flirty?'

'Definitely flighty, I wrote it down, but it's similar, isn't it?'

'Hmm. Flighty could be just unreliable or erratic, flirty suggests – well – flirty! Come on, let's get inside and see if the others have come up with anything.'

Sam didn't reach her office. Waiting for her in reception was Ben Chapman, who stood when she approached and hurried towards her. 'Can we talk, detective inspector?'

'Yes, of course.' Sam led him through the swing doors, closely followed by Jenny. They entered the first vacant interview room and she asked Ben to sit, taking the seat opposite him, Jenny at her side. 'What can we do for you, Ben?'

'I want to be kept abreast of the investigation. I rang Geoff last night to say how sorry I was and ask if I could help, but he won't let me in. He said it has nothing to do with me – although he did add *unless you killed her* – and he wouldn't let me speak to the girls. Can he do this? Val was my mother. Don't I have a right to know what's happening?'

'Yes, Ben, you do and I'm sorry this has happened. Geoff's hurting now. He may feel differently later. Jenny, could you rustle up some coffee, please?' Jenny left the room to arrange the drinks.

'There's very little to report yet. The investigation is still in the early stages, but we will keep you informed. The CSI will soon be finished at the house, although I don't know if the family are moving back in. Perhaps it would be better if you didn't contact them for a while; it's a difficult time for all of you and emotions can run high.'

'But the girls might want to see me. We get on well and even if Geoff doesn't like it they're my sisters.'

'Yes, but I'm asking you to give him a little time and the girls are old enough to contact you themselves if they want to.'

Ben nodded and ran his fingers through his hair. 'Are you any closer to knowing who did it?'

'I can't discuss details with you yet. As I said, it's still early days. When the CSI reports come in, they might provide clues and the autopsy will tell us the cause of death. I'll let you know the results as soon as I do.'

'But after you've told Geoff?'

'Yes. Geoff was Valerie's husband, her next of kin. He'll be notified first, then you.'

'He wasn't much of a husband, though, was he?'

'I don't know. You tell me.' Sam's interest was piqued.

'Val said he had no time for her. The marriage was dead, and I'm pretty sure she was planning to leave him.'

'Did she tell you that directly?'

'No, not in so many words, only the odd hint – things like, *I'm not putting up with him for much longer* – but she wouldn't be pressed on what she meant. I assumed she was planning to leave him, which didn't surprise me. The girls were old enough to cope and she was clearly unhappy.'

'Is there anything else Valerie said which could be relevant?'

'Like what?' Ben looked puzzled.

'Do you think there was someone else?'

'I wouldn't blame her if there was, but no, there was no mention of anyone else, so I don't think so. The way she talked, it was as if her life was about to change for the better, and there was a sort of excitement about her.' Ben looked at his watch. 'Look, I have to go but you will keep me in the loop, won't you?'

'Yes, Ben, I will, and thank you for coming in. If anything else comes to mind, please get in touch.'

As Ben left, Jenny was approaching the interview room

with three coffees. Looking at his retreating back, she shrugged. 'Well, that's good. I can chuck this stuff down the sink where it belongs. Fancy some decent coffee from the deli, boss, and then you can get me up to speed?'

Sam smiled her approval and went upstairs, leaving Jenny to dump the machine excuse for coffee and nip to the deli.

EIGHTEEN

'There's something you should see, boss.' Paul Roper greeted Sam as she entered the incident room.

'I hope it's good...'

Paul raised a quizzical eyebrow and led the way to his computer. 'This is taken from a camera at a house around the corner from the Turners. You'll see the date and time in the corner, Saturday at 10.40am.' Paul set the footage running and Sam moved in closer to peer over his shoulder. A supermarket delivery van was blocking most of the pavement and from behind it a lone figure walked across the road heading towards the Turners' street. Although grainy, the image was clear enough to identify the figure as Anna Turner as she turned her face towards the camera to check for traffic.

Sam's heart sank. She'd cited Anna as a possible suspect and even described a scenario in which the girl figured – but Sam didn't want to accept what she saw. 'If Anna's heading home, why wasn't she picked up on other cameras closer to the house?'

'Look at the direction she's walking. It's likely she turned into the lane to enter the house at the back. She moved out of camera range at that point and wasn't picked up on the other videos we've viewed – this is the only lead we've got.'

'What have I missed?' Jenny entered the room with two take-out coffees and joined the little huddle around the computer, her eyes widening as she gawped at the screen. 'Is that Anna?'

'Yes, at 10.40am, when she claimed to be in town. Thanks, Paul. It is a lead, although not one I particularly wanted.' Sam went to her desk, followed by Jenny. 'Damn it. Could Anna have killed her mother? If so, why did she break the glass in the door?

'To make it appear to be a burglary?'

'I didn't have her down as that calculating.'

'Is this enough to make an arrest?' Jenny frowned, clearly not relishing this any more than her boss.

'It's enough to bring her into the station for questioning under caution. I'll have to inform DCI Kent; he'll want to know there's been a development, and then we'll bring her in. See if you can get an appropriate adult to sit in. Even though she's sixteen, I want someone there for her. And preferably not a family member.'

DCI Aiden Kent's voice boomed, 'Come in'when Sam knocked on his door. 'Ah, Samantha, how are you?' He removed his glasses and laid them on the desk, giving Sam his full attention.

'Very well, sir. Thank you. There's been a development in the Turner case, and I'm about to bring someone in to question under caution.'

'Excellent news, good work. Who is it?'

'It's the victim's sixteen-year-old daughter, sir. In her original statement, Anna claimed to be shopping in town with her sister, but her sister has since admitted that they split up to go their separate ways. DS Roper's been trawling neighbours' CCTV and Anna is seen heading home at 10.40am, which fits our time frame.'

Aiden Turner stroked his chin thoughtfully. 'Does this surprise you, Samantha?'

'Yes, it does. There's friction in the family but I didn't think it sufficient to warrant murder. Anna doesn't strike me as capable of such an act. Perhaps it was an accident.'

'You're right, you have to bring her in. It's the only way forward.'

Sam returned to the incident room. Suddenly, this case wasn't the distraction she needed – it was getting to her. A young girl murdering her mother? Surely not.

Jenny bustled over as she entered the room. 'I've got a member of the youth justice team on standby. Do you want me to send a car to pick Anna up now?'

'Yes, but ask Kim to go too. A familiar face might make it easier. Then can you get the team together to see if there's anything else to go on?'

Ten minutes later a car was on its way to bring in Anna Turner, and DI Freeman was addressing her team. After updating them, she asked if there was any news from forensics.

'Nothing of interest. They've taken DNA samples from the victim's fingernails, clothing and a ring she was wearing but there's a backlog for processing – twelve days I'm afraid.' Layla grimaced while imparting the news.

'Twelve days will slow us up considerably. Can you have another word, Layla and see if it can be fast-tracked?'

'The twelve days is for fast-tracking, but I'll have another try.'

'Thanks. Anything from the CSI search? They must be nearly finished by now?'

DC Tom Wilson coughed and raised his hand. 'They'll be finished by this evening.' He glanced at his notebook. 'There's no sign of a murder weapon and nothing appears to be missing, so a burglary looks unlikely. The only thing out of place was a candlestick near the body. They've taken prints, but there was no blood, so it can't be the weapon; maybe the perpetrator took whatever it was with him?'

'Thanks, Tom, well done. What about the autopsy? Is it still on for this afternoon?'

'Yes, boss. It's 3.30pm if you want to be there.' Paul answered.

'Or I could take it?' Jenny was quick to offer.

'I'll be fine for 3.30. We should be finished with Anna by then.'

NINETEEN

'You do not have to say anything, but it may harm your defence if you do not mention something when questioned that you later rely on in court.' Jenny recited the words to their very pale suspect, and then the four people in the room took their seats. Jen announced their names for the tape: herself, DI Freeman, Andrea Mason from the YJT, and Anna Turner.

'Thank you for coming in this afternoon, Anna. I hope you're feeling better than this morning.' Sam smiled at the girl, hoping to ease some of the tension in her face. Anna shrugged and appeared to shrink even further down in her seat. 'If you'd like a solicitor present, we can arrange for one of the duty solicitors to come and advise you.' Another shrug. 'Anna, you need to speak your answers out loud for the tape – it's to help protect you as much as us. Would you like a solicitor?'

'No. I'd like to get on with this and go home.'

'Do you know why you've been brought here?'

'Yeah. Lizzie admitted she'd told you we weren't together on Saturday morning. I'm sorry I lied, but she didn't want anyone to know she was seeing a boy.'

'This isn't the only reason we asked you to come in. I want to show you a video clip from a CCTV camera near your home and then I'd like you to explain it to me.' Sam swivelled her laptop to face Anna and tapped the screen. The image of herself walking along the street captured Anna's attention immediately. Her mouth dropped open, and her face paled even more. When the short clip finished, Samantha turned it off and looked at Anna, who promptly burst into tears.

'I think we might need a break, detective inspector.' Andrea Mason whipped out a packet of tissues and passed one to Anna, sliding her arm around the girl's shoulder.

'I'll organise some tea,' Jenny said as she and Sam left the room.

Kim Thatcher caught them up in the corridor. 'Geoff Turner's here. He wants to know what's going on and why you're interviewing Anna.'

'Why doesn't that surprise me?' Sam sighed. 'You see to the tea, Jen, while Kim and I talk to Geoff.'

Geoff Turner was pacing the interview room where Kim had left him. 'What's going on?' he barked as they entered.

'Please sit down and we'll tell you.' When they were seated, Sam continued. 'We have evidence to prove that Anna lied to us in her statement...'

'I know. Lizzie told me she'd covered for her so she could meet a boy, but why bring her here? The girl's just lost her mother!'

'It's more than that. Our evidence places Anna near your home at 10.40am on Saturday morning.'

'No, that can't be right. She was still in town even though Lizzie had left her!'

'Not according to the footage we have and which Anna has seen.'

'I want to see her! Where is she?'

'She's in an interview room with a member of the Youth Justice Team. Anna's been cautioned and has declined to have a solicitor present. We're giving her a break so she can re-consider.'

'Too right she needs a solicitor! I don't want her answering any questions until she has one.'

'I agree. Would you like a solicitor of your choosing, or shall I organise a duty solicitor?'

'I don't know any solicitors other than those Val worked with – will you sort it?' Geoff's anger was abating. His face reflected pain and confusion. Sam wondered what was going on in the man's head.

It was nearly an hour before the interview could resume. When the duty solicitor arrived, Andrea Mason was no longer needed. After allowing Anna time to speak to her solicitor, Jenny reminded her that she was still under caution.

The girl had clearly been crying. Her face was blotchy, her eyes red and swollen. 'Are you okay to continue now, Anna?' Samantha was concerned for their suspect, but her solicitor, Deana Jones, spoke for her.

'Anna would like to make a statement. She regrets misleading you before, and once you hear her explanation, I think you'll understand why she lied.' Deana nodded to Anna, whose hands trembled on her knees. The girl looked terrified but managed to look Sam in the eyes as she spoke.

'I'm sorry I lied but I was afraid. I didn't intend to go back to the house, and I wish I hadn't, but I was angry with Mum. Lizzie wanted to meet her boyfriend but Mum would have gone ballistic if she'd known, so we said we were going shopping. I meant to stay in town too, but Lizzie had been going on about how strict Mum was and that she treated us like babies – which is true – and we'd both had enough. So I thought I'd go back and have it out with Mum once and for all. She was at home alone, and I knew Dad wouldn't be back for ages, so it seemed like a good opportunity.

'I was angry. Mum had been acting strange lately. The only one who could do anything right was Ben. I sometimes thought she preferred him to us. Mum was always mad at Dad and us, but never with Ben. I thought I could talk to her, just the two of us, and tell her how we felt, how she was being unfair to us and Dad. I nipped down the back lane and in through the garden and noticed the glass panel in the door was smashed. I was scared but everything was quiet so I went inside, thinking Mum had had an accident and broken the glass – and then I saw her on the floor in a pool of blood. I tried to scream for help but couldn't. My legs felt like jelly and I thought I was going to be sick. It was weird. Mum was clearly dead. I went a bit closer to make sure, it was horrible!' Anna blew her nose on a crumpled tissue, sniffed and then continued.

'After that, it's all a blur. I remember running out of the back door. Part of me knew I should get help but I also knew it was too late to save her and I felt guilty. Having gone home to confront Mum, to have a row if necessary, it seemed that she was dead because of me. I know that's stupid, and honestly, I didn't kill her – I wouldn't, but I'd had such terrible thoughts about her lately. I loved my Mum, but at times, I hated her, and it felt as if she was dead because of me... I caught the bus back to town and wandered around aimlessly, waiting until it was time to meet Lizzie. I lost track of time, and then DS Newcombe rang to tell me I had to go home.'

Tears streamed down Anna's face as she spoke, and she wiped it with a crumpled tissue. Sam and Jenny remained silent while the story unfolded. It was being recorded, and they could question Anna later if necessary.

When the girl appeared to run out of words, Sam said, 'Thank you, Anna. We'll have another break and bring you some more tea.' She switched off the tape.

'Can't I go home?'

'Not yet. Perhaps you can have a chat with Ms Jones while we make some decisions.'

TWENTY

'Come in!' Déjà vu swept through Sam as, for the second time that day, she stood outside DCI Kent's office, this time with Jenny beside her. Having briefly discussed the startling interview, they agreed it was appropriate to consult the DCI before taking the action they favoured.

'Have you interviewed the girl?' he asked. The DCI quickly put down his pen and a frown crossed his brow.

'Yes, sir,' said Sam. She could tell her boss didn't like the idea of the daughter being involved any more than she did. 'Anna's admitted returning to the house, claiming she wanted to discuss family problems while her mother was alone. Anna insists the back door was already smashed, and she found her mother dead on the floor. Panic set in, and as she wasn't supposed to be there, she fled.'

'And your thoughts on this revised version of the truth?' He rested his elbows on his desk and steepled his fingers.

'I believe her, sir.'

'And I concur,' Jenny added.

'Anna was an unlikely suspect from the outset, and even with their family problems, it doesn't strike me as sufficient motive for a sixteen-year-old girl to turn to murder. I've had Layla Gupta speak to her school this morning, and the impression they give is of a well-balanced student with no trouble in her background and the potential to do well in her exams.'

'Hmm. So, what do you want to do?'

'I'd like to release her without charge. I believe the family are staying indefinitely with the grandparents, and I don't see her as a flight risk.'

'But she is your only suspect?'

'Not quite, sir. There are other alibis we're checking. However, it's early in the investigation, and I'm hopeful forensics will come back with something. The autopsy is this afternoon.'

'Right. Keep me posted. And, Samantha, are you all right?'

'Yes, sir. Thank you.'

Once outside the DCI's office, Sam clicked her tongue against her teeth. 'That's the second time he's asked if I'm okay today. I wish people would stop fussing.'

'They're concerned, Sam, that's all. We're your friends as well as work colleagues. We care.'

'I know. Sorry for being grumpy. And now I have the dubious pleasure of an autopsy to attend. I'm running late, so I'll leave you to explain to Anna and her dad what's happening, okay?'

'Yes, boss.'

'And ask Kim to visit the Turners on her way home this evening. I'd like to know what the mood is among the family after this afternoon's revelations. Tell her to ring me if there's anything to report.'

Rick Fielding, the pathologist, greeted Sam with a smile as she entered the autopsy suite ten minutes later, ready for the summing up. She felt relieved that the days of detectives attending the full autopsy were in the past. Her time and the force's budget were better spent elsewhere.

'Are you okay?' was the first thing Rick said. Sam remembered Jenny's words and, resisting the urge to hit him over the head, thanked him and answered in the affirmative even though a knot was forming in the pit of her stomach.

The smell of death in the room seemed more pungent than usual, and Sam breathed through her mouth to lessen the odour. As she moved closer to the examination table, her head spun, and she wondered if she could do this.

Most of Valerie Turner's body was covered in a white sheet and Sam frequently needed to look at her face to remind herself it wasn't Ravi's body on the slab. The woman looked peaceful and quite beautiful, her matted hair the only clue to the vicious attack which killed her. Sam thought she could have been sleeping if it wasn't for the Y-incision visible above the sheet.

Rick switched to professional mode and reeled off his findings. 'It's pretty much as we thought.' He turned the cadaver to reveal a bloodied wound on the left side of her head, visible where her hair had been cut away. 'Death was caused by a blow from a heavy instrument, something smooth and probably heavy. The resulting depressed fracture would have caused immediate death. Judging from the angle, our victim must have been facing her attacker, who was right-handed. The murder weapon was wielded with considerable strength.'

'What about the possibility that she fell and hit her head on the work surface?'

'I'm afraid not. The locus of the injury rules out that scenario. The wound would have been at the back of the cranium rather than the top.'

Sam was deflated but required more information. 'Does the force indicate a man?'

'Or an angry woman, but someone reasonably tall or with a long reach, I would guess.'

'How about a golf club?'

'Yes, I could see that. A steel golf wedge could fit the bill.' Rick raised an imaginary golf club over his head and brought it down hard. 'You'd do some damage with a blow from one of those.'

Samantha flinched as his hand came close to her head. 'Anything from forensics yet?'

'Now, Sam. You know better than that. They're working flat out on this one and you'll be the first to know.'

Rick dipped his head again and continued his report. By the time he'd finished, Sam was almost frantic to get out. It was all too much. Samantha felt nauseous, and when Rick finished his summation, she was the first to leave the room, hurrying out to fill her lungs with fresh air.

Outside, the night was closing in, and the encroaching darkness and early evening sounds of traffic and people going about their routines seemed almost comforting.

Samantha decided to head straight home, where she could gather her thoughts, hopefully, get some rest, and pick up the investigation with a clearer mind the following morning.

TWENTY-ONE

DC Tom Wilson was in the incident room when Sam arrived the following morning. 'Tom, I want you to ring Geoff Turner and ask him where his golf clubs are. When you find out, get them and bring them in for testing as a priority: we could be looking at our murder weapon.'

'Yes, boss.' Tom grinned, clearly relishing his role on the team. Samantha moved off to find Jenny so they could return to Valerie Turner's place of work.

Portland Street was busy on Tuesday morning as Samantha and Jenny headed towards Hammond, Birch and Fox, solicitors. Sam had spoken briefly to Alex Hammond on the phone to inform him of Valerie Turner's death, and now they were visiting the office for the second time with the aim of interviewing those who worked closely with their victim.

Jenny still insisted on driving and muttered to herself when it was clear she'd have to park in the multi-storey. The last time she'd used the concrete edifice, she'd scraped the side of her car, an expensive blunder. Finding a space on the third level, Jenny parked with extra care, and they set off towards the solicitor's office.

Standing in the lobby waiting for someone to allow them entry, it appeared a different place to their visit on Saturday. Through the glass doors, people scurried in all directions, and when they were finally let inside, the foyer seemed smaller than previously. Although the detectives hadn't made an appointment, Mr Hammond knew they would be coming and had agreed that Tuesday would be a good time to catch him and his colleagues in the office. It was a day they reserved for their partner meeting.

After they had waited for a few minutes in the foyer, a secretary arrived and invited them to follow her to Mr Hammond's office.

Alex Hammond stood to greet them, crossed the spacious office with an outstretched hand, and after shaking hands with them, offered a seat. Samantha noticed the plush carpet into which her feet sank and the leather-topped desk beneath a large picture window. The firm must be doing well. The walls held prints of Stubbs horse paintings and framed professional certificates of Hammond's achievements. Several golf trophies were displayed on a wall of shelves among thick tomes of legal books. Alex Hammond was a tall, slim man in his early to mid-fifties, Sam guessed, with receding grey hair and green eyes.

'What a terrible business.' He shook his head in disbelief. 'Val was such a large personality and an excellent office manager. She'll be greatly missed here.'

'I'm sorry for your loss, and thank you for seeing us, Mr Hammond.'

'It's no problem – anything at all we can do to help, just ask.'

'Thank you. How long have you known Mrs Turner?' Sam took him at his word.

'Actually, only for a few months. I moved to New Middridge last summer, before which I was based in Carlisle. The opportunity arose for me to buy into the firm here, and I took it, so I haven't known Val for very long. Perhaps James Birch can tell you more. He's the longest-serving partner and knew Val when she started here as a junior accountant.'

'Maybe we can see Mr Birch next?'

'Certainly. I'll get my secretary to tell him you're here. I'm sure he'll make himself available. We all want to help in any way we can.' Hammond gave the instructions through an intercom.

'What were Mrs Turner's responsibilities in her role as office manager?'

'Val was responsible for supervising and monitoring the work of our administrative staff. She managed the office budget, processed invoices and maintained procedures and office systems. Oh, she also organised induction programmes for new employees. Val knew the workings of the firm inside out.'

'So, Mrs Turner would know all of the staff here?'

'Absolutely. She'll be difficult to replace.'

'Did she get on with her colleagues? Was she well-liked?'

'Generally, yes. As I say, I haven't known her as long as the others, but she appeared to work well with everyone.'

'Are you aware of any tension between Mrs Turner and any other members of staff?'

'Not at all.' Hammond blinked as if surprised at the question. 'She was very professional with a great work ethic. I don't think Val socialised with any of the more junior staff. It wouldn't have been appropriate. When you're in a managerial role, you have to maintain a certain distance, which she achieved successfully. As far as I was aware, Val was respected and well-liked.'

Samantha nodded her understanding. 'Thank you, Mr Hammond. Perhaps we could talk to Mr Birch now, and then some of the staff who worked more directly with Mrs Turner?'

'Yes, certainly. I'll get my secretary to show you the way and then feel free to talk to the admin staff. You'll probably find some of them on their break in the staff room soon.'

Mr Birch's office was smaller and more welcoming than Hammond's ostentatious décor. He was an older man, sixtyish, with a pleasant, ruddy face and deep-set eyes. His smile was wide when he greeted them. 'Please sit down. Terrible business this. I still can't quite believe it. Who would want to kill Valerie, the poor girl? How are her family coping?'

'With difficulty, as you can imagine, but they have help. Thank you for seeing us, Mr Birch. I believe you've known Valerie longer than your partners have?'

'Yes. I'd just been made a junior partner when she started here as a clerk. It didn't take long for Val to learn the ropes, and she very quickly became an invaluable member of staff. Such a bright young woman – terrible to end up like this.'

'Did Valerie have any particular friends here?'

Mr Birch frowned. 'Do you know, I can't say she did. She was pleasant enough but a stickler for propriety, which could have made her appear somewhat aloof. Val wasn't much for socialising, either. It was all work as far as she was concerned, which was good for us. She kept the place running like clockwork.'

'What involvement did she have with your clients?'

'Not much, certainly not face to face, although she would be the one to prepare invoices. Val's work was all behind the scenes, but if you're looking for suspects on our client list, you won't find any. As you probably know, we don't handle criminal law. Peter Fox and I deal mainly with family law, and Alex specialises in corporate law.'

'So, can you tell us anything that might help our investigation?'

James Birch paused as if considering his next words. 'Well, I don't know how relevant it is, but Val had spoken to me recently about drawing up divorce papers for her.'

Sam's eyes widened. 'And had you done so?'

'No. She only asked last week and I suggested she think it over and maybe discuss it with her husband. I don't believe she'd told him then, but of course, she may have done since.'

Samantha thanked Mr Birch for his time, and then he directed the two detectives to the staff room where, as Alex Hammond had predicted, three of the secretaries were taking their coffee break. Samantha and Jenny accepted the offer of coffee and began an informal chat with the three employees who had worked under Valerie Turner's supervision.

TWENTY-TWO

'Grandad doesn't usually go shopping with Gran, does he? Do you think they wanted to get out of the house, away from us?' Lizzie looked solemnly at her sister.

'If so, I can't say I blame them. It's not much fun having three extra people in the house. There's barely enough space to breathe as it is. Even the bloody weather stops us from getting out, although there's nowhere to go, is there?'

'I don't think I'll ever want to go home again!' Tears welled in Lizzie's eyes. 'Was it very awful, you know, seeing Mum like that?'

'Of course it was awful! What do you expect?' Anna had a catch to her voice. 'I've never seen a dead body before, and for it to be Mum...' She turned away from her sister to hide her tears. 'Let's not talk about it, eh?'

'But it's all I can think about! I was out with Craig enjoying myself, and I'd lied to Mum! I feel so ashamed.' The tears flowed freely.

Anna turned to hug her sister. 'It'll be okay. Dry your eyes before Dad comes in. He has enough to worry about. We have to be strong for him.'

Lizzie sniffed and blew her nose. The doorbell interrupted their conversation, and Anna went to answer it.

———

'Hello, Anna. How are you this morning?' DC Kim Thatcher followed the girl into the lounge and smiled at Lizzie. 'Is your dad in, or your grandparents?'

'No. Dad's driven them to the shops; he should be back soon. Have you any news?'

'Sorry, there's nothing yet.'

'DI Freeman rang Dad last night to tell him the autopsy results. He said they confirmed it was murder... is that right?'

Kim looked pained. If only there was something positive to offer. 'I'm afraid it is. The pathologist is convinced your mum's injuries couldn't have been caused by a fall.' Before they could talk further, the doorbell rang again, and Anna jumped up to answer. Returning to the room with a smile on her face, Ben Chapman followed behind.

'Ben!' Lizzie jumped up and threw herself into Ben's arms. More tears flowed as the siblings hugged each other, and it took several minutes for them to compose themselves enough to sit down. Ben was introduced to Kim and shook her hand before turning his attention to his sisters.

'How are you managing?' Ben looked from Anna to Lizzie.

'Not well. The police are saying it was murder – there's no way it could have been an accident.'

'Yes, I know. DI Freeman rang me last night. Where's your dad?'

'He's out. He'll be back soon.' A knowing look passed between Anna and Ben, which didn't go unnoticed by Kim Thatcher. The sound of a car on the drive caused them all to turn towards the window. Lizzie shrank back in her seat, and

Anna chewed on her fingernails. The car door slammed, and the front door opened. Even Kim wondered what Geoff Turner's reaction to seeing Ben would be.

'What the hell are you doing here?' Geoff's face was scarlet.

Ben jumped to his feet, his chin lifting in a defiant attitude. 'I wanted to see the girls.'

Geoff swivelled to face Anna. 'Did you tell him we were here?' He growled.

'Yes. Ben has lost his mother, too, and we wanted to see him!'

Geoff took two steps forward and grabbed Ben's shoulder, dragging him towards the door. Ben pulled back and was rewarded with Geoff's fist connecting to his jaw. Kim Thatcher moved quickly. 'Stop this!' She ordered, stepping between the two men so they couldn't continue the fracas. 'Ben, I think perhaps you should leave. Your presence isn't helping. Maybe you could see the girls another time?'

Ben, rubbing his bruised chin, nodded, threw a black look at Geoff, and headed for the door. Anna pushed past her father to follow him, with Lizzie close behind.

'Hey, come back!' Geoff shouted, but the front door slammed behind them, leaving only Kim and an agitated Geoff in the room. 'They can't just go off with him like that!' he bellowed.

'If you're unhappy about him coming to the house, perhaps you could give them a little space. The girls are old enough to meet with him elsewhere, and I'm sure they'll be sensible – trying to stop them from seeing their half-brother will probably make the situation worse. Look, I'll make us a cup of tea and we can have a chat.' Kim left Geoff with his head in his hands. In the kitchen, she leaned against the worktop and sighed. Ben's visit could have turned into a nasty incident – Kim was glad she'd been there.

Returning with the tea, she noted that Geoff hadn't moved. Kim handed him a steaming mug and sat opposite him on the sofa. 'I'll ring Anna before I go and see if they want a lift home. Is that okay?'

'Yes.' Geoff lifted his head and muttered thank you. Kim noticed he'd been crying.

'I understand why you don't want the girls to see Ben, but perhaps it's the wrong time to tackle this problem. Ben might still be a novelty, but you're their dad. They need you on their side more than ever now.'

'I'm sorry. Flying off the handle was a stupid thing to do, but I don't trust Ben. I don't know why Val made such a fuss of him or why the girls do – there's something off about him.'

'As I say, having a big brother is probably still a novelty.'

'No, there's more to it, you don't understand... when he came along, Val didn't seem to want me or need me anymore. She changed. He completely took the three of them in, and I didn't seem to figure in Val's life anymore. Yeah, it might sound like jealousy and I suppose it was, but she listened to him, someone she'd known only a few months, and she never listened to me – I was always in the wrong. I'd known for ages that Val didn't love me anymore, yet since Ben arrived on the scene, it was more obvious. Life was becoming bloody impossible; he made me feel like an outsider in my own home, and I didn't know what to do about it.'

Tears rolled down Geoff's face as he spoke, and Kim shuddered, wondering if he was on the verge of confessing to killing his wife. He was talking so much more openly than before. Simultaneously excited and fearful, Kim puzzled over what to do. She could hardly call the DI and interrupt his flow. Should she surreptitiously attempt to record his words? No, he'd notice and clam up or even become violent. Her only option was to listen and see where the conversation led. Kim sipped her tea and remained silent, trying to arrange her features into an open, empathic expression.

'Val was the strong one in our marriage. Hell, I often felt like one of the children, certainly not an equal *partner*. She wasn't averse to putting me down in public, either. I'll admit she had the brains, but superior intelligence is no excuse to ridicule others. And Val knew how to get what she wanted, and not just from me.

'My mother always said she was a flirt, which I knew, yet I never thought she'd act on it. But she bloody did! Val had an affair with Steve Green, of all people, and he was supposed to be a friend! I didn't blame him entirely; if Val wanted something, she went all out to get it. When I found out, she laughed in my face – said I wasn't man enough for her, so she had to go elsewhere! Yet she was the one making me sleep in the box room – it wasn't my choice!

'Hell, she could be a frustrating woman, but I still loved her. Who would kill her, Kim, and why?' Geoff looked pleadingly at Kim as if she could answer his questions.

'I don't know, Geoff, but we're doing our best to find out.'

TWENTY-THREE

After James Birch's surprising revelation and an enlightening conversation with three of Valerie Turner's colleagues, Sam and Jenny returned to the station. They broke their journey only to grab a take-out sandwich and coffee each.

Eating in the corner of the incident room, they discussed the morning's visit. A thoughtful Jenny asked, 'I wonder if Geoff had any idea Val wanted a divorce. More importantly, would it be a motive for murder?' Sipping her coffee, she waited for her boss's comments.

'A crime of passion, maybe? If Valerie had chosen Saturday morning to tell him she was filing for divorce, it could have caused a row, one which escalated into violence.'

'And if we can't find Geoff's friendly dog walker, he hasn't got an alibi.'

'Exactly. Val's turning out to be something of an enigma – well-liked by the partners, yet those she had charge of had reservations. I got the impression she wasn't popular, perhaps even a bit of a bully if they made a mistake. Val may have run a tight ship, but it didn't make her any friends, and did you notice that phrase again, *not a warm character*?'

Jenny nodded in agreement. 'Yes, they were polite, but it seemed to be a case of not speaking ill of the dead. I don't think Val will be missed or that many tears will be shed among the staff she was responsible for.'

As they downed the last dregs of coffee, Tom Wilson approached them. 'Turner's golf clubs are with forensics. I caught him just before he took his parents shopping and they were in his boot. Having half-expected some resistance, he surprised me by handing them over without question. Forensics say they'll get straight onto it.'

As Tom left, a swagger in his gait, a somewhat flushed Kim rushed into the incident room. 'You'll never guess what happened at the Turners' house this morning!'

'You're right, I won't so spit it out.' Jenny grinned.

'When I arrived, Anna and Lizzie were alone. I'd hardly got inside before Ben Chapman turned up, and the girls were all over him. Their relationship seems very close, but things sort of soured when Geoff arrived home. He was livid and grabbed Ben to throw him out. Ben got a whack on his chin for resisting, and I had to step in to stop the violence from escalating. Ben agreed to go, and the girls followed him out. I made tea and took the opportunity to chat with Geoff. At one point, I thought he was going to confess to killing his wife – but he didn't. He admitted to problems in their marriage, things he hadn't said before, like them sleeping in separate rooms – and Val having had an affair with Steve Green!'

'Steve Green? I thought there was something they weren't telling us. No wonder the friendship had cooled.' Samantha nodded at Kim to continue.

'Geoff said he was aware Val no longer loved him, that she was the strong one and the brains of the marriage. He also claimed she belittled him, even in public, but despite all of this, he maintains he still loved her and wanted the marriage to work.'

'What was your opinion of these revelations?'

'I believed him. Geoff was quite emotional, and what he told me must have been hard to admit, but my gut feeling is that he was telling the truth. It's as if some form of coercive control was in play within their marriage. I've always thought of it being a man thing, but in this case, it was clearly Val who held the upper hand.'

'Good work, Kim. Did the girls come back?'

'Yes. I intended to ring Anna to check their whereabouts, but they returned home before I left. The mood was heavy; they were angry with Geoff, but he apologised, and I left them sitting together, attempting to sort out the situation. I think Geoff realises he'll have to pick his battles carefully and maybe allow them to see their brother.'

'Right. We need a team update.' Sam's chair scraped loudly on the floor as she hurriedly stood to call the team together.

'New developments, folks.' She smiled briefly, her mind computing what Geoff's revelations meant. 'It appears that Val and Geoff's marriage was in trouble. Kim has learned they were sleeping in separate rooms, and Val had had an affair with Steve Green, the neighbour. Naturally, this pushes the Greens up the suspect list – a spurned lover or a jealous wife? It gives them both a motive.

'We also discovered this morning that Val had spoken to a solicitor about a divorce. It appears she was popular with the solicitors as she ran a tight ship, but not with those she had responsibility for. The consensus was that Val could be a bully, but it's unlikely we'll find sufficient motive among the staff at Hammond, Birch and Fox... Although Layla, could you check out the list of employees? Paul, I want you to do a full background check on Steve and Hayley Green. Jenny, I think we need to pay another visit to Mr and Mrs Green.'

TWENTY-FOUR

As Sam and Jenny were about to leave, the sergeant at the front desk rang to say a Mr and Mrs Edwards were in reception asking to see the detective in charge of the Turner case.

'I'll be down in a minute.' Sam threw her coat back onto her chair, shrugged at Jenny and indicated to her DS to follow her.

Robert and Bella Edwards were seated in the reception area, looking anxiously around. Their eyes settled on Samantha, and Bella's face turned white. Mrs Edwards was a petite, frail woman with a long, pale face that seemed almost ghostly in the artificial light. She was pressed against her husband as if seeking warmth or strength, her slight frame nearly disappearing into his side. Mr Edwards, though equally lean, towered over her, his wiry frame accentuated by a shock of thick, unruly grey hair that defied the solemnity of the moment. Both were impeccably dressed in woollen coats, their neat attire at odds with the grief that clung to them. There was a stiffness about them, not in posture, but in how sorrow seemed to hold them rigid as if bracing against a tide of emotion too great to bear.

'Mr and Mrs Edwards? I'm DI Freeman. How can we help you?'

The couple rose to their feet and Robert offered his hand. Sam shook it and smiled, a smile which faded with the man's next words.

'We've come about Valerie Turner. We're her parents.'

To say Sam was shocked was an understatement. 'Right, okay...' She quickly recovered her composure and asked the pair to follow her to an interview room.

Jenny opened the swing doors for them to pass through and whispered to her boss, 'The family room's vacant. It might be more comfortable in there.'

Sam nodded and led the way. When they were seated, Jenny offered coffee, which was accepted, and left the room to find someone to organise it. On her return, Bella Edwards was wiping her eyes with a cotton handkerchief.

Sam updated Jen. 'I've just explained to Mr and Mrs Edwards that we were unaware Val's parents were still living. It appears they lost contact with Val when she was eighteen and haven't seen or heard from her since.'

'I'm so sorry.' Jenny sat down. 'And how did you find out about her death?'

'From the newspapers. Her picture was on the front page... it was such a shock.' Robert Edwards' eyes grew watery.

'It would be and I'm sorry you had to find out like that. It would be helpful if you could fill us in on what happened with Valerie when you last saw her.'

'Yes, of course.' Robert cleared his throat and sat up in his chair. 'Valerie had always been a difficult child, and in her teenage years, things grew worse. We tried to be understanding but Val was unreasonable, wanting to be grown up before her time, as most teenagers do, I suppose.' Bella Edwards held her husband's hand as he spoke and nodded in agreement, occasionally dabbing her eyes with a tissue.

'At fourteen, she started dating boys. We weren't too happy about it, yet we encouraged her to bring her friends, boys and girls, home so we could meet them. She refused and rarely told us where she was going when she went out, ignoring any time limits we set for her to be home. I know it sounds trivial, but it was often one in the morning when she came home, and sometimes she smelled of alcohol and cigarettes. We were out of our minds with worry. Then we heard from the school that she was truanting – a shame because Val was such a bright girl. She could have gone far.'

Bella nodded enthusiastically. 'She'd been at the top of the class in most subjects until then.' Her husband patted her hand and continued his story.

'The social services became involved, but she wouldn't listen to them, and their visits eventually dropped off. They said if she refused to engage, there was nothing they could do unless the situation escalated. Those four years were the worst of our lives. We tried to understand, to be lenient, to get alongside her, but the more we tried the further away Val seemed to drift. It got to the point when she was sixteen or seventeen that she was staying out all night, coming home only to change her clothes and eat.'

The door opened, and a PC brought in a tray of coffee. When he left and closed the door, Jenny passed the cups around, and they waited until Robert was ready to continue.

'After years of constant rows, we were worn down. Valerie turned eighteen and her lifestyle didn't change. One day we came home from shopping to find she'd gone – packed her things and moved out without even a note to say where she was going.' Robert paused again. His wife sat alongside him, silently weeping.

'Thank you for sharing this with us. It must have been difficult. Was that the last time you heard from your daughter?'

'It was. We contacted the few of her friends we knew about but they could tell us nothing.'

'Did you report her as missing?' Jenny asked.

The couple exchanged a look and Bella spoke quietly. 'Valerie hadn't only packed her things; she'd taken some of ours. The television, my jewellery, an amount of cash we kept in the house. We were devastated and didn't know what to do. If we went to the police, there'd be awkward questions. Val was still our daughter, despite what she'd done, and we didn't want her to be dragged back home as a criminal. Besides, she was eighteen and had left by her own free will...'

Robert picked up the narrative again. 'Over the following few days we realised the scale of Val's deceit. She'd taken Bella's debit card – we didn't miss it at first as Bella hardly uses it. By the time we cancelled it at the bank, she'd managed to withdraw most of our current account. She'd also taken our building society passbook – which we hadn't thought to check, and by the time we discovered it was gone, Val had somehow managed to withdraw our savings.'

Samantha was appalled by the Edwards' revelations. 'I'm sorry you've been through such a difficult time, and thank you for telling us. It can't have been easy. Do you think Val left because of her pregnancy?'

'Pregnancy? What pregnancy?' Two stunned faces turned towards Sam who reached over to grab the cup from Bella's hand before it fell to the floor. The woman was trembling, tears falling freely.

Sam's heart went out to this couple as she explained, 'Valerie had a son when she was eighteen. She gave him up for adoption, but in recent times, they've been reunited.' To learn of their daughter's death and her pregnancy must be hard to process.

'So, are you saying we have a grandson?' Bella's voice cracked with emotion.

Jenny looked at her boss, who nodded. 'You also have two granddaughters, Anna and Lizzie. And a son-in-law, Geoff.'

Bella put her head in her hands and wept. Samantha stood. 'Would you like some time alone? We'll come back in ten minutes or so?'

'Yes, thank you.' Robert held his wife as she wept.

'Wow!' Jenny rolled her eyes, 'Is there no end to the lies that woman has told?'

'It seems not, and I'm inclined to believe everything they've said. It looks like our visit to the Greens will have to wait until tomorrow, Jenny. You and I could be in for a long evening.'

Samantha's words proved accurate. They spent another hour and a half with Robert and Bella Edwards before, after more talking, more tears and more disgusting coffee, the exhausted couple left the station to return to the Travel Lodge, where they'd booked a room.

TWENTY-FIVE

Hayley Green was taking a batch of scones from the oven when the doorbell rang. A frown creased her brow as she hoped it wouldn't wake Steve. He was still sleeping after another night shift, and her husband didn't take kindly to being disturbed.

Hayley was surprised to see the two detectives on her doorstep. 'Oh, hello. Did you want to come in?' She hesitated briefly, then stood aside to allow them to enter.

'Is your husband at home, Mrs Green?' Samantha asked.

'Yes, but he's sleeping. Steve was on night shift last night. Can I help?'

'Hopefully, yes, but we'll still need to speak to your husband.'

Hayley showed them into the lounge. Wary and wondering why they were in her home again after they'd answered all their questions yesterday, she decided not to offer coffee in the hope the visit would be short. She waited for the detectives to speak.

'Have you thought of anything else which may be relevant to our investigation?' Samantha looked directly at Hayley, who appeared surprised.

'No, nothing. As I told you yesterday, I didn't see anyone on Saturday morning, so I can't help you.'

'Did you know your husband and Valerie Turner had been having an affair?'

Hayley was shocked by the detective's directness and wished Steve was with her now. How had they found out? Surely Geoff wouldn't have told them. She lifted her chin in a slightly defiant attitude. 'Yes, I knew, but I also knew it was over – Steve made a mistake which he bitterly regrets, and we've put it behind us now.' Hayley watched Samantha nod slowly and dithered over what else to say. 'Perhaps I should wake Steve?' *Damn it! He should answer these awkward questions – it was down to him – why should I have to suffer the embarrassment of discussing our private life with the police?*

'Yes, that's a good idea.'

Hayley left the room and ran up the stairs, pausing at the top to take a few deep breaths. Steve's snores could be heard before she reached the bedroom door, and feeling justified in waking him, she barged in. This was his mess, and he should sort it out. Shaking his shoulder, Hayley waited for her husband to open his eyes and wake properly.

'What time is it?' He rubbed his eyes.

'Time to get dressed and come downstairs. The police are here, and they know about your affair with Val. You need to answer their questions, not me!' Hayley's nostrils flared.

'What the hell do they want? We told them we didn't see anything.'

'Aren't you listening? They know about you and Val – that makes you a viable suspect – and probably me too!'

Steve threw the covers back and reached for his trousers. Pulling them on, he swore under his breath. 'Didn't you tell them the fling was over?'

'It was your *fling*, you tell them!' Hayley left the room and went downstairs, hovering in the hallway rather than returning to the lounge. When Steve came thumping downstairs, she opened the door and they entered the room together.

'Good afternoon, Mr Green. Sorry to have woken you but we have a few questions that won't wait.' Hayley and Steve sat down as Samantha continued. 'Why didn't you mention your affair with Valerie Turner when we spoke yesterday?'

'Because it's a private matter which has nothing to do with her death.' Steve Green scowled as he fought to control his anger.

'In a murder enquiry, nothing is private. Something like an affair could be significant, and it makes me wonder why you didn't tell us yesterday.'

Hayley was feeling uncomfortable, like a stranger in her own home, and furious with her husband for landing them in the middle of a murder investigation. Although the decision not to mention the relationship was a joint one, they'd assumed the police wouldn't discover it. As Steve appeared lost for words, Hayley tutted and stepped in. 'The affair was over weeks ago and we're trying to put it behind us. It's not the sort of thing to bring up in conversation, and as we knew it was irrelevant, we decided not to mention it. It was over very quickly. Steve regrets it and was trying to save me from the embarrassment of it becoming public knowledge.'

'It would have been better to be honest and tell us – an affair which turned sour could be a motive for murder. Surely you can see how your silence looks.' Samantha threw in the inflammatory suggestion.

Steve, now fully awake, snarled angrily. 'That's absurd! And we told you we were both here. I was asleep, and neither of us left the house all morning.'

'If you were asleep, how do you know your wife was at

home? And Mrs Green, I presume you didn't sit with your husband while he slept?'

'That's a ridiculous suggestion. You'll be saying we planned it together next!' Steve balled his fists and shuffled uncomfortably in his seat.

'Did you?' Samantha's eyes flashed from one to the other, her face unreadable.

'No!' They spoke simultaneously.

After a few more questions, the detectives left, and Hayley turned to her husband. 'We're suspects now, thanks to you!'

'But we know we didn't do it, so what the hell does it matter?'

'I know I didn't do it!' Hayley was almost screaming with frustration. 'But for all I know, you could have!' She'd tried to forgive her husband, yet the anger was resurfacing again – all the pain and humiliation – some friend Valerie had turned out to be.

Hayley didn't think her husband would have sneaked downstairs, left the house and murdered Valerie... Or did she?'

TWENTY-SIX

Discussing the interview with the Greens on the way back to the station, Samantha and Jenny agreed it was highly unlikely that Steve or Hayley had killed Valerie Turner, but when they walked into the interview room, Paul greeted them with some interesting background information on Steve Green.

'At the age of fourteen, he was something of a teenage tearaway, a joy-rider. After two cases of taking without consent and involvement in an off-licence raid, he spent twelve months in a youth offenders centre. His behaviour there was aggressive, and his name cropped up as the instigator of a couple of protests, near riots, really. Once released, Green appeared to change his ways. We have nothing on him since those early years.'

'Thanks, Paul. Presently, they're alibiing each other, although I suspect our visit this morning may have stirred things up a little. We'll see if anything develops.'

Samantha had a meeting scheduled with the Edwards for lunchtime. During the previous day's interview, the detectives discovered that the Edwards resided in Merseyside, where Valerie had been born and lived until she was eighteen. Jenny had made comprehensive notes, both detectives hoping this new information would provide some much-needed leads to follow. Jenny had stayed late to transcribe her notes onto the system after the Edwards left.

Samantha glanced at the date at the bottom of her computer – the digits appeared to jump out at her and she groaned inwardly. She was feeling down and knew why, but pushed her thoughts to the back of her mind and concentrated on work. After a quick sandwich in the canteen, Sam and Jenny headed to the family room where Robert and Bella Edwards were already waiting.

'Can we see Geoff and our granddaughters?' Bella asked as soon as they were seated.

'I'd rather you left it until we've spoken to them. This will be another shock for them to absorb, and they're still grieving Val's loss.'

'But maybe our presence will help? And there's Ben, too. We'd like to meet him.'

Sam could guess how the conversation between the couple had progressed after the revelations of the evening before – it appeared they were seeking the positives in the chaos of emotions a murder inevitably triggers.

'It's not quite as simple, Bella, and I'll have to ask you to be patient. Our enquiries are ongoing, and news like this will cause ripples. I'd like to tell the family about you myself before you meet them...'

'But why?' Bella interrupted.

'It's difficult to explain. I must establish if they knew the truth about your daughter's background. It may not be relevant, although we don't know at this time. Their reactions to learning about you will give me some indication, so I must ask you to allow me to approach them first. When I'm satisfied your meeting will have no bearing on the case, we'll take you to meet them.' It was the best Sam could offer, and she was confident it was the right way forward. The elderly couple reluctantly accepted her decision, and as they had no way of contacting the Turners or Ben Chapman, Sam promised to move towards the introduction as soon as possible.

When the Edwards left, Samantha worked on her reports for an hour before calling it a day. Even with this new development, frustration with the lack of progress on the case hung heavily on her, and depression was threatening to set in. Sam wouldn't allow it. Saying goodnight to the team, she headed home determined to do something physical, even if it was only a thorough cleaning of her house.

Pulling into the drive, Sam noticed her mother's car opposite her home. Her eyes rolled. The last thing she wanted tonight was company. She chided herself swiftly. Brenda had been a brick over the last three months, and Sam knew she wouldn't have survived without her.

'Hi, Mum. Can I smell cooking?' Sam wandered into the kitchen and kissed her mother. 'You don't have to do this, you know.' Brenda had clearly been batch-cooking.

'I know, but I wanted to. There's a cottage pie for tonight, some individual steak pies for the freezer, and a tin of ginger cookies.' Beaming at her daughter, Brenda's eyes widened when Samantha flopped down at the little kitchen table and burst into tears. Brenda sat beside her and wrapped her arms around Sam's petite frame. Words seemed inadequate, so she waited for the tears to stop.

'Sorry, Mum!'

'Don't be sorry. Let it all out. You'll feel better for it.' Brenda reached for the kitchen roll and tore off a couple of sheets for her daughter. Sam put her head on her mother's shoulder and sobbed loudly.

When the deluge ended, Brenda released Sam from her grip and looked at her.

'Did you realise what day it is?' Sam asked. Brenda nodded. 'He would have been thirty-five today; it doesn't seem fair.' Sam blew her nose loudly.

'Life isn't always fair, love. But Ravi enjoyed his short life, which was mainly due to you. He loved you very much and would hate to see you so unhappy. I know it's only been three months, but you're still alive, and Ravi would want you to live!'

'I can't just forget him as if he hadn't existed!'

'No one's asking you to forget him. It's important to remember, to keep him alive in your heart. But you're still young, and there's more to life than work. I'm not suggesting you start dating or anything, just make more of an effort to enjoy life. With the type of work you do, it's important to have a life outside of the station. Now, there's enough cottage pie for two, so give me half an hour to do some veg, and we'll open a bottle of wine to wash it down.'

'Mum, you're driving!'

'I'll only have one; if I lose count, I'll stay in the spare room. Your dad won't notice I'm gone until the football's finished.'

'I love you, Mum. Thank you.'

'That's what mums are for. Now scoot, get a shower or something, and I'll call you when it's ready.'

After their meal, Sam received a phone call and was surprised to hear from Ravi's mother, Divya. Feeling guilty, Sam thought she should have perhaps rung them; this would be a difficult day for them, too. After a minute or so of general chatter, Divya asked Samantha if she and Arjun could visit her the following evening. Samantha agreed, a time was set and the call ended.

'Divya and Arjun want to visit tomorrow.' Sam found her

mum washing up in the kitchen and picked up a tea towel to dry.

'They must miss him too.' Brenda's smile was wistful. 'He was a lovely man. He leaves a huge hole in many hearts.'

The remainder of the evening passed pleasantly. Mother and daughter talked easily about Ravi, with Brenda asking questions to prompt Sam's happy memories. Too much wine was consumed, so Brenda rang home to say she'd stay overnight. Then they opened another bottle and talked until midnight.

'Thanks, Mum. You're a tonic, but I must get some sleep. I've another early start tomorrow.'

'Is the case moving forward?' Brenda asked.

'Not as quickly as I'd like. We've had very few breaks with this one, but I'm hoping that's about to change. It's quite the enigma and the more we dig the more the mystery deepens.'

'You'll get there in the end, love. You always do.'

They retired to their rooms, and Sam immediately fell into a deep sleep.

TWENTY-SEVEN

When Samantha woke, the smell of coffee reminded her of her mother's presence, and the tempting aroma encouraged her to go downstairs. Sam was refreshed, a feeling she'd not experienced since Ravi died. It could have been due to a good night's rest or, more likely, having sobbed without reserve on her mother's shoulder, finally giving way to her emotions without feeling guilty for not coping.

'Good morning!' Brenda Freeman greeted her daughter. 'Did you sleep well?'

'Yes.' Samantha smiled; it was good to have someone else in the house. 'The wine may have had something to do with it, although your company was very welcome, Mum. Thank you for coming over.'

'Anytime. You know I'm always up for a girly night, even if things do get a little maudlin. Do you want some coffee?'

'Yes, please. Sorry for all the histrionics last night, but I feel much better this morning.'

'There's no need to apologise and I'm pleased you're feeling the benefit.' Brenda pushed a steaming mug of coffee across the table to her daughter. 'If you'd like me to come round again tonight for a bit of moral support when Divya and Arjun come, I'm happy to do so.'

'What, and leave Dad having beans on toast for the second consecutive night? Thanks, but I'll be fine. Divya and Arjun are easy to get on with. I want to keep in touch with them; they're lovely people, and we'll always have Ravi in common.'

'Good for you. Now, how about a bacon sandwich? You've plenty of time; something on your stomach will help you get through the day.'

Normally, Sam would jump at the chance of a bacon sandwich, but the smell of the bacon her mother had under the grill suddenly made her feel nauseous. Jumping up from the table, she ran to the downstairs loo, where she was violently sick.

Returning to the kitchen, Brenda's eyes studiously followed Sam. 'Are you okay?'

'Yeah, it must have been the wine. I'll stick with coffee and then get off to work.'

'Samantha, you're not pregnant, are you?'

'What? Goodness, no.' Sam sat down and wrapped her hands around her cooling mug, trying to work out when she'd last had a period. 'I think you could be right, Mum. We weren't trying for a baby and I've never been very regular. I assumed stress was affecting my monthly cycle...' The women looked at each other, the tension broken by a smile on Sam's face. 'Do you think I could be?'

'Get yourself dressed while I pop out to the chemist – we'll soon find out.' Brenda's smile matched her daughter's as she grabbed her coat and bag and hurried to her car.

Samantha hardly dared move. If she was carrying Ravi's baby, life would have purpose again, something other than work. She whispered a silent prayer to God, asking for what she'd previously thought would never be possible – to have Ravi's child.

Pulling herself together, Sam showered and dressed, by which time her mother was back, charging through the doorway, waving a pregnancy testing kit in her hand.

'I've never bought one of these before, but I don't think the chemist thought it was for me!' She giggled while tearing the box open. 'Right, time to wee on a stick. Here's the instruction leaflet, off you go.' Brenda almost pushed her daughter towards the stairs.

Samantha obediently returned to the bathroom from where she could hear her mother clattering around downstairs. It was typical of Brenda, who needed to be active when stressed or excited.

A couple of minutes later Samantha almost galloped downstairs with the plastic wand in her hand. 'We should know in another two minutes. The leaflet said the test is 99% accurate.' Mother and daughter grinned at each other.

'Have you had morning sickness before?' Brenda asked.

'No, but I've got out of the habit of eating breakfast. A slice of toast, maybe? I've not much of an appetite, which I thought was part of the grieving process.'

'Anything there yet?' Brenda leaned over Sam's shoulder. 'Oh, look, a couple of faint lines, just like a covid test!'

'Mum! I'm pregnant!' Sam laughed – and cried. It was the best possible news. Ravi would still be with her in this new life growing in her body. Yet it was also bittersweet. Ravi would never see his child, never hold their baby in his arms and Sam knew he'd have been a wonderful dad.

Glancing at the clock, Sam was hauled back to reality. 'Heck, I'm going to be late for work!' While she scrabbled to find her bag and shoes, her mother stood grinning.

'You don't have to be first in every day, and today is special. Are you going to tell Divya and Arjun tonight?'

'Do you think I should?'

'Absolutely! A grandchild will be good news, and they could use some of that. Tell them; they'll be grateful if you do.'

'You're right, Mum, as always. They'll want to share the news and the baby, too!'

'We grandparents have rights, you know – I'll be expecting to be hands-on with this child.'

Samantha hugged her mother tightly. Pulling away, she said, 'Being hands-on is a given! Sorry to leave you to clear up. I'll ring you later. And thanks, *Granny*, you're the best!'

TWENTY-EIGHT

It was rare for Samantha to struggle with concentration. Generally, at work, her mind was focused on the task at hand, giving one hundred per cent to the case. Since returning to work after Ravi's death, this focus kept Sam going – her professionalism carried her through each day. Today, the awareness of Ravi's baby growing within her brought comfort, a seed of hope and the possibility of future happiness. Focus today would be difficult, but Sam would do it and think of the baby this evening when she could share the news with Ravi's parents.

'What are you smiling about?' Jen's voice startled Samantha. 'Something good come up?'

'Yes.' Sam's smile widened. 'But not with the case.'

'Come on, spit it out.'

'Not here. Let's go over to the deli for a coffee.'

'But it's only 9.15am.'

'Do I have to pull rank?' Sam grinned.

'You're the boss!'

They grabbed their coats and headed out of the office. With

large skinny lattes in front of them, Jenny tapped her fingers on the table. 'What's going on, Sam?'

'I'm pregnant!' she blurted out, a radiant expression reflecting her delight. Jenny reached over the table to hug her.

'And you've only just found out?' Jen released Sam from her bear hug.

'Yes, this morning. Mum stayed over last night and when I was sick at the sight of her bacon sandwich, she guessed. I haven't been eating well, and sleep is erratic, but I assumed it was due to missing Ravi.'

'But you must be at least three months. You'll have to see the doctor, go to antenatal classes and everything. Can I be Auntie Jenny?'

'You most certainly can! I'd like to keep it quiet for a little longer until it's officially confirmed. Only Mum knows, and tonight Divya and Arjun are visiting, so I'm going to tell them.'

'Wow, they'll be delighted. I'm so pleased for you, Sam. You deserve some good news.'

'Thanks, now drink up and let's get back to work. We still have a murder to solve.'

A team meeting presented the opportunity to discuss Valerie Turner's lies to her family about her past but otherwise established nothing new. Forensics had been super quick with checking Geoff's golf clubs and found nothing. It was highly unlikely that Geoff would have killed his wife with one of his clubs and then cleaned it sufficiently well to leave no trace. Unless one was missing.

Samantha delegated duties to incorporate more digging and more interviews. Kim Thatcher was tasked with returning to the Turners' house to see how things were with the family. Sam was impressed with the way Kim was shaping up. The young DC had good instincts and was proving to be a valuable team member.

Layla and Paul were keen to dig deeper into Valerie Turner's background. Now they knew her parents were alive and she'd lived in Merseyside during her childhood, this new information could prove useful.

Sam and Jenny were to visit Hammond, Birch and Fox again to interview Mr Fox, who hadn't been available on their last visit. At the solicitors, Sam asked Jenny to take the lead which she did with competence and alacrity. Sam was grateful; other things were buzzing around her mind.

The solicitor, a small middle-aged man, answered their questions in a clipped manner. Although polite, he gave the impression that they were wasting his time. He had no new information or insights to offer and the interview lasted only a few minutes.

At this stage, it seemed to the detectives that they were duplicating tasks already performed, yet without any fresh leads, it was all they could do.

The afternoon dragged, and Sam spent it writing reports. It was an aspect of police work no one particularly enjoyed but a necessary part of the investigation. She was also obliged to present an update to DCI Kent before daring to allow her thoughts to return to her changed situation and the visit of Ravi's parents that evening.

Driving home, Sam smiled. It was a silly thought, but it felt as if the huge void Ravi had left in her heart was somehow being filled with another love, Ravi's child. A baby would never replace him, and Sam knew she'd always miss him like crazy, but now there was a reason to continue living, a wonderful, exciting reason that she couldn't wait to share with Divya and Arjun.

TWENTY-NINE

On impulse, Samantha had offered to cook a meal for her visitors and was somewhat relieved when Divya had graciously declined; it was one less thing to worry about. Instead, she bought a good bottle of red wine and would offer wine or coffee, whichever they preferred. It was times like these when she wished Ravi was at her side. Divya and Arjun were lovely people, but Sam feared the conversation would be strained. Ravi was all they had in common, yet an evening talking about him would be surreal and maybe even distressing, although her news would surely be welcome.

Brenda had left the house immaculate as always, so Sam showered and changed before her guests were due, then paced the floor, anticipating how the evening would play out. Should she jump straight in and tell them about the baby? It would be a great way to open the conversation. *Guess what? I'm pregnant!* but perhaps it would be better to wait and see how things panned out.

The doorbell chimed at 7.30pm precisely, and Sam jumped, even though they were expected. Opening the door, she ushered her visitors inside out of the cold, damp evening. Arjun carried a large bouquet, which he presented to Sam with a kiss on her cheek, a genuine sign of affection, but Sam shivered at his proximity, momentarily taken aback as she recognised the same cologne Ravi wore. Divya stepped forward and enfolded her in a warm embrace, blinking back tears and forcing a smile.

Taking coats and offering drinks occupied the first ten minutes, but once settled with coffee, all three looked to their drinks for inspiration. Sam's heart pounded. It was unfair to keep them in ignorance any longer.

'There's something I'd like to share with you – some good news.' Smiling shyly, she paused as Divya and Arjun stared wide-eyed at her. 'I'm having Ravi's baby.'

'Oh, my dear, that's wonderful!' Divya was on her feet and hugging Sam again, this time allowing her tears to flow – tears of happiness.

'I've not seen the doctor yet, but I've had a positive test.' Sam waited for the couple to say more, but words seemed to have deserted them. Even Arjun looked overcome, his deep brown eyes – Ravi's eyes – glistening with tears. 'I'll book an appointment with the doctor as soon as possible,' Sam continued. 'But I've been experiencing morning sickness too, only I didn't recognise it as such.'

'Samantha, this is the best news you could give us.' Divya glanced at Arjun and nodded. 'It makes what we have to tell you even more important. Arjun, will you explain?' Her husband cleared his throat and turned to look at Sam.

'We heard from the solicitor on Tuesday. He's completed probate for Ravi's will, so there are some papers for you to sign, which the solicitor will happily take you through. Essentially, Ravi's shares in the family business will pass to you. I can advise you on the best way to proceed and explain what dividend you can expect from them, but there's no hurry.' Arjun smiled at Samantha's bewildered expression.

'I'm sure you were aware that yesterday would have been Ravi's thirty-fifth birthday. Ravi had a trust fund and family money which was due to become available to him on that date, and in the terms of his will, he left the proceeds to you. It's in the region of £500,000, but we can discuss the finer details another time.'

'What? I didn't know...' Sam was stunned, 'Ravi didn't tell me any of this!'

'He probably didn't expect to be leaving us so soon. With your wonderful news of the baby, his planning has been perfect. You won't have to worry about finances when the baby's born – the trust fund and the share dividend will give you all the security you need. This offers you choices, and we couldn't be more delighted for you.'

Sam was unsure, confused. 'But if it's family money, shouldn't it pass to you or his brother?'

Arjun smiled. 'Samantha, you are family! Ravi was deeply committed to you, and there's a baby to consider now, Ravi's heir. I don't have to remind you that we don't need the money; we're truly happy for you, and it's what our son wanted.'

'Tell us more about the baby, Samantha.' Divya clearly wasn't interested in the financial details and Sam needed time to process it.

'There's not much more to tell. As I said, I've only just found out. I feel rather stupid for missing the signs – I assumed them to be the effects of grief or depression. As soon as I've seen the doctor I'll let you know. I'm so glad you're pleased about the baby, and naturally, your involvement will be welcome. I want my baby to know as much about his father and his heritage as possible, if it's okay with you?'

'Thank you, Sam, you're very kind.' Divya dabbed daintily at her eyes.

Ravi's parents didn't stay much longer, needing time to

process the news. Once alone, Samantha debated whether to ring her mother but decided against it. The bottle of wine in the kitchen crossed her mind. No, now that she was pregnant, alcohol was strictly off-limits – a mug of hot chocolate, some mindless television and an early night would suffice if she could stop herself from churning over the very recent and exciting news.

THIRTY

Before leaving for work on Friday morning, Samantha logged on to her laptop and searched for her GP's website. Being generally very healthy, she'd had little reason to visit her GP and rarely saw the same one twice. There were very few free appointments, and although it wasn't an emergency, Sam was keen to set her antenatal care in motion and took the first one available the following Monday. Then, she logged off and set off for work.

There were no fresh insights into the murder during the early team meeting, although they now had fingerprint evidence back from the CSIs. Once family members were eliminated, only a few were unaccounted for. Samantha tasked DC Tom Wilson with visiting the Greens to request their fingerprints. Having both been visitors to the property, they would also need to be eliminated.

'Ask if they'll give a voluntary DNA sample while you're there, Tom. If there's any resistance, that in itself will tell us something. And can you call at number 19 as well? They've apparently been away on a skiing holiday but should be home now, and they have CCTV, so if you could ask to see Saturday's images, that would be great.' Tom smiled, clearly pleased with his task.

––––––––

The curtains were closed at number 19, so DC Tom Wilson crossed the road to the Greens' home. The sound of raised voices from inside greeted him. Pausing, he listened, hoping to distinguish what was being said, but the words were muffled, so he decided to interrupt the apparent argument. The shouting ceased when he rang the bell, yet it was almost two minutes before anyone answered the door and only after a second ring.

Steve Green looked suspiciously from the doorway. 'Not you people again! Can't you leave us alone? We can't tell you anything else.'

Tom was used to being an unwelcome visitor and found the best way to deal with it was by politely stating his purpose. 'My apologies for interrupting, sir. Could I have a few minutes of your time?' Tom looked hopefully at Steve, expecting an invitation inside.

'What for?'

'Perhaps we can discuss it inside?' Rain was falling and Tom didn't wish to stand outside getting wet any longer than necessary.

'I asked what for?'

Tom reluctantly explained that he wished to take fingerprints to eliminate them from their investigation. 'And if you would be kind enough to allow me to take a DNA sample, that will help, too,' he added.

'Are you arresting me?' Steve kept his shoulder behind the door as if expecting Tom to force an entry.'

'No, sir. It's entirely voluntary – to assist our investigation.'

'Then the answer is no!' Steve Green slammed the door leaving a startled DC wondering what he'd done wrong.

Returning to number 19, Tom received a much better welcome. Invited in from the rain and plied with coffee and biscuits, the young couple were pleased to show him their CCTV. Nothing of interest appeared, but Tom asked them to send the footage to his phone to be scrutinised in more detail at the station. The couple were aware of their neighbour's death and keen to talk about it. Thinking it prudent to listen to their impressions of the Turner family and of the Greens, he did so as he enjoyed his coffee.

On his return to the station, Tom approached Samantha with his news. 'The Greens were clearly having an argument when I arrived, which probably accounted for their bad mood. Perhaps I can try again tomorrow or next week?'

'Did you see Mrs Green at all?' Sam asked.

'No.' Tom realized he should have checked on her safety. 'Should I go back?'

'Maybe not. You say you heard her, so we'll assume she was okay. It's best not to go in heavy-handed; they seem antagonistic towards us as it is, although I'd love to know what they were arguing about. We'll leave them until Monday and have another try.'

'I've got the footage from the CCTV outside number 19, although an initial look doesn't offer anything new. I'll send it on to DS Roper for him to double check. The young couple were keen to talk. He works from home and has an office overlooking the Turners' property. Graham Smith, his name is, and he notices everything. Although they don't know the family well, he's an observant sort and can relate the comings and goings of most of his neighbours. I know they were away last Saturday, but they might be worth a second visit.'

'Good work, Tom. I'll get someone to call again. We've

precious little else to work with until we get the forensic reports back, and even then, there may be little of use.'

It appeared the weekend would yield little more in the way of leads. Samantha needed time off: it had been a long two weeks since her return to work, and her body was crying out for rest; and there was a baby to think of now, a very precious baby. A weekend off was the sensible option. Other members of the team who'd worked through their rest days could also do with some rest. They could always be contacted if anything cropped up, and if not, they'd return to the investigation on Monday, rested and hopefully better equipped to make progress.

THIRTY-ONE

The GP's waiting room was full. Sam squeezed into a corner seat, aware of much coughing and sneezing around her. The doctor she was due to see bore an unfamiliar name, Dr Marie Moorhouse, but Sam didn't recognise many of the doctor's names. Having no siblings and no children in her wider family, she felt unprepared for this pregnancy. Brenda had offered to accompany her, but as much as she loved her mum, she didn't want to take her to antenatal appointments.

A ten-minute wait seemed much longer, although from the snippets of conversation (or perhaps grumbles) she'd heard from other patients, waiting times were usually much longer. Navigating her way down a narrow corridor, Sam found the room with Dr Moorhouse's name on it and knocked.

'Come in!' the cheerful voice said, and as Samantha entered, she experienced her first surprise of the day. The women looked at each other and smiled. 'Samantha Freeman! I haven't seen you since sixth form prom. How are you, if that's not a stupid question?'

'Marie Everton!' Sam grinned. 'I'm fine, how good to see you!' It was good. Samantha was embarking upon a new experience, a road to be travelled alone, and a familiar face was welcome. 'I don't need to ask what you've been doing since school – and married too, I presume?'

'Yes! Years of hard work and study, but I'm home now, married to Peter Everton, with two little Evertons at home. And how about you?'

'I didn't go the university route and joined the police force as soon as they would take me. DI Freeman now, and I'm here because I'm pregnant.'

'Wow, congratulations.' Marie's smile faded. 'It is good news, I hope?'

'Yes, the best!' They could both smile again.

'Well, we'd better get on with it then. Have you brought a urine sample?'

Sam produced one from her bag.

'Great, now hop up on the couch and we'll have a feel of your tummy.'

While Sam shuffled onto the couch and readied herself for examination, Marie tested the urine sample. 'Yes, congratulations are in order.' She approached Sam, smiling. 'Sorry if the hands are cold.' The doctor pressed Samantha's abdomen and then listened through her stethoscope. 'All seems well and good. I think you could be as far on as three months. Is there a reason why you didn't come sooner?'

Samantha tidied her clothing and sat beside the doctor. 'I became engaged before Christmas to another police officer, Ravi Patel, although we weren't trying for a baby. On 28th December, Ravi was killed in a motor accident.'

Marie reached out and squeezed Sam's hand. 'Oh, Samantha, I'm so sorry!'

'Thank you. I've found it tough at times, you know, sleeping, eating, it all seemed pointless, so I didn't even notice I'd missed my periods, or if I did, I ascribed it to the grieving process.'

'Understandable.' Marie smiled. 'I can't begin to understand how awful this must be, but if you're happy about the baby, you have another little being to consider. You're looking after two now, Sam.'

Samantha wiped away an escaping tear and nodded. 'It's good to see an old friend. Will you see me through the pregnancy?'

'I'll certainly oversee the next few months. We offer shared care with the maternity hospital and have some antenatal classes here at the surgery. For your first appointment, we'll book you in at the hospital for the twelve-week scan. I'm generally around during antenatal classes, so if you ever want to see me or ask anything, tell one of the nurses, and they'll get me.'

'Ooh, special treatment for being an old friend of the doctor, eh?' Sam smiled.

'Absolutely. Anything I can do, any time. Have you had any cravings yet?' Marie smiled.

'Yes, quite early on actually. While I was shopping I felt an urge to buy a couple of jars of pickled gherkins – something I never usually eat.'

'Hah, that's a new one. With my first, it was blancmange and then raw swede with the second.' Marie laughed. It felt good to Sam to have a normal conversation. Meeting Marie was a blessing for which she was grateful.

Samantha returned to work feeling almost cheerful. Marie hadn't been a close friend at school, but they'd always got on well. It was comforting to know a friend was in the background if needed.

As expected, Jenny was waiting to give her boss the third degree. 'Well, what happened? Did you have a scan or anything?'

'No, but the doctor, who I happened to go to school with, did a test and confirmed it. She thinks I'm about twelve weeks, but I'll be getting an appointment for a scan at the hospital to confirm.'

'If you need anyone to hold your hand...' Jenny grinned.

'It might be more important for you to hold the fort here, or better still, to solve this murder. Did anything turn up this morning?'

Jenny shook her head. 'I'll get back to the grindstone, boss.'

Samantha fired off two texts, both saying the same thing.

> Pregnancy confirmed, about 12 weeks on!
> Speak later x.

One text winged its way to her mother and the other to Divya, while Sam imagined the smiles on the two grannies' faces before she, too, returned to the grindstone.

THIRTY-TWO

It was time to visit Geoff Turner and inform him that his wife's parents were alive and well and wished to meet him. In fairness to the Edwards, Sam could no longer leave it. As yet, this startling news had had little impact on the investigation other than to underscore that Valerie Turner was a well-practised liar.

Sam had spoken to Geoff earlier in the day and they'd agreed to meet at 5pm at his parents' home. Geoff assured her he'd be in alone and Sam was pleased to see his car in the drive when she pulled up a few minutes early for their appointment. Although she was keen to get home and ring her mum and Divya, this interview took priority.

Sam followed Geoff to the kitchen, where the kettle was boiling. A pan of soup was on the cooker, and a loaf of bread sat waiting to be attacked. He waved his hand to take in the scene, 'I'm not much good in the kitchen, but the girls are helping so we'll not starve and Mum does her best although I don't like to put on her.'

'Good. How are the girls doing?'

'Okay, I think. Anna doesn't say much and goes out with her

friends more often than not, but Lizzie talks to me. It helps us both – to remember the good times – you know?'

Sam swallowed, aware she was about to drop another bombshell on this man who was still reeling from the events of the last week. 'I'm afraid there's something else I have to tell you.'

Geoff's shoulders slumped as he finished pouring tea and slid a mug towards her, a raised eyebrow prompting her to continue. 'Valerie's parents came to the station last week. It appears they're both alive and well.'

Flopping down on the chair, Geoff's face paled as his tea slopped over the table. Ignoring the mess, he stared at Sam, 'You're not serious, are you? Val told me her parents were dead.'

'I realise that, but we've checked them out, and they're genuine. Valerie left home without warning when she was eighteen and Robert and Bella Edwards have heard nothing from her since. They saw her photograph in the paper and came to see me on Wednesday.'

'Where are they now?'

'Still in New Middridge. They're staying on for a while, hoping to meet you and the girls.'

'What! After they threw her out! When Ben turned up, Val told me they threw her out when she became pregnant, and she hadn't seen them since. How dare they!'

'Geoff, I think you'll find there's another side to the story. When I mentioned Val's pregnancy, they were stunned. I believed them when they said they knew nothing about it.'

'Bloody hell. Did they never look for her? She may have been eighteen, but she was still a child!'

'They have their reasons why they didn't report Val as missing, which I'll leave them to tell you about if they wish to. I do think they're genuine and they were left in no doubt that Valerie didn't want to be found.'

Geoff looked pained. He put his hands over his face and sighed, 'I don't think I ever truly knew my wife, did I?'

Samantha couldn't argue. Valerie Turner was a woman with secrets who apparently lied when it suited her purpose. Was it someone she'd lied to who killed her? 'Will you tell the girls?'

'Yes, they're old enough to know, although I don't think they'll understand. Hell, I don't understand the woman. Why so many lies? What did she hope to gain?'

Sam could offer no answers. 'As I said, they'd like to meet you, Anna and Lizzie. How do you feel about a meeting?'

'The girls will need to decide for themselves, although I can't see them refusing – this couple are their grandparents as much as my mum and dad. I think I want to meet them too, to ask a few questions if nothing else. What are they like?'

'They seem a really pleasant couple. I'd put Robert in his mid to late sixties and Bella a few years younger. They've been very open and honest with us, and I'm inclined to believe them. They've no reason to lie. Can I give you their number?'

'Yes, but I'll not ring until tomorrow. I'll have to speak to the girls tonight. Have the Edwards met Ben yet?'

'No, and I haven't told Ben about them yet. I'll do so tomorrow. Naturally, they'd like to meet him as well. I'd suggest a separate meeting.'

'Agreed. Thanks for telling me first, I appreciate it.'

Samantha left to go home. Geoff had taken the news better than expected, and it was positive that he was open to meeting his parents-in-law. As she drove home, Sam reflected on what a strange case this was turning out to be. They were learning more about their victim but still didn't have a clear suspect with a sufficient motive to want to kill her. *What was it that we're missing?*

THIRTY-THREE

Robert and Bella Edwards were excited and nervous about meeting their grandchildren. They were grateful to Geoff for agreeing and inviting them to his home yet spent a troubled night worrying about how the meeting would go. Arriving promptly, Geoff invited them into what had been their daughter's home. There was no sign of Anna and Lizzie.

'I thought it best for us to have a chat before the girls join us. They're upstairs.' Geoff offered coffee, which was declined; nervous energy made such social niceties seem inappropriate.

'Thank you for letting us come, Geoff. We realise what a difficult time this is for you all.'

'That's okay. We're certainly discovering another side to Val, and I must admit to being shocked when I heard of your existence. When did you last see or hear from her?'

Robert inhaled deeply and commenced his semi-prepared speech. 'Val left home not long after her eighteenth birthday. Her teenage years were difficult, and she was a very strong-willed child. We had no prior warning and returned from a trip out to find her and her possessions gone. Clearly she must have been planning to leave but it was a shock to us; quite devastating.'

'Did you go to the police?' Geoff looked from his wife's father to her mother, a frown on his face. 'It's the first thing I'd have done if it was Anna or Lizzie.'

Robert and Bella exchanged a look. They'd realised that for Geoff to understand their reasons, they'd have to tell him the whole truth. 'Valerie stole from us. She took some of Bella's jewellery, money, and, we found out later, a bank card and building society passbook. If we'd gone to the police, she'd have been branded a criminal, which we didn't want.'

Geoff shook his head sadly. 'The more I learn about Val, the more I think I've never really known her.'

Robert gave a sympathetic nod and continued. 'Initially, we tried to contact the few of her friends we knew, but it appeared she'd severed all ties and we believed them when they said they didn't know her whereabouts. We spent hours searching the streets of Liverpool, thinking that's where she might have gone – a fruitless exercise which we eventually abandoned. We hoped she'd come home of her own accord, that maybe when the money ran out–'

Geoff interrupted. 'DI Freeman told me you didn't know she was pregnant. Is that true?'

'Absolutely!' Bella wrung her hands, the memories almost too much to bear. 'If we'd known about the baby, we'd have supported Valerie. It might have been the makings of her, something to bring us back together.' A sob hindered Bella's words, and Robert took her hand.

'We've never stopped loving our daughter, Geoff. To learn of her death was a shock to us, softened only by the knowledge of our grandchildren. We'll understand if you don't want us in your lives, but we'd appreciate the chance to get to know the girls, and Ben.'

'I can't speak for Ben, although Anna and Lizzie are prepared to meet you. Be warned, they may ask a few awkward questions.'

'Yes, I appreciate that. If it can be avoided, we'd rather not tell them about Val stealing from us. Their memories of their mother shouldn't be tainted any more than they already are.'

'I understand, Robert, although the things we're discovering have left us all somewhat puzzled. I'll call the girls down now, shall I?'

Learning they had maternal grandparents had been a momentous surprise for Anna and Lizzie. Having no reason to doubt their mother's version of her past, they wanted to quiz Robert and Bella Edwards out of loyalty to their mum, if nothing else.

Lizzie and Anna entered the lounge in a subdued mood, unsure what to say. Anna spoke first. 'Hi, I'm Anna and this whole situation is absolutely weird. Are we supposed to call you gran and granddad, or what?'

'Hello, Anna.' Bella smiled. 'It's a bit weird for us too. You can call us Robert and Bella if it's easier for you. I know you have other grandparents.' Bella couldn't take her eyes off the two girls as if drinking in all the years she'd missed by not knowing them. 'You look so much like your mother did at your age, Anna. And, Lizzie, you have her beautiful eyes. I always thought they were her best feature.'

Robert chipped in. 'You probably have a ton of questions to ask us, so fire away.'

The girls hesitated. They had a list in their heads, but it now seemed rude to ask Bella and Robert personal questions so soon after meeting them. Lizzie found something interesting to study on the carpet while Anna looked at her dad, silently pleading for assistance. Geoff attempted to ease the tension.

'Robert and Bella have explained to me how your mother

came to leave home and they've assured me they had no idea she was carrying Ben. They'd have helped her if she'd confided in them, but your mum, headstrong as always, wanted to do things her way. We don't have to go into all the details now. Today's a time to get to know your grandparents. Why don't you get some of your photographs out, and I'll make us that coffee now, shall I?'

Anna rolled her eyes and Lizzie ran to fetch the albums. When Geoff returned with the drinks, his daughters appeared relaxed and were chatting happily to their visitors. Bella smiled at Geoff, tears filling her eyes. 'Thank you for your kindness in allowing us to come to your home. You'll never know how wonderful it is to meet you all and seeing these photos is a real joy. We never stopped loving Valerie and we've missed her every day since she left.'

An hour later, Robert and Bella left with promises to keep in touch. Once they met Ben, they'd be travelling home. Bella was particularly delighted when both of her granddaughters spontaneously hugged her and Robert. The elderly couple left in an emotional fug, with a solid hope of building relationships in the future.

THIRTY-FOUR

Samantha rang Ben Chapman on Tuesday morning to arrange a meeting. Ben offered to come to the station, which she gratefully accepted, and at 2pm, a conversation similar to the one with Geoff Turner the previous day took place in an interview room.

'I don't understand. Val told me her parents threw her out, disowned her when she was pregnant, and that they never had a chance to make it up as they were killed in an accident a couple of years later!' Ben's expression mirrored that of Geoff when he'd heard the news. 'So that means I've got grandparents too?'

'Yes, and they're keen to get to know you. How would you feel about a meeting?'

'Are they for real? Do you think they're telling the truth?'

'I do. They strike me as a genuine couple, and I hate to say it, but it was Val who lied about them.' Samantha didn't reveal details about Val's treatment of her parents. It was up to Robert and Bella to tell their grandchildren as much or as little as they wanted.

Ben agreed to Sam passing on his phone number and left bewildered, yet with a hint of a smile.

The rest of the week proved uneventful and frustration was rife among the team with their lack of progress. It was Thursday, the second week of the investigation, and despite chasing up forensics, it appeared results would only arrive when they arrived, and no squawking and pleading could bring them sooner. The only good news was that the coroner released the body so the family could finally make arrangements for a funeral. The coroner's verdict was unsurprising – unlawful death by a person or persons unknown. The cause of death – a severe blow to the head.

Unsure whether the news she was about to impart was good or bad, Samantha set off to visit Geoff Turner. The family were still staying with his parents, probably causing problems, yet Sam could understand their reluctance to go home. Kim Thatcher accompanied her. The young DC seemed to have developed a rapport with the family, who appeared to trust her.

Geoff answered the door with his usual expectant expression and the same two-word question. 'Any news?'

'May we come in?' Sam smiled as Geoff stood aside. His mother hovered in the hallway, wearing a matching expression of anticipation. No one spoke until they were in the lounge where Donald Turner sat reading the newspaper. Anna and Lizzie were absent from the room, so Samantha took the opportunity to tell them that Valerie's body was being released.

Geoff sat forward on his seat. 'Does that mean we can arrange the funeral?'

'Yes, it does. The coroner is satisfied with the cause of death being from the blow to Valerie's head, so no further examinations will be necessary. He'll send what we call a "pink form" to the registrar stating the cause of death so you can register the death and go ahead with your arrangements. The investigation will continue with the inquest paused for now.'

Silence flooded the room; there were no more questions from the adult Turners, so Kim asked after the girls.

'They're with Ben – their choice, but I've given up arguing over him. They'll eventually see him for what he is.'

To change the subject, Sam enquired how the meeting with the Edwards had gone.

'Okay, I think. I'd warned the girls not to ask too many questions but they still went in with both feet. Having believed Val's version of leaving home, I think they felt disloyal to accept their grandparents' version without question. Still, it is what it is. They've both had to grow up rather quickly of late.'

With little else to discuss, Sam and Kim took their leave, and Mary Turner walked them to the door. Once away from the house, Kim suggested it was probably for the best that Geoff Turner appeared resigned to his daughters seeing their half-brother.

'Yes, he has enough on his plate without facing confrontation. I wonder why he's so set against Ben, though.'

'Maybe he has regrets. Things with his wife clearly weren't good and can never be put right now. Geoff seems a little more subdued, I think.'

Sam was quick to change the subject. Regrets were frequently a bugbear to her. 'While we're in the area, we'll return to Juniper Grove. I'd like to speak with the neighbours at number 19.'

After only a short journey, they were invited inside Graham Smith's home and offered coffee. 'My wife's at work but I work from home – a blessing or a curse, I can't decide!'

Sam smiled. 'Please don't worry about coffee. We won't keep you long; it's simply a follow-up visit from your chat with DC Wilson.'

'Ah, yes. Was the CCTV footage any help?'

'Sadly, no, but I wondered if you've thought of anything else since then. Even the slightest incident can prove useful, and now you've had time to settle back in from your holiday?'

'I must admit the murder's been on my mind quite a bit lately. You don't expect such an event in a quiet neighbourhood like this. Trish and I have talked about it often, and I mentioned the car to her. It was before the murder and I thought it might be of interest but Trish said it was probably nothing.'

'What car is this, Mr Smith?' Sam asked while Kim pulled out her notebook.

'It was a Peugeot 208 Coupe Cabriolet convertible. I noticed it because it's the kind of car I aspire to, yet sadly Trish insists our hatchback is more practical. It was electric blue and parked just below my window the first time. Come upstairs, I'll show you.'

The detectives followed Graham upstairs to his office. A cluttered desk was positioned beneath the window and Sam wondered how he could ever work on such an untidy surface, and surely the window would be a distraction.

'See. We're almost opposite number 22 and the car was parked just down there.' He pointed to the road directly beneath the window.

'And did you notice anyone get out, perhaps to visit the Turners' house?'

'No. That's the funny thing. The car remained there for about fifteen minutes and the driver didn't leave. The top was up too, so I'm afraid I didn't get a good look at who was inside.'

Sam wondered where this was going. 'And why did you think this was unusual? Have you seen the car before?'

'That was the first time, and it came back the next day, but very early. I noticed it when I got up and opened the curtains. It was parked a little further down, and again, I didn't see who was inside, and no one exited even though it was there for about fifteen minutes. Trish said he was probably taking a phone call or something, although I thought it odd that he should stop in the same place two days running.'

Kim was scribbling in her notebook. 'I don't suppose you can remember which days these were?'

'Actually, yes!' Graham reached for his desk diary and flicked through the pages. 'It was 21st February, Friday. I remember because I was on an international call and the car rather distracted me. The second time was the following day, Saturday, but then we went on holiday so I wouldn't know if there were any more visits. Do you think it might be significant?'

'It could be. At this stage in the investigation, we consider every piece of information available, so this will be logged with everything else. Did you notice the registration number?'

'Sorry, no. As you can see, it was directly below me, so not visible. I'll let you know if I see it again.' Graham's face reflected his excitement at having been of help. 'Wait until I tell Trish you were interested.'

'Absolutely. And if there's anything else you can think of, please give us a ring.' Samantha and Kim left the house.

'He's a proper little Miss Marple,' Kim mumbled, climbing into the car. 'It could have nothing to do with the investigation.'

'But it could have everything to do with it. Don't ignore anything, Kim. It's often the detail that wins the day, and we could do with a few more Miss Marples. Give Paul a ring, will you, and ask him to go through our suspects and Valerie's contacts at work to see if a blue Peugeot is registered to anyone on our radar.'

Kim did as she was asked, both detectives wondering if this would be another dead end.

Friday was another uneventful day. The team at New Middridge were growing restless with the lack of any solid evidence to work with. Paul completed his search into all known contacts of Valerie Turner, including her work colleagues and not one of them owned a Peugeot 208 Coupe Cabriolet convertible. Frustrated scratching of heads, metaphorically and at times physically, frequented the incident room until Sam decided to send her team home early. The ones who were on a weekend off, including herself, would hopefully return with a fresh impetus on Monday. It was to be hoped they would also receive some forensic results next week – they were overdue some kind of break.

THIRTY-FIVE

Samantha was late to work on Monday morning due to her first antenatal appointment. In an attempt to dissuade her mother from accompanying her, she'd opted for the earliest available appointment, telling Brenda Freeman that she'd be dashing off to work immediately afterwards, an excuse but also true.

It had been a week since she'd seen the doctor, and Sam was grateful for a quick appointment as she was already past the three-month stage and an ultrasound scan was due. Morning sickness was still a problem, though she wasn't a great breakfast eater at the best of times. It was easier to take an apple and a cereal bar to work and eat them when she could. This morning, even coffee hadn't appealed. Sam chalked it up to nerves, or was it excitement?

An unattractive mushroom colour adorned the walls of the waiting room – not the best choice for those suffering from morning sickness – and coupled with the charcoal grey bucket seats, the space was altogether uninspiring. The only relief was a splash of colour in the corner of the room, a dedicated space for toddlers. Bright-coloured chairs screened off the corner, and boxes of toys designed to keep siblings occupied littered the floor. Sam smiled at a little girl with wispy blond hair who clung onto the doll she'd been playing with as her exasperated mother tried to persuade her to leave it and accompany her into the examination room. The child won and hugged the doll to her chest like a trophy while being dragged away from the toy corner.

A small boy clung to his mother's legs, watching the goings-on with wide brown eyes. Sam sympathised; she was also apprehensive. For perhaps the first time, the thought of what her and Ravi's baby would look like crossed her mind. Seeing the little boy's brown eyes, she hoped her child would favour Ravi in looks, whether a boy or a girl.

Her doctor, Marie, said there might be a chance she'd learn the sex of her baby today. A warm feeling rushed through her veins as the thought nestled in her mind. Sam wanted to know for herself and to tell her parents and Divya and Arjun. It would provide a welcome focus for them all and hope for the future. She might even leave with one of those grainy photographs to show off.

When her name was called, an impossibly young nurse led her into an examination room. 'First baby, is it?'

'Yes.' Sam replied, noticing the ultrasound scanner and unsure what would happen next. Her nervousness must have been obvious as the nurse enlightened her about what would happen during her appointment before examining Samantha. With a huge smile, the nurse declared everything to be *cooking nicely*

'Okay, we'll do the scan now.' The nurse pulled the machine towards the bed and smothered gel on Sam's neat little bump. 'We can't always be accurate about the sex at this stage; if I can tell, do you want to know?'

'Yes, please!' Sam held her breath, and the nurse smiled.

'Just relax, and if you look at the monitor, you'll see your baby.'

As the nurse moved the ultrasound probe over her abdomen, Samantha was engrossed and stared at the monitor, fascinated with how well-formed her baby was.

It was a bittersweet experience. A deep longing to have Ravi at her side sharing in this magical moment tugged at her heart, yet a feeling of almost gratitude to be carrying his baby balanced the pain. A tear dripped silently onto the pillow.

'Amazing, isn't it? Are you sure you want to know the sex?'

Sam nodded, blinking back the tears.

'It's a boy. This will be confirmed at your next scan, although the equipment is good and eighty-five per cent accurate.'

A boy! Samantha would have been delighted with either gender, but a boy might grow to look like Ravi. It was a precious gift, a part of Ravi to keep, to love and cherish. Her attention was pulled back to reality as the nurse spoke again.

'I'd estimate the gestational age at fourteen or fifteen weeks and I'm confident there's only one baby in there.'

'Gosh, I'd not thought about twins!'

'Many new mums hope for twins – to get it over with in one pregnancy. One will be enough for me when my time comes!' Passing Sam a handful of tissues to clean the gel from her abdomen, the nurse continued. 'Okay, we'll take some blood now and then you can make another appointment at reception on the way out.'

Soon, Samantha was outside in the fresh air, clutching information leaflets in one hand and three amazing pictures of her baby in the other. It felt surreal – she was going to be a mother, the greatest responsibility of her life – and it was going to take some working out. Yet thanks to Ravi, she had choices and was financially secure. Her baby may not have a daddy, but he'd be surrounded by love and would want for nothing.

Trudging across the increasingly busy car park, Sam reflected on how different her career was from that of the young nurse who clearly loved her job. Sam dealt with violence, death and some of the dregs of society, while maternity care was the complete antithesis, although she wasn't so naïve as to think there wouldn't be times of sadness too. Life and death could be so wonderful and so cruel, giving and taking away indiscriminately.

THIRTY-SIX

Sam's emotions were all over the place. Yesterday's antenatal appointment felt like a dream, but the evidence of her pregnancy couldn't be denied. She found herself holding her slightly swollen belly and smiling to herself. It was so good to have something to look forward to, an event to anticipate with joy instead of the constant dread she'd experienced since Ravi's death and a reason to go on living. Having shared her news with Divya, Arjun and her mum, Sam now showed the image to Jenny and was thrilled by her friend's squeals of delight. However, today she must concentrate on work, focus on a case that continued to puzzle the team, and pursue the few leads that only seemed to steer them in circles.

Samantha read and re-read everything they'd discovered so far, searching for something they might have missed, something to give them the break they needed.

The *something* arrived at 10.20am just as Sam was considering making her second coffee of the morning. A flushed Jenny Newcombe approached her desk waving a thin blue file. 'Forensics!' she grinned and Sam almost grabbed the document from her. Jenny summarised the salient points before Sam could read them. 'DNA taken from Valerie's dressing gown has a twenty-five per cent match to someone we have in our data base.'

Sam ran her finger down the page, stopping at a name and address. 'Simon Prentis, 8 Thorndale Road, Belmont, Durham. So, a twenty-five per cent match – a familial connection. He might not be our man, but he's the best lead we've got. What is it, Jen? You look like you've seen a ghost.'

'There's something you should know about him. Simon Prentis is a DC at Aykley Heads. He's one of our own.'

Sam was silent as she processed this information, then her instincts kicked in and she jumped up. 'Gather the team. A twenty-five per cent match means he has a close relative who is now our chief suspect, not that he's involved himself. If there's half a chance of seeing Prentis today, you and I are going on a trip to Aykley Heads this afternoon.'

While Jen hurried to gather the team, Sam took out her phone to ring Aykley Heads. Although Ravi had been based there, Sam had only visited a couple of times; New Middridge was part of North Yorkshire Constabulary, while Aykley Heads was Durham Constabulary. Eventually, Samantha was connected to DI Helen Jarvis, Simon Prentis's senior officer. Stressing the importance of her need to speak to Prentis, Sam revealed her reasons but asked Helen to say as little as possible to Simon, who was on leave. Helen agreed to contact him and ask him to come in. A time of 3pm was decided.

As the team gathered in the incident room, Sam asked Jenny to summarise the forensic report, which the DS did, ending with the shocking fact that the familial DNA was a match for a serving police officer. 'As well as this familial DNA match on Valerie's clothing, there were tiny amounts of trace DNA. But they were so small that it was impossible to distinguish if they were secondary transfers as opposed to primary deposits. So, the only lead we have for the moment is DC Simon Prentis, who lives in Durham.' Jenny finished her summary and gazed around the room at the stunned faces of her colleagues.

Samantha felt it necessary to clarify the facts. 'Remember, familial DNA simply identifies *potential* relatives of an alleged perpetrator. We're not looking at Prentis as a suspect – don't be labelling him a bad cop – he simply has a familial relationship with a possible suspect. DS Newcombe and I will visit Aykley Heads this afternoon and will be meeting Simon Prentis at 3pm. This news will probably be as much of a shock to him as it is to us. For now, continue with whatever you're working on, except for Paul. I'd like you to do a full background check on him – his history with the force, siblings and parents. And see if he has a Peugeot 208 Coupe Cabriolet convertible registered in his name.'

While Paul returned to his computer, Sam and Jenny headed to the canteen for coffee. 'If the A1's not too busy, it shouldn't take much more than an hour,' Samantha said, choosing a tuna salad sandwich. She didn't want it but felt she should try to eat.

Jenny grabbed a cheese toastie. 'I'll drive.' She flashed a *don't argue with me* look at her boss.

'You're a good friend, Jen.' Sam returned the smile. 'Let's enjoy this and then see what Paul has discovered.'

THIRTY-SEVEN

P aul Roper checked the DVLA register first to see if a Peugeot Coupe was registered to Simon Prentis. The answer was no, but then, Paul thought, he was a copper, and the 2010 Nissan Micra registered in his name seemed a better fit for the salary of a DC.

Moving on to search the man's history felt uncomfortable. As the boss had reminded them, a familial match doesn't make him a criminal, but the investigation's focus was shifting to this unsuspecting DC's family links.

Prentis had joined the force at eighteen and spent three years in uniform before being accepted into CID. Paul accessed the original police vetting form and the disclosures Prentis would have to make regarding his financial situation and any police record.

Details of any family and friends with a record or behaviour which may be of concern and leave an officer vulnerable to extortion or blackmail also need disclosing. Everything looked good. Prentis had no siblings; his only family at the time was his parents. His credit checks were as would be expected, and social media searches threw up nothing of concern. The DC had married at about the same time he moved to CID and all checks on his wife, Christine, were positive.

Paul leaned back in his chair and sighed. He could have been reading his own record, average with nothing of interest.

A few more clicks of his mouse changed his opinion completely, and as Paul stared at the screen wide-eyed, he exclaimed, 'Bloody hell!'

'We'll call this an early lunch, shall we?' Samantha wiped her mouth with a napkin. 'I'm curious to see what Paul's turned up, and then we'll get on the road.' She paused for Jen to finish the last dregs of coffee before they left the canteen to return to the incident room.

The first thing they noticed on entering the incident room was Paul Roper sitting in front of his computer, leaning back in the chair, running his hands through his hair, and shaking his head in apparent disbelief.

'Have you found anything of interest, Paul?' The DS swivelled his chair around and looked at Sam and Jen.

'You're not going to believe this!'

The two detectives scurried over and peered over his shoulder. It was patently clear to all three that their investigation had taken a surprising twist.

THIRTY-EIGHT

DC Simon Prentis was enjoying a few beers on a lazy Tuesday off work. With a week's holiday ahead of him, relaxing had been yesterday's and today's priority and having played the dutiful dad and taken his two-year-old son, Noah, to the park to give his wife a break, Simon was feeling quite virtuous as he arrived home. After enjoying the pie and chips Christine had prepared for lunch, he planned to watch the horse racing on TV.

Christine was upstairs, settling Noah for his afternoon nap, and Simon put his feet on the coffee table and took another swig of beer. As he reached for the TV remote control, the phone rang, and muttering a word Christine didn't like him to use, Simon answered it. It was his boss, DI Helen Jarvis. 'Simon, sorry to disturb your day off, but I need you to come in this afternoon.'

'But boss, this is the first week I've had off for ages. What's happened?' He couldn't honestly say he had plans, but the call wasn't welcome.

'It's not a case; we just need you here to clear something up,' Helen sounded evasive, piquing Simon's curiosity. He didn't intend to interrupt his week's holiday without good reason. Helen sighed. 'A DI is coming from New Middridge. It appears you can help them with one of their current cases, a homicide, and that's about all I know. Can you get to Aykley Heads for 3pm?'

'Who is this DI and what's his case?'

'It's a female. Samantha Freeman, and as I said, it's important. The DI was quite insistent.'

Simon recognised the DI's name and frowned while reluctantly agreeing to attend the appointment. Ending the call, he wondered what on earth DI Sam Freeman could want from him.

Christine entered the room and flopped exhausted onto the sofa. 'Noah's finally asleep. I think he was overexcited from your trip to the park. Is anything wrong?'

'Can you remember Ravi Patel?'

'Of course. Such a tragedy, a waste of life.'

'He was engaged to a DI from New Middridge, Samantha Freeman and for some reason she wants to see me this afternoon concerning one of her cases.'

'But Ravi's only been gone a few months. The poor girl must be devastated. Should she be back at work so soon?'

'Well, she is, and it's bloody awful to land a murder investigation so soon after Ravi's death.'

'It can't be right to give her a murder investigation after all she's been through...'

'I wouldn't be surprised if Sam insisted on taking the case and it might be exactly what she needs to help her over her grief. Still, I'm at a loss to know why she wants to see me.'

Ravi had been a popular and respected DI at Aykley Heads, who Simon liked and respected. He remembered the excitement in Ravi's face when announcing his engagement and his smile as he listened to his colleagues crack the usual jokes about tying the knot – the usual copper's banter. To hear of Ravi's death just a few days later came as a shock to the whole of Aykley Heads – a tragic accident that stunned them all and prompted the desire for them to hold their own loved ones that little bit closer.

Christine broke into his thoughts. 'It won't affect our plans for the rest of the week, will it? Your mum and dad are expecting a day with Noah tomorrow while we go to the Metro Centre; you hadn't forgotten, had you?'

'No. It's probably nothing important and I am *so* looking forward to a day's shopping!' Simon didn't actually mind shopping, and a civilised meal out without an independent toddler who insisted on feeding himself would be a treat.

'That's good. This week's all about our time together – and Noah should be asleep for at least another hour...' Christine moved to sit on her husband's knee, her skirt riding to the top of her thighs as she wound her arms around his neck. All thoughts of shopping, Ravi, and murder cases suddenly flew from Simon's mind.

THIRTY-NINE

'No! That's Ben Chapman!' Jenny voiced what they were all thinking, her eyes swivelling from Paul's screen to the photo of Chapman on the whiteboard. She crossed to the board and took the photo down, bringing it to Samantha, who held it next to the screen to compare the images.

'It looks like the same man to me.' Paul folded his arms. 'Although they say we all have a doppelganger. Could they just be very alike?'

'Or could he be a twin?' Samantha leaned in closer to compare the two faces. 'Does it say in his file if he was adopted, Paul?'

'What? Are you suggesting that Valerie Turner had twins who were adopted separately?' Jenny looked aghast.

'It's a more likely scenario than having a double – and it would be too much of a coincidence for two look-alikes to have a connection to our murder case.'

'There's no mention of Prentis being adopted, but then he may not even know himself. It does say he has no siblings.' Paul laced his fingers behind his head. 'This is getting more bizarre by the minute. What do you think it means for our investigation?'

'It means that if I'm right and these two are twins, Ben Chapman is back in the frame for his mother's murder, and Simon Prentis is in for the shock of his life this afternoon. Jenny, I'm going to update the DCI, and then we'll get off to Aykley Heads.'

'So, you're telling me we have a colleague who's a familial match to DNA found on the victim, and you think he may be the victim's son, given up for adoption as a baby?' DCI Aiden Kent tilted his head to the side and looked quizzically at Samantha.

'That about sums it up, sir.'

Kent nodded thoughtfully. 'And you have an appointment to meet this DC this afternoon?'

'Yes, sir. At Aykley Heads. Clearly, if he is the son of the victim and the twin of Ben Chapman, then Chapman will become our chief suspect. It won't be quite so cut and dried, as the DNA could have legitimately transferred to Valerie's clothing; Ben was a frequent visitor to the house. Yet it was on her dressing gown, which in itself is suspicious.'

'Okay, Samantha. It appears you're in for an interesting afternoon – let me know how it goes.'

Sam left the DCI's office wondering if she should have used the opportunity to tell him she was pregnant. No, it was still early and he fussed over her enough as it was, although today's encounter was the first time he hadn't asked if she was all right.

Within ten minutes, Samantha and Jenny were on the way to Aykley Heads, Jenny at the wheel. 'I always thought when babies were given up for adoption, they kept siblings together, and with twins, it's even more important to maintain the bond, surely?'

'Yes, you'd think so, wouldn't you? Perhaps it's difficult to find adoptive parents prepared to take on twins.'

'Did you ever see that film, *Three Identical Strangers*?' Jen asked. Samantha shook her head. 'It's a true story of triplets given up for adoption and intentionally separated as a sociological experiment – a sort of nature versus nurture thing. They discovered each other when they were nineteen and two of them ended up at the same university. It must have been a hell of a shock.'

'And it's going to be quite a shock for Simon Prentis when we tell him why we want to see him unless he knows he's a twin, which I very much doubt.'

'Would you have been pleased if you were carrying twins, Sam?'

Samantha thought for a moment. 'Yes, I think I would. It would be hard work but I'd have welcomed the news. As it is, I'll only ever have one child to keep Ravi's memory alive.'

'Sorry, that was a personal question. I shouldn't have asked.'

'Don't apologise. In a weird sort of way, this pregnancy has changed my thinking about so many things. I'm even remembering Ravi without quite so much pain now. Although I can no longer share all my thoughts and feelings with Ravi, I keep thinking of things I must tell his son when he's old enough.'

'That's great. Maybe you should write them all down for him? If you're anything like me, you'll forget.'

'You're right, Jen, I'll do that. Next left here, just a couple more miles now.'

FORTY

Jenny manoeuvred into a vacant visitor parking spot, they exited the car and headed to the entrance. They were deliberately early, hoping to speak to Prentis's colleagues before meeting the man himself. It was busy for mid-afternoon, and everyone seemed to know where they were going except the New Middridge detectives. With directions, they found DI Helen Jarvis' office and introduced themselves. Helen was a tall woman with a long face split by a wide smile as she greeted her visitors.

'It's good to meet you, DI Freeman. Ravi often spoke of you. I'm so sorry for your loss; he was a much-loved colleague.'

'Thank you, and it's Samantha.'

'Let's find a comfortable place to sit.' From her office, she led them into a large interview room, probably a family room, and they settled on low, bench-style sofas. 'Can you tell me any more about why you wish to see Simon?'

Samantha understood the DI's interest. Prentis was part of her team and any suggestion of criminal involvement would be of grave concern. As she began a more detailed explanation than she'd given over the phone, Sam emphasised that Prentis's

DNA was only a familial match and, therefore, they were not considering him a suspect. She also related her suspicions that he had been adopted at birth.

'So, your victim was Simon's birth mother?'

'That's our theory. Did you know he was adopted?' Jenny asked.

'No, he's never said as much, but as far as I know, his parents are both alive and live locally. He has a small child and has occasionally mentioned grandparents babysitting for him.'

'What's he like? Not only as an officer but as a person.'

'He's very likeable. Simon's been on my team for over a year now and has proven to be a reliable, competent team player. I've been encouraging him to study for his sergeant's exam – he's got a bright future ahead of him in the force. He's happily married. I've met his wife, Christine, and they clearly dote on their son.'

Samantha thought the DI's voice held a protective note – a good thing and a positive testimony to Prentis' character. Helen clearly liked him. 'Thank you. It's nearly three, I assume he'll be here soon?'

'Yes. I asked my DS to keep him in the office until you're ready for him. Shall I see if he's here and maybe organise some coffee?'

'That would be amazing, thank you.'

Helen left the room.

'She has a motherly attitude towards him.' Jenny observed. 'Strange, isn't it, how your team can become as close as family?'

'Yes, I got that vibe too. I'm feeling rather sorry for him before we even meet. We may not be accusing him of anything, but our news will almost certainly come as a shock. Finding out who his birth mother was and that she's been murdered, possibly by someone with a familial DNA match, is a lot to take in.'

Helen entered the room once more with Simon Prentis

behind her. Sam and Jenny stood to greet the man, both stunned at the likeness to Ben Chapman. 'I'll see to the coffee and leave you to talk.' Helen tactfully retreated.

Samantha paused to draw a deep breath before thanking Simon for meeting with them and apologising for breaking into his holiday.

'That's okay. We didn't have plans for today, but we do tomorrow.' Simon was clearly fishing to see if this would be a one-off interview.

'I'm hoping we can clear things up today.' Sam smiled reassuringly.

'So, how can I help?' Simon's eyebrows arched as he looked from one detective to the other.

'This may seem a strange question, Simon, but are you adopted?'

His chin lifted slightly, and his brow furrowed. 'Yes, I am, but what's that got to do with anything?'

'We're investigating the murder of a Mrs Valerie Turner. She was killed in her home and we've discovered a familial DNA match to you. I'm sure you know that you're on the DNA database, and what this means?' Sam paused. Simon didn't answer. His face was pale.

A knock on the door interrupted them as a PC brought in a tray of coffee. Placing it on the table in the centre of the room, she spoke quietly, 'The DI says she's in the office if you need her.' She closed the door quietly behind her and Jenny served the coffee, spooning sugar into Simon's without asking.

'This must be difficult to process.' Jen smiled as she passed his coffee. 'Do you need a few minutes alone?'

'No. I'd like some answers, please. I understand that the DNA must come from someone related to me, but as I've confirmed, I'm adopted, and as I haven't any idea who my birth parents are or any other blood relatives, how can I help you?' He took a sip of coffee as Sam leaned forward in her seat.

'We do actually have a suspect, but first I need to tell you that we believe Valerie Turner may have been your birth mother.'

'No, damn it! You come in here telling me things I've never wanted to know! Why? Why the hell do you need to involve me? Yes, I knew I was adopted, which meant my so-called birth parents didn't want me, and for that reason, I've never had the desire to seek them out! This Valerie Turner, whoever she is, has nothing to do with me. I have wonderful parents, the only ones I need or want. Do I have to stay and listen to more?'

Samantha ached for the man. 'There's something else I think you should know.' She paused, waiting for a reaction before continuing. Simon remained seated and held eye contact, which she took as permission to continue. 'It appears you have a twin brother. An identical twin.'

Simon covered his face with his hands. Sam, unsure if he was crying or laughing, waited for him to speak.

He lowered his hands and banged them on the table. The coffee cups jumped. 'This is crazy. I don't believe you!'

Jenny reached into her bag and pulled out a photograph of Ben Chapman, which she passed to Simon. Taking the photo, he stared at it, mouth open and head shaking slowly. After a full minute, Simon lifted his head to meet Sam's eyes.

'Okay, I'm sorry, I'm not taking this well. Can I have a few minutes alone?'

'Of course.' The New Middridge detectives stood and left the room. 'We'll be outside when you're ready.' Jenny said, closing the door.

FORTY-ONE

Simon Prentis stared at the image of a man with his face. He could have been looking in a mirror; identical was an understatement. Even this stranger's hair was cut similarly to his own; the cow's lick he hated featured in this man's hair, too. The eye colour was the same, the shape of his nose, chin, and cheekbones... it was uncanny, chilling to see someone who looked like him.

Simon's adoption had never been a secret, and he couldn't recall a time when he didn't know. His parents handled it well – not making it a big deal – just stressing their love for him and how much he was wanted. As a boy, he'd longed for a brother or even a sister would have been acceptable, but he recognised it wasn't to be, and they were happy as a family of three. Now, it appeared he had a brother, a twin.

Had he ever wondered about his birth parents? The answer would have to be yes. Curiosity is a powerful emotion in a young boy, and although he didn't want to wonder, naturally, he did. Each time the mystery of his origin crossed his mind, Simon felt mixed emotions – sadness as he assumed he hadn't been wanted by the couple who created him and anger that they'd given him away. Being a sensible boy, he soothed his hurt by reminding himself of the parents he did have, the couple who loved him unconditionally and would do anything for him. His childhood had been happy, idyllic almost, and thoughts of his birth parents troubled him only occasionally.

Simon also felt blessed to have Christine and Noah. When his son was born, he again wrestled with his adopted status, but not for long. Having a child of his own changed Simon's outlook on life. He was more considerate and liked to think that being a father had made him a better person and a good police officer. But now he'd learned he was also a twin – he had a brother. Looking at the photograph left no room for doubt in his mind.

DI Freeman had clearly met his brother and believed them to be twins, but why had they been separated? Simon's mind buzzed with more questions than answers. Questions for the New Middridge detectives, for his parents, for his twin. Did his twin know about him? Could he meet him?

Simon gulped down the remains of his cold coffee and stood to open the door. The detectives were talking to his boss at the end of the corridor. Damn, what would his colleagues think? This was life-changing – he motioned to the detectives that he was ready to speak to them again, and they walked back towards the room, Helen Jarvis with them.

When they were seated, Helen spoke first. 'Simon. DI Freeman has outlined her case to me and what she's discovered about your connection. I want you to know that this will go no further. None of your colleagues will learn anything from me. I'll leave you to talk some more, but if I can help, just ask.' She stood to leave the room. Simon nodded his thanks, relief that one aspect was covered; he dreaded being the source of gossip, even well-meant gossip among friends.

Samantha leaned forward, looking earnestly at Simon. 'I know we've dropped a bombshell on you, and it will take much more than a few minutes to process this information. From our point of view, now that we've confirmed you were adopted, we'll be looking again at your twin brother and asking for a DNA sample.'

'What's his name? You haven't told me.'

'Let's just call him Ben for now.'

'Does he know about me? Did he know our mother– Oh hell, he must have if you think he killed her!'

'We don't think that yet; he's a possible suspect, one of several. We're a long way from solving this murder yet.'

'Does he live in New Middridge? Did my mother live there? And what about my birth father? Who is he, and are they still together?' The questions tumbled from his mouth, his mind spinning with endless scenarios and a sudden desire for information.

'I can't tell you where Ben lives, Simon.' Samantha spoke softly. 'He'd searched for Valerie after his adoptive parents died and found her last summer. They were building a relationship but she claimed not to know who your father was, a brief affair when she was young, apparently.

'Can I meet Ben? Are there other family members I don't know about?' Simon knew what the answer would be but had to ask.

'No, I'm sorry you can't. As you're a serving police officer, and he's a suspect in an ongoing case, that would be imprudent. And yes, there are other family members. You have two half-sisters and grandparents. Clearly meeting them will also be unwise until after the case is concluded We'll keep you informed of any developments.' It was inadequate but the best she could offer.

'Can I keep this photograph?' Simon still clutched the image of his twin, unsure if he was pleased or horrified to have learned of his existence. DI Freeman paused for a minute before answering, exchanging a look with her colleague.

'You can keep it as long as you give me your word that you won't use it to try and trace him.'

'Yes. I understand, and I certainly don't want to do anything to jeopardise my job.' Simon meant it. As much as the questions were stacking up in his mind, he wouldn't do anything stupid. He had too much to lose.

'Thank you, Simon and I'm sorry again to have been the bearer of such shocking news.'

The journey back to New Middridge offered the chance to share thoughts and ideas about how the interview with Prentis had gone. 'I like him,' Jenny stated. 'He's clearly well thought of among his colleagues and comes over as a good, honest cop. It must have been one hell of a shock for him.'

'Agreed. I can't imagine how he feels after such a revelation, and I'm sure he'll be asking his parents some difficult questions.'

'I wonder if they knew he was a twin when they adopted him. I gave him my number, as you suggested, in case he wants to talk. I'll be interested to know what his parents have to say. Do you think he'll keep his word about finding Ben?'

'Yes, I do. Simon seems sensible. If he does try to use facial recognition, there'll be nothing on the system as Ben doesn't have a record, but I think he'll keep his word. He has a lot to lose. I'm going to ring DCI Kent. He was keen to know how we got on. Then I'll update Paul and the team, and as it's 5pm, we can call it a day. Tomorrow, we'll decide how to proceed with Ben.'

'That should prove interesting!' Jenny concentrated on her driving and left Sam to make her calls.

FORTY-TWO

DI Helen Jarvis caught up with Simon as he hurried, in a surreal daze, to the exit of Aykley Heads. She wanted to offer any help he might need and reminded him of the counselling service the force provided.

'Thanks, boss. I'll get over it. I just want to get home and try to make sense of all DI Freeman told me.'

'Okay, and try to enjoy the rest of your week off.' Helen tactfully left him to make his way home.

'Christine!' Simon shouted as soon as he opened the door. He'd driven home far too quickly and was pale and sweating despite the cold outside.

'What?' His wife appeared from the kitchen, the aroma of chicken curry wafting in her wake.

'Come and sit down. I need to tell you something.' Simon grabbed her hand and almost dragged her into the lounge, where Noah played with his favourite Duplo bricks on the carpet.

'Hey, what's happened? Are you okay?'

'No, I'm not!' He threw his coat onto the chair and almost fell onto the sofa.

Christine stared at this distressed version of her husband. 'What is it? What's wrong?'

Trying to catch his breath, Simon began to explain what the interview with DI Freeman had been about. His wife sat silently, a bewildered expression on her face. When he told her about his DNA match to a suspect who could be none other than an identical twin, she shook her head. 'That's ridiculous! Something must be wrong with the test results.'

Simon reached for his coat and pulled the photograph from the pocket. 'Here!' He pushed it under her nose. 'They let me keep this, but all I know is that his name is Ben.' Christine stared at the image of a man who was identical to her husband and was lost for words.

'Apparently, I have grandparents and two half-sisters as well! Hell, Chris, I didn't want any of this, it's so confusing.' Pulling his phone from his pocket, Simon jabbed at the buttons. 'I'm going to ring Mum and Dad. I need to know if they were aware I had a twin brother when they adopted me.'

'Surely they wouldn't have known!' Christine said, unable to take her eyes off the photograph.

'We'll soon find out!'

'Simon! How lovely to hear from you. You're not ringing to cancel tomorrow, I hope?' Elaine Prentis sounded pleased to hear from her son.

'No, Mum, I'm not, but I need to ask you something.'

'You sound very serious, is anything wrong?'

'Yes. I can't explain everything but I've found out today that I have an identical twin brother. Did you and Dad know about this when you adopted me?'

'What? Are you joking, Simon?'

'No. I've never been more serious in my life.'

'Of course you didn't have an identical twin! You know your history – we've never kept anything from you from the time you were old enough to understand.' A few moments of silence ensued until Elaine asked. 'Simon, are you still there? What's this all about?'

'I'm sorry, Mum, it's to do with work, so I can't say too much. I've spoken with a detective from New Middridge today who's working on a case where they've discovered DNA, which is a partial match to mine. She came to see me and showed me a photograph of a man who can only be my identical twin.' Simon listened to his mother's gasp on the other end of the phone. Perhaps he should have spoken to his father first. 'Don't worry about it, Mum. It will all be sorted out soon. I just had to check that you knew nothing about it.'

'Oh, Simon, we didn't! If we knew you had a twin, we'd have adopted you both. Was he adopted too?'

'Yes, but he's recently been reunited with our birth mother.'

'And are you trying to tell me this is the way you're going – you want to find your birth family? Because if you do, you know we'll support you, don't you?'

Simon sighed. 'It's not as simple as that. My birth mother has been murdered, which is how the police came across the DNA.'

'Oh no! How appalling! Are you okay, Simon?'

How typical of his mum, always worrying about him. 'It's been a shock, and I still need to get my head around it all, but I'll be fine. Christine's with me. I'm not sure we'll stick to our plans tomorrow – can I let you know in the morning?'

'Yes, of course you can. But if you're not up to your shopping trip you could still come here, or we'll take Noah off for the day. Whatever you want to do is fine by us.'

'Thanks, Mum. You're an angel.'

Simon ended the call and turned to Christine, who'd been beside him, listening and rubbing his back in a comforting gesture. 'I should have known they wouldn't have kept something this momentous from me. Mum sounded as shocked as I was. Let's eat now, and then we'll decide what to do tomorrow.' Simon felt calmer than he'd been since meeting Sam Freeman. He had a great family – they'd get through this together and he couldn't resist Christine's chicken curry.

FORTY-THREE

Even with the case playing on her mind, Samantha slept surprisingly well after her visit to Aykley Heads. Up with the dawn chorus, she couldn't face food and skipping breakfast, set off early for work, keen to use the latest developments to progress the case.

She and Jenny had mulled over their next steps the previous evening on the drive home and decided that Samantha would call Ben Chapman early in the morning and ask him to provide a DNA sample. If, as they now suspected, he was involved in Valerie Turner's death, they anticipated a refusal. A refusal, together with the familial DNA from his brother, would give them sufficient grounds to apply for a warrant to obtain a sample by force if necessary.

It was 7.30am and Sam decided it wasn't too early to call Ben Chapman. His phone rang several times before a sleepy voice answered. Sam kept her tone cheery and light. 'DI Freeman here. Sorry to disturb you so early but we have a new development which you may be able to help us with.'

'Oh, okay, er, what is it?'

'The forensic samples are back from the lab, and I was wondering if you could provide us with a DNA sample for comparison.' Sam held her breath, waiting for some excuse or an outright refusal.

'Yeah, that's fine. I'm coming to New Middridge later this morning to meet Anna and Lizzie. Shall I come to the station?'

Sam was taken aback. This wasn't the reaction they'd anticipated. 'Yes, that would be very helpful, thank you. Maybe you could come before you meet with your sisters?'

'Yes, no problem, I'm awake now anyway.'

'Sorry about that. If I'm not in the station, just ask at the desk and someone will see you straight away. Thank you, Mr Chapman.'

When Sam finished speaking, she waved to catch Jenny's attention. Her DS had arrived during the call and was hanging up her coat.

Jenny greeted her boss. 'You're an early bird again.'

'Yes, but I don't think I've caught a worm.'

'Why, what's wrong?'

'I've spoken to Ben Chapman and asked him to come in to give a voluntary DNA sample.'

Jenny looked interested. 'Ooh, and what did he say?'

'Yes. He's coming in later this morning.'

'What, really? No argument, no procrastination?'

'None. He seemed happy to do so.' Sam rubbed her hands over her eyes. 'That sort of changes our theory, doesn't it?'

'Not necessarily. Maybe he's confident he can explain away any DNA match. He was a fairly frequent visitor to the house, and Valerie was his mother. He could claim any matches were legitimate, couldn't he?'

Sam sighed. 'Yes, I suppose so. But maybe he's not the one.' Sam felt deflated. As she looked up she saw the others of her team arriving. 'When everyone's here, gather them together for a briefing and we'll update them on yesterday's events and toss some ideas around.'

By 8.30am, the incident room was silent as the team listened to Jenny's account of their meeting with Simon Prentis the previous day. The buzz of excitement was almost tangible as each one processed the information Jenny shared. Questions followed.

'Did Prentis know he was a twin?' Layla asked.

'No. And as you can imagine, it was a huge shock.'

'What's your opinion of him, boss?' Paul was next to enquire.

'I liked him. There's no doubt in my mind that he's a genuine guy who's caught up in our investigation through no fault of his own. By all accounts, he's a good copper and a well-liked family man. I think Jenny's opinion is the same?' Sam looked to her DS, who nodded in agreement.

DC Kim Thatcher had listened to these developments in awe, her eyes wide with excitement. 'So does this mean that Ben Chapman is now our chief suspect?'

'That would be the natural assumption. However, I rang him requesting a voluntary DNA sample. I was fully expecting him to be evasive, which you'd expect from a guilty man, but he wasn't. He readily agreed to come in this morning to provide a swab. So, now I'm not so sure. Naturally, we'll take the swab and get it tested ASAP, but his reaction makes me doubt he's our man.'

Paul interjected, 'Won't Anna and Lizzie's DNA be a familial match to Simon Prentis? He is their half-brother, the same as Chapman.'

'Good point, Paul. The problem with a match from her daughters is that it would almost certainly be considered legitimate. It appears the DNA sample may be useless, so I think it's time to request voluntary DNA samples from all the principals in this case. We need to concentrate on all threads of the investigation – keep working on the slightest lead. This case is far from over.'

FORTY-FOUR

Lizzie Turner wasn't happy. Without consulting her and Anna, her dad had decided that it was time to return home, an event she'd dreaded yet knew was inevitable. Packing her bag, mixed feelings muddled her thoughts.

Lizzie had missed her things as she hadn't taken much to her grandparent's house and was fed up with wearing the same few clothes, so in some ways, she was ready to go.

It was also a squash in the bungalow, with no privacy, and her gran was always following her around the house, asking what she was doing or how she was feeling. She loved her gran, but living with her was stifling and sharing a room with Anna wasn't ideal either. Anna cried most nights, which Lizzie understood; she often cried herself, but Anna had been the one who'd seen their mother's body, and she kept talking about how gross it was, which was pretty tough to hear. Going home was the next big step.

As the car pulled up outside 22 Juniper Grove, its three occupants were silent, each lost in their own thoughts. It appeared they were all reluctant to exit the car, or more accurately, to enter their home.

Geoff made the first move, and Lizzie watched his strained expression turn to determination as he swung his legs out of the car and stood, slamming the door behind him. He moved round to open the boot and called to the girls. 'Come on, get your lazy bones moving and give me a hand.' Geoff's attempt at light-heartedness didn't fool his daughters.

Lizzie gathered her bags from beside her and slowly climbed out of the car to help her dad. Swinging her backpack over her shoulder, she grabbed a couple of carrier bags and heaved them from the boot. Anna reluctantly hovered by the car, waiting for her dad to lead the way. Lizzie linked her arm as they followed him to the front door. She could feel her sister flinch as the key turned in the lock and the door swung open. Lizzie purposefully steered Anna to the staircase.

'Take your bags upstairs while I help Dad with the rest of the stuff.' She smiled at Anna. Lizzie was aware that her sister and dad had seen her mum dead in the kitchen – she hadn't. Did that make her the lucky one? If she concentrated on Anna and Dad, maybe it would make the ghosts of the house easier to face.

When the car was unpacked, they gathered in the lounge. No one had yet entered the kitchen. 'Shall we have fish and chips for lunch?' Geoff asked.

'Great.' Lizzie replied. 'I'll warm the plates and make a pot of tea.'

As Geoff left the house to fetch their dinner, Lizzie forced her legs to go into the kitchen. Everything looked the same. 'Give me a hand, Anna,' she called to her sister. Anna stood in the kitchen doorway, her eyes fixed on the floor.

'It's probably best not to think about it. We had to come back, and I, for one, was fed up with being at Gran's.'

'You're right,' Anna said, lifting her head and stepping over the threshold. We should act normally for Dad's sake.' Lizzie hugged her sister on impulse as Anna sniffed away the building emotion, refusing to entertain the dark thoughts edging into her mind.

By the time Geoff returned, his daughters had laid the table and made a pot of tea. Geoff took the fish and chips into the kitchen, and Anna unwrapped the parcel. 'It smells good. I'm famished,' she said.

The worst was over. Father and daughters had confronted the scene of Valerie's death and, by acting normally even though it felt anything but, they managed to survive the first of many hurdles.

Another hurdle to be faced the same day was a visit from the undertaker. Valerie's funeral had been arranged for the following Wednesday and it was time to make plans.

Geoff had asked the girls if they wanted any involvement in the service, such as reading a poem or talking about their mum. The very thought terrified them. Lizzie knew she would never be able to keep her emotions in check and as they were expecting a large turnout, she declined. Anna also said no, but they were both keen to assist with the planning and that afternoon was the appointed time.

The undertaker was prompt. A thin, wispy-haired man with a too-large nose for his small head, he entered the lounge and introduced himself as George King. His manner was sympathetic but his sentences were punctuated with sniffs, an annoying habit which hardly endeared him to his clients. George King opened a notebook to go through the formalities, adhering to a scrawled list that Lizzie could see but not read.

A coffin was to be chosen; flowers discussed; an order of service... Lizzie wanted to be anywhere other than in that room, thinking about her mum lying dead in a coffin and talking about her funeral.

'Do you want a photograph displayed on the coffin?' King

smiled. 'We can have one of your favourites enlarged and framed for you.' Lizzie thought he was probably totting up the pounds as he ticked off the boxes.

'What do you think, Anna?' Geoff looked to his elder daughter, whose response was a shrug. 'I think it would be a good idea.' Geoff decided. 'Lizzie, would you go and have a look for one? I think there are some albums in the bottom drawer of the tallboy in the bedroom or maybe in your mum's wardrobe.'

Lizzie took the chance to escape, to breathe easier, and hurried upstairs, pausing momentarily outside her mother's bedroom. Pushing the door open as if it might break, she peered inside, half hoping to see her mum putting on her make-up at the dressing table. *Stupid girl!* Lizzie chided herself and marched into the room with a purpose.

A faint smell of her mother's favourite perfume hung in the atmosphere. Lizzie padded across the room, a heavy lump forming in her chest as she wondered how long it would linger. The bottom drawer of the tallboy was stiff to open; something was jamming it. Lizzie wriggled her fingers as far in as she could and pressed down on the offending item. With her other hand, she pulled the drawer open. It was crammed with albums, some old and tatty – she wouldn't find a recent photo in those. Lifting them out, Lizzie spread them on the carpet and, choosing the newest-looking one first, searched for a suitable photo of her mum. There were several that might do; she'd take them down to let her dad choose.

As she was about to replace the albums, Lizzie noticed the bottom of the drawer was loose. Pressing it with her palm made it see-saw as if something was underneath the base. Prising it out with her fingernails, she pulled out a thickly padded A4-sized envelope. It wasn't sealed and when she lifted the flap, Lizzie was stunned to see it was full of money. Notes of ten, twenty and fifty pounds in value filled the envelope; there must have been hundreds, maybe thousands of pounds.

Why would her mother have so much cash in the house, and why was it hidden away? Lizzie's mind whirred with theories, some of them not so good. She was aware that her dad had been sleeping in the spare room and things had been strained between them, so did he know of the money? Probably not, as it was Dad who'd sent her up here to look in the tallboy. Could there be more stashed in other hiding places? If so, why? And what did this tell her about her mum?

Lizzie faced a dilemma. Should she mention this to her dad? There could be a simple explanation – saving for a surprise holiday, perhaps? Her instinct was to think about it before making a decision, so she carefully replaced the money, laid the board on top, put the albums back in place and took the chosen photographs downstairs.

FORTY-FIVE

Wednesday and Thursday proved to be frustrating in the New Middridge Police Station, with the Valerie Turner case no nearer to being solved than two weeks ago. The DNA familial match to Simon Prentis had caused an excitement which had almost completely fizzled out. It wasn't as relevant as they thought, and then, when Ben Chapman willingly offered a DNA sample, it created doubt in Samantha's mind as to whether he was involved. He may not have an alibi, but neither did he have a strong motive, unless he'd harboured a grudge at being given up for adoption – something Sam considered but dismissed, even though Jenny reminded her people had killed for less.

Sam couldn't see Ben as a murderer, although if his DNA sample proved a 100 per cent match, they'd have to look more seriously at him. Yet his reaction when he heard of Val's death had seemed genuine, and he'd clearly formed a bond with his half-sisters. Would he murder their mother? Unlikely.

The team had spent the last few days collecting DNA samples with no problems other than Steve Green, who continued to refuse their request. He'd also persuaded his wife against cooperating. Was he hiding his guilt or simply making a point because he could? The couple alibied each other, but Sam wanted to speak with Hayley Green again when her husband wasn't around – and maybe vice versa, too. Hayley probably had a stronger motive to kill Valerie than her husband; she was the wronged wife.

DC Kim Thatcher had been at Hammond, Birch and Fox solicitors all morning, supervising the collection of DNA samples with a couple of uniformed officers. She returned to seek out her boss, who wasn't in the office. Taking the chance to visit the ladies' loo, Kim found Samantha or rather heard her, vomiting in a toilet cubicle.

'Are you okay, boss?' Kim tapped on the cubicle door.

'Will be soon. Just give me a minute.'

Kim took the hint and returned to the office. Ten minutes later, Samantha approached her. 'Sorry about that. How did you get on with the solicitors?'

'Okay. A couple of office staff were off, one on long-term sick leave and another with flu. Alex Hammond was also on holiday, apparently in Mauritius.'

'Lucky for some. Get the samples to the lab, will you, Kim?'

'They're already there, but they say it'll be next week before they're processed. Do you want me to visit the staff who were off?'

'Not today, Kim. Enjoy your weekend off. You've worked hard and need some downtime.' Sam watched as her DC left with a smile on her face and was grateful the girl hadn't asked about the episode in the toilets. Surely the sickness should be over by now? Perhaps it was time to make her pregnancy official and tell the DCI. He was out of his office and she decided that if he came back before she left, she'd tell him, and then the others could know.

Sam's due date was 8th September, so her son must have

been conceived in early December when she and Ravi hadn't a care in the world – when she didn't know that her heart would be ripped out in such a sudden and cruel way. It was now 2nd March. Sam put her hand on her abdomen and smiled. This baby was her future; all she had left of Ravi.

A figure climbing the stairs in the corridor caught Sam's eye. The DCI was back. After waiting a few minutes, Sam followed Aiden Kent to his office. His door was open, and he was packing his briefcase, preparing to leave for the weekend.

'Can I have a word, sir?' Samantha stood in the doorway.

'Yes, come in!' He turned and smiled. 'How's the case going?'

'Slowly I'm afraid. We're currently collecting DNA samples, but it's not the case I'd like to speak to you about.'

'Sit down, Samantha. How can I help?' His face adopted a concerned expression with eyebrows raised in a quizzical fashion.

'I'm pregnant, sir.' Sam smiled, an intentional indication to her boss that this was good news.

'Congratulations! And how are you coping?'

'Oh, the morning sickness has been a pain, but hopefully, I'm getting past that stage. Generally, I feel fine, and I can assure you that this will in no way affect my work.'

Aiden Kent smiled. 'Sam, I know you well enough to realise that, but you've been through a difficult time, and whatever you need, just ask. Time off, lighter duties – whatever.'

'Well, there will be antenatal appointments but they'll quite easily fit around work, and I shouldn't need time off. I'm generally quite healthy. This isn't going to affect my performance.'

'Yes, I'm sure. But you need to take care of yourself, Sam. Speaking as a friend, not your boss, you know you can come to me if there's anything at all I can do, don't you?'

The DCI's words shouldn't have been a surprise, yet they touched Sam, who swallowed hard and nodded her understanding.

'You're not working this weekend, are you?'

'No, sir. I'm off until Monday unless there are any developments.'

'Good. Make the most of it, and again, congratulations! My wife will be thrilled when I tell her – it is all right to tell her, isn't it?'

'Yes, sir. I've told Jenny and it's time to tell the rest of my team.' She left the office to do just that.

FORTY-SIX

It was four days since the return to Juniper Grove, four days since Lizzie had discovered the stash of money in her mother's drawer, and she was still undecided as to what to do. Having spent an uncomfortable weekend dithering over the dilemma, it was time to make up her mind. Geoff was going to the supermarket to stock up on essentials and asked the girls to go with him. Keen to get out of the house, Anna jumped at the chance. Lizzie declined, wanting time to think and to get her ducks in a row.

Her dad frowned. 'I don't like leaving you at home alone...'

'I'll be fine. It's not like you'll be gone for hours, and I have a headache; the supermarket's the last place I want to go.'

'Okay, but ring me if you need me.' Geoff grabbed his coat.

Anna was ready and looked at her sister as if she'd never seen her before. 'Are you mad?' she hissed. 'Why would you want to stay here alone after all that's happened?'

'I'm fine. A bit of time to myself is all I need; I'll probably have a lie-down.' Lizzie hated lying; she'd learned her lesson about the consequences of lies, but she wanted to search her mother's room again and needed to be alone to do so. As soon as

Geoff and Anna left, Lizzie ran upstairs. Her dad had moved back into the main bedroom and the scent of his aftershave replaced her mother's perfume. His clothes were strewn on the unmade bed – her mother would have been fuming at the mess.

Carefully prising the bottom drawer of the tallboy open, Lizzie removed the albums and put them to one side. With her fingernails, she grappled with the loose board until she managed to remove it and then carefully lifted out the envelope. Her heart was pounding; guilt made her clumsy as she took out the notes to count them. Sitting on the carpet, Lizzie counted the fifty-pound notes into one pile, the twenties into another and the tens into a third pile.

Holding her breath, she was stunned to discover there was over ten thousand pounds sitting in neat piles on her Dad's bedroom floor. Where had such an amount come from? Lizzie knew they weren't poor, and during the pandemic, they'd cut back on many little luxuries, so how did her mum have such a sum as this? And more importantly, what on earth should she do about it?

Regretting her curiosity, Lizzie put the piles of money back in the envelope and replaced it in her mother's hiding place. Checking the time, she decided it was safe to have a quick search of the rest of the room. Her mother's wardrobe held nothing but clothes and shoes – her cupboard stored her handbags, scarves and other accessories – nothing hidden away there.

The jewellery boxes were next. Lizzie's mum had loved her jewellery and owned several boxes, none of which appeared to hold any strange envelopes of money. A quick look in the ottoman to check if that, too, might have a false bottom revealed nothing; all was as it should be.

With nowhere else to search and time running out, Lizzie left the room and went to her bedroom. Taking a few deep breaths, she sprawled on her bed and buried her face into the pillow. Her head really was aching now. Lizzie dearly wished she'd never found the money in the first place.

Trying to think methodically, she listed where such an amount could have come from. Her mum saving for a family holiday would be the best scenario, but Lizzie somehow doubted that, suspecting it was a more sinister reason.

She and Anna knew things weren't good between her parents, and the more Lizzie thought about it, the more she became convinced that her mum was planning to leave her dad – but was she also leaving her daughters? A tear escaped and trickled down her cheek. Mum had been strict, and they argued like any other family, but she loved them and wouldn't leave them all… would she?

Lizzie rolled over and stared at the ceiling. Should she tell her dad? It would be hurtful for him to know his wife had a secret stash of money, but then he'd find it himself sometime. Mum's things would eventually be sorted out; they were only waiting until after the funeral to tackle that job.

The funeral was something else Lizzie dreaded. They'd received dozens of sympathy cards, which were all over the house, and it was clear there'd be a big turnout at the funeral. Anna said it was always the same when someone young died, and because it was a murder, there'd be lots of people coming out of curiosity, rubberneckers, Anna called them. Perhaps even the press would be there to take photographs; Lizzie wished she could wear her hoodie and hide inside its folds but doubted Dad would allow her. It was on Wednesday, two more days, but even then, this nightmare – their current normality – would continue until the police discovered who'd killed her mum.

It had been surreal learning they had another set of grandparents. Lizzie didn't know what to think of her mother now; she'd lied about her parents and Ben, and this stash of money was concerning. Why would she claim her parents were dead? They'd returned to Merseyside but were coming back for the funeral, and Lizzie was looking forward to seeing them again. On their first meeting, she and Anna had asked several questions, and her grandparents answered as many as possible. When the girls talked afterwards, they agreed that the Edwards had been telling the truth. They both liked them and would be happy to see them again.

Life was surreal and Lizzie felt she was hanging onto her sanity by a thread. It was like being caught up in a television soap, yet this was their new reality. Maybe she shouldn't decide what to do about the money until after the funeral – they had enough to worry about until then. Yes, that was probably the best plan – when in doubt, procrastinate, someone had once told her jokingly.

A noise downstairs warned Lizzie that her dad and sister were home. Relief washed over her – being alone in the house wasn't as easy as she'd expected it to be and she'd be glad of their company.

FORTY-SEVEN

In the days leading up to Valerie Turner's funeral, her family argued over many things. Geoff had arranged a church service, after which they would travel to the crematorium to say their final farewell. Anna accused him of being hypocritical as neither he nor Val had been in any way religious. Claiming she'd be uncomfortable in a church, she'd only backed down when her grandmother intervened and told her to think about her dad rather than herself.

'If a church service brings him comfort, then you should agree to it and hold your tongue!' Mary Turner chastised her granddaughter. Lizzie entered the debate and declared that she would like a church service, so Anna backed down.

When they discussed who should travel in the funeral cars, both the girls wanted Ben to be with them but Geoff said a firm no, and again, his wishes were overriding. Anna rang Ben to apologise but he understood and even agreed with Geoff, saying it wasn't a day for confrontation and he'd be happy to follow in his own car. Geoff did concede and allowed them to invite him to the pub afterwards, where they'd booked a private room and a buffet reception. The Edwards were coming to the funeral but insisted on making their own way there.

It was a typical March day. Heavy grey clouds scudded across the sky, and the wind blew bitterly cold rain almost horizontally at the mourners as they exited the car to enter the church. As expected, the pews were full, with some unfamiliar faces among the many known to the family.

Lizzie was surprised to see DI Freeman and DS Newcombe waiting outside the church. Kim Thatcher stood with them and nodded to Anna and Lizzie when they looked her way. Lizzie squeezed her dad's hand – trying to control her feelings by thinking of his as they followed the coffin into the church.

The atmosphere was solemn, and the air smelled of damp, furniture polish and lilies. Simon and Garfunkel's 'Bridge Over Troubled Water' played as they walked to their seats. It had been one of Valerie's favourite songs, and the haunting melody released the tears that Anna and Lizzie had been holding back.

As the service progressed, the girls wept quietly, Lizzie occasionally lifting her head to look at the coffin – unable to believe her mother was actually inside it. How she longed to feel her mum's arms holding her right now. Yes, they'd argued lately, and Lizzie had said some awful things which she bitterly regretted. But she'd loved her mum and wished she was still alive.

Three rows back, Robert and Bella Edwards sat stoically clasping each other's hands, their thoughts battened down tightly, emotions resolutely under control.

The vicar's calm, clear voice broke into Lizzie's thoughts. 'Even though I walk through the darkest valley, I will fear no evil, for You are with me; Your rod and staff, they comfort me.'

Lizzie had heard those words before in an assembly at school. They were from the Bible, Psalm 23, she thought, and described exactly how she was feeling. Walking through the darkest valley, and surprising even herself she silently prayed that God would be with her and comfort her.

The day dragged. The service proved emotional as the vicar spoke of Valerie's life, throwing in a few anecdotes which Geoff had provided. Even he wept openly at one point. When the coffin was finally carried out of the church, it was to Simon and Garfunkel's 'Sound of Silence'. The family walked sombrely to the waiting car.

Lizzie thought she'd never experienced such sadness in her life. The committal at the crematorium was unreal; she moved robotically as if in a dream and afterwards recalled very little of what had happened.

Talking with Anna later, they agreed that the worst part of the day had been the wake at the pub afterwards. Neither of the girls wanted to be there. They couldn't believe how people could eat and drink and talk to each other about mundane things. An odd burst of laughter had startled and sickened Lizzie – how could people laugh on a day like today? It had been the first funeral the girls had attended. Would they get used to death as apparently these people had?

That same evening in Belmont, Durham, Simon and Christine Prentis watched the local news and were surprised to see a report on the funeral of the murder victim in New Middridge. Simon's head realised it was his birth mother's funeral but it somehow didn't register in his heart. The cameras panned in on the family as they exited the car, and Christine tutted. 'They have to try to capture people's grief, don't they? Why can't they leave them alone? Haven't they suffered enough?'

Simon nodded his agreement, his eyes fixed on the screen. 'Look,' he exclaimed, 'That's Samantha Freeman standing by the wall, the one on the right.'

Christine looked at the small figure with short-cropped hair and large, sad eyes. 'She looks so young and fragile, as if a gust of wind would knock the poor girl over.'

'Don't let looks fool you. Sam's known as an excellent DI and something of a terrier at work. When she gets her teeth into a case, she won't let go. Now that I've met her I can see how she earns her reputation. We could do with more detectives like her.'

'Oh my goodness, there's your brother!' Christine grabbed his arm and pointed to the screen as the camera swept past a man who was the image of Simon. Her husband gasped and pressed the pause button on the remote. Staring wordlessly, his stomach seemed to flip over, and if he hadn't been seated, he was sure he'd have fallen over.

'Ben – his name's Ben. Hell, there's no room for doubt, is there?' They stared in silence at Simon's newly discovered twin brother.

'His hair's a bit longer than yours,' Christine eventually spoke, weaving her fingers through her husband's and squeezing. 'Are you okay, love?'

'I don't know. It's weird. I thought it wouldn't bother me, but it does! I want to talk to him, to hear his voice and ask him so many questions...'

'Can't you arrange a meeting?'

'No. DI Freeman was clear there's to be no contact until the case is over – he's still a suspect.' Simon suddenly shivered. 'I wonder if Mum and Dad have seen this?'

FORTY-EIGHT

Lizzie had so far kept silent about the money she'd discovered in her mother's room and was troubled in case it had any bearing on her mother's death. Maybe someone had known the money was there, come to steal it and killed her mum? Her dad had been despondent since the funeral; they all had, but Geoff was intending to return to work after the weekend, and she and Anna would go back to school.

Finally, she decided to confide in Anna and found her moping in her bedroom. 'Can we talk?' Lizzie hovered uneasily in the doorway.

'Course, we can come in and close the door.' Anna's room was a mess. Clothes were strewn all over, several dirty mugs littered her desk and bedside table, and the bed was unmade, looking as if it had hosted a wrestling match. Anna was sitting cross-legged on the floor, an open book beside her, and music playing too loudly.

'Can you turn that down?' Lizzie asked.

Anna rolled her eyes but did as she was asked. 'What do you want to talk about? I don't want to discuss the funeral again. It's best forgotten. We have to move on.'

'No, it's not the funeral. Do you remember when the undertaker was here and Dad sent me upstairs to find a photo of Mum?' Anna nodded. 'Well, that's not all I found. In the bottom drawer where all the albums are, there was an envelope with some money in it.'

'So what?'

'There was about ten thousand pounds.'

'Ten thousand!' Anna sat up straighter, suddenly interested. 'Are you sure?'

'Yes. I counted it later when you and Dad were out shopping. The envelope was hidden under a false bottom in the drawer. I don't know if I should say anything to Dad. What do you think?'

'He might already know about it.'

'Yeah, I wondered if he did, but he and Mum were sleeping in separate rooms at the time. It was in her drawer.' Lizzie looked hopefully to her sister for some pearls of wisdom, some direction she could take.

'Maybe Mum was saving up for something?'

'D'you think she was saving up to leave Dad – and us.'

'Never – she wouldn't!'

'That's what I thought. Maybe someone had known the money was there and had come to steal it, found Mum in the house and killed her. Should we tell the police?'

'Not without telling Dad first, he'd go ape! This could be important, but if Dad already knows about the money, then it has nothing to do with the police. Let's go down and tell him.'

Geoff Turner was in the kitchen endeavouring to prepare lunch when his daughters came in and asked if he could sit down to talk. 'Sounds serious?' He half smiled. Anna nudged Lizzie for her to tell her story.

'I don't want you to think I was snooping, but when I went to find a photo of Mum for the undertaker, I noticed the bottom of the drawer was loose, and there was an envelope under it, with quite a bit of money inside.' Lizzie watched the frown appear on her dad's face and had her answer. He didn't know about the money. 'I thought if you didn't know, then it might be something we should tell the police – a motive for whoever broke in and killed Mum.'

'How much money are you talking about? Some loose change or a hundred quid?'

Lizzie shuffled uneasily on her chair. 'About ten thousand pounds.'

'What!' Geoff was on his feet and heading upstairs before his daughters could say more. 'Which bloody drawer, Lizzie?' He yelled as his feet thundered on the stairs. Running after him, Lizzie and Anna followed him into Valerie's bedroom where Lizzie pointed to the bottom drawer of the tallboy. Geoff yanked it open and threw the photographs and albums onto the floor. Placing his palm on the false bottom, he rocked it until he found purchase with his fingernails and lifted it out. Grabbing the envelope, he tipped the contents onto the bed.

'Where the hell did she get this much money?' His question was hypothetical. Geoff didn't expect the girls to know any more than he did.

'So you didn't know it was there?' Lizzie asked the obvious.

'No way! And I don't know where it's come from either.'

'Do you think we should tell the police?' Anna almost whispered as Geoff Turner slowly nodded his head.

FORTY-NINE

Samantha sighed. Yet another team meeting, and they were no further forward with this frustrating case. As the officers gathered, an excited Kim Thatcher hurried towards her boss. 'The DNA results for Ben Chapman are in!' She passed a sheet of paper to Sam, whose eyes raced over the words.

'A twenty-five per cent match to the DNA on Valerie's clothing, meaning it wasn't him. We're back to square one.'

'Doesn't it put Anna or even Lizzie back in the frame?'

A second sigh left Sam's lips. 'I'm fairly sure their DNA results will show one of them to be our match, which renders the sample useless. It's entirely possible for their DNA to be found legitimately on their mother's dressing gown.'

'Forensics are sending more results later this morning. Maybe something will turn up then?' Kim looked hopefully at her boss.

'We'll see. You've worked well on this case, Kim. Well done.'

During the team meeting, Sam relayed this latest news. Ideas and suggestions were tossed around, some helpful, others not. 'Realistically, the DNA samples aren't going to solve this crime. We keep returning to Steve and Hayley

Green, the only principals who have refused to provide a sample. Why is that, and what are they hiding? Paul, will you and Tom visit Steve Green's place of work and ask a few questions? We've nothing to suggest it's him or his wife, although their alibis for each other are a bit weak. Maybe if we rattle his cage a bit, he'll cooperate or make a mistake. Any other ideas?' Blank faces answered her question and when Kim's phone rang, Sam took the opportunity to thank the team and dismiss them.

'Boss!' Kim caught Sam's attention. 'It's Geoff Turner on the phone. He wants to know if we can go and see him?'

Sam's eyes widened as she nodded vigorously. 'Tell him we're on our way.'

Lizzie Turner was watching from the window as the detectives pulled up outside number 22 Juniper Grove. Sam gave a friendly wave and smiled, curious as to why they'd been summoned when their visits were generally unwelcome intrusions. Lizzie opened the door and led them into the lounge.

Anna, who was sitting beside her father, jumped up when they entered. 'Can I make you a coffee?' she asked.

'Thanks, but no. How are you doing?' Sam had seen the family at the funeral but not to talk to and wondered if something had happened at the wake which they wished to tell her.

'It's better now that the funeral's over. I'm returning to work on Monday and the girls will go back to school.'

'Probably the best thing to do. And why did you want to see us today?'

Geoff pointed to a thick envelope on the coffee table, his face in a grimace as if there was a bad taste in his mouth. 'Lizzie found this in Val's drawer. There's ten thousand pounds in there, and I don't know where the hell it came from. We thought you should know in case it's relevant.'

Sam put on a pair of nitrile gloves, picked up the envelope, and peered inside. 'Have you counted it?'

'Yes. Lizzie counted it shortly after she found it and I have today.'

'And do you know how or why Valerie would have such a large amount in cash?'

'Absolutely not. Since I found it, I've checked our savings accounts passbooks to see if she'd taken any from there, but she hadn't. Even if Val emptied all our savings and the current account, she'd have been hard pushed to total ten grand.'

'Did Valerie have any accounts in her name only?'

'Not that I knew of, but I'm beginning to think I didn't know my wife very well. I would have happily boasted that we didn't have secrets from each other until Ben turned up and then the thing with Steve Green and her parents.' Geoff blinked hard and sniffed. 'It makes me wonder what else I don't know.'

Samantha held her breath for a minute. Geoff would have to be told that his wife had given birth to twins at some point and it would be another shock for him, but she wasn't inclined to reveal that information just yet. It was too early. 'So, you can't think of where the money might have come from or for what reason Val had hidden it?'

Geoff looked at Lizzie, then at Anna. 'The girls were aware things weren't great between Val and me... and maybe... she was planning on leaving. I honestly don't know.'

'Then it's possible she was saving up? Do you think it's feasible for Val to have saved such an amount without your knowledge?'

'No... I don't know what to think any more.'

Lizzie spoke up, 'Maybe whoever broke in knew about the money and was looking for it?'

'It's certainly something to consider, Lizzie. Geoff, thank you for telling us about this. I'm afraid I'll have to take the money away as evidence and pass it on to forensics, although I doubt it will tell us much. I'll leave a receipt, and if it turns out to be legitimate savings, you'll get it back.' Samantha stood to leave and all three of the Turners walked her and Kim to the door.

On the way back to the station, Kim asked. 'Do you think the money's relevant?'

'Yes. One thing Geoff hadn't considered is whether Val had amassed the money by fraudulent means and her position as office manager may have given her the opportunity to do exactly that. Perhaps it's time to look more closely at Hammond, Birch and Fox.'

FIFTY

'No, we'll take my car this time. I'm fine, you know. The leg's healed well, and I have no qualms about driving. I've been back at work for a month; you don't have to coddle me any longer.' Samantha smiled as she spoke to her DS, not wanting to offend and grateful for Jenny's support and concern.

Climbing into the Mini Cooper, Jen wouldn't give in too easily. 'But there's the baby to consider as well.' She raised her hands in mock surrender as Sam flashed her a look of reproach. 'Okay, you win, I'll back off!'

'That's good. Pregnancy isn't an illness, and I fully intend to work for as long as possible before the birth.'

'Any plans for afterwards?'

'Not yet. It's not an easy decision – I love my work, but this little boy is so precious.'

'There's plenty of time to think about it. Your news went down well in the office, although I think Layla was slightly jealous. If she starts to get broody, Paul might have to commit to a wedding date.'

'Maybe I should tell her about the awful morning sickness – put her off the idea?'

'Nah, I won't admit to saying this but we women are wired to get broody at a certain age. Perhaps I should get myself a man before my clock ticks any louder. That last idiot has rather put me off men, but there must be someone out there worthy of me!'

'Ha! You're right, Jen, but you have to get yourself out there to find him. Stop putting in for all the overtime going and get yourself a social life.'

'Yeah, maybe when we solve this case, eh?'

Pulling up outside the offices of Hammond, Birch and Fox, the detectives exited the car and entered the lobby. A smiling Maddie greeted them, inviting them into the foyer to wait while she checked which partner was available to see them. 'Mr Hammond is still on holiday, although I think he's at home now, having a few days to himself before returning to work. Mr Fox is in today and Mr Birch too. If you'd like to wait here, I'll see if either of them is free.' She disappeared through the swing doors toward the partners' offices.

Two minutes later Maddie was back. 'Mr Birch is available to see you now. Can I bring you some coffee, ladies?'

'No thanks. We don't want to take up too much of your boss's time.' Sam and Jenny followed Maddie to James Birch's comfortable office, where he greeted them warmly. 'Good morning. How can I help you, detectives?' He motioned for them to be seated and took his place behind his desk.

'Good morning, Mr Birch, and thank you for seeing us without an appointment.' Sam stated the reason for their visit without any preamble. 'I'm afraid I have to ask if you've had any financial irregularities in the firm of late? A strange question, I know, but there's a suggestion of fraud playing a part in Valerie Turner's death, and we wondered if you've had any problems recently?'

'If you're suggesting Valerie was somehow embezzling funds, I don't believe it!' James Birch's eyes widened in surprise.

'I've known her for years and there's never been the slightest irregularity. Valerie was an excellent and trusted employee.'

Samantha sat forward and frowned slightly. 'My apologies, Mr Birch. I don't mean to cast aspersions and I wouldn't be asking such a sensitive question if it wasn't necessary. A large amount of cash has been found in Valerie's home, which can't be accounted for. I'm not accusing her of stealing this money but we have to consider that someone may have known it was there and broken in to take it. Or even the possibility that she was holding the money for someone else. Can you assure me that Val didn't have access to a significant amount of cash here at work, and then we can look elsewhere?'

'Well, I suppose she did have access to cash. Most of our transactions are by bank transfer, but we do have clients who prefer to use cash, and Valerie would have been responsible for banking whatever we received.' James Birch scratched his balding pate. 'I find the suggestion most upsetting, although I understand your position, DI Freeman. I suppose I can have our auditors review the books to check for abnormalities, but I'd have to consult my partners first.'

'That would be most helpful.' Sam smiled, but James Birch hadn't finished.

'I'd need to know what time period to cover and the amount of money we're talking about.'

'I'm afraid I don't know the answer to the first part of your question. The sum is in the thousands, but it could have been gathered over months, even years.'

'So, not an easy task then?'

'No. Do you think we could talk to Mr Fox about it? And I believe Mr Hammond is on holiday?'

'Yes, that's right. Alex is back in the country but not due into work until next Tuesday.' Mr Birch stood up and turned towards the door. 'I'll just see if Peter's free to join us.'

When he left the room, Jenny gave a low whistle. 'Gosh, this is a tricky one. We're asking them to look for something which might not be missing or could have been squirrelled away over a period of years, and by doing so, we're besmirching the reputation of a woman he clearly admired.'

Jenny grinned. 'That just about sums it up, boss.'

James Birch took ten minutes to return, time which Sam and Jen assumed he was using to brief Peter Fox. When the two men entered the office, they both wore solemn expressions.

'James has told me of your request. I'm a little hesitant about calling in the auditors, which in itself will raise a few eyebrows. Can you give us a little time to consider our position? Maybe we'll consult with Alex and get back to you?'

'Yes, of course and thank you. Perhaps you could call us as soon as you decide?' Sam smiled and stood to leave. Peter Fox walked the detectives to the door.

Once outside, Jenny huffed as she lowered herself into Sam's Mini. 'We should have expected as much from solicitors. They play their cards close to their chests at the best of times. Probably worried about their reputation.'

'Well I hope they play ball. If we don't hear from them over the weekend, maybe we'll pay Alex Hammond a visit at home.' Sam switched on the engine and manoeuvred out into the traffic.

FIFTY-ONE

D S Paul Roper flashed his new warrant card at the man at the office reception desk and asked to speak to the manager. A little thrill ran through his body when he introduced himself as a DS rather than a lowly DC. Tom Wilson stood beside Paul, attempting to look stern.

The man looked them both up and down, finished scribbling on the form he was busy with and ambled lazily further into the office. The detectives watched him knock on a door at the far end of the room before disappearing inside.

Steve Green had worked at Bartlett's Haulage for the last ten years, driving HGVs all over the country and occasionally on the continent. Paul's mission was to find out a little of the man himself – whether he was popular with colleagues, if he caused any trouble, or had a temper – gossip really – and the reason was to ruffle Steve's feathers.

A rotund man walked towards them, in no more of a hurry than his colleague. After further introductions, Paul asked if there was somewhere they could talk privately. The manager, who'd introduced himself as Melvin Jones, asked them to follow him to his office, an untidy mess of a room with the smell of cigarettes hanging heavily in the air.

'We're here to ask about Steve Green. Just some background about him, your impressions of his character and such like.' Paul sat in the chair opposite Jones while Tom stood; there were only two chairs.

'Is this to do with his neighbour who was murdered?' Jones leaned over the desk, alert and eager to talk.

'It's a formality. We're looking into all family friends and those close to them. Did Steve tell you about the case?'

'He said he's fed up with your lot hounding him. Came in the other day complaining he'd had no sleep with you turning up to ask questions all the time. Is Steve a suspect?'

'He's a close neighbour and a friend of the victim. Did he ever mention the family?'

Jones sat back, a playful look in his eyes. 'He might have done. If she was a looker, then Steve would be interested. He has an eye for the ladies. I saw her photo on the news. Shame, such a waste.'

Paul was glad Layla wasn't with him on this interview. Melvin Jones was what she would describe as a slimy little man. His attitude toward women would have riled Layla to the point of saying something she might regret. The question was, did Steve Green share this attitude toward women, and could he trust Jones to give a true account of Green's personality?

'Does Steve have any colleagues he's particularly close to? Maybe I could talk to them.'

'Nah. The men come and go. They don't hang around here much after they've had a long drive. Barry on the front desk knows him as well as any of us. You could have a chat with him on the way out.'

Paul was itching to get out of the stuffy room. He thanked

Melvin Jones and left to see if they could glean more information from Barry.

'Steve's an okay sort if you're on his right side, but he's got a bloody temper on him if he's crossed,' Barry confided. 'What's he been up to then?'

'Nothing. These are just general enquiries in a current case. Thanks for your help. I shouldn't think we'll need to trouble you again.'

Paul and Tom left the haulage company, both glad to be out in the fresh air. 'Not much to go on there,' Tom commented.

'No. But Steve Green will hear we've been asking questions, which will stir him up a bit. He'll either go bananas or roll over and give us a DNA sample. My money's on the bananas!'

FIFTY-TWO

Samantha spent the weekend painting the little bedroom allocated as the nursery. She wanted to do it early before her tiny baby bump became restrictive – it seemed sensible, but she didn't mention the decorating to her parents, knowing their views would differ from hers. It was only a matter of rolling on fresh emulsion as the room was in good order. Sam found it therapeutic, and the pale blue colour was soothing.

Once finished, she intended to order a new carpet and nursery furniture. Shopping on the internet filled in the rest of her time as she planned the transformation of her baby's room.

Sam still preferred to spend her free time at home and only went out to visit her parents or do the necessary grocery shopping. Jenny tried to encourage her to socialize more, but Sam wasn't quite ready and only occasionally joined her friend for a curry. She did make an exception to attend Paul's promotion celebration at the pub but left after an hour, returning to the comfort of her solitude at home. Sometimes, Sam wondered if it was possible to fully enjoy life again without Ravi. Planning for their son became her only positive focus outside of work.

On Monday, Sam and Jenny intended to visit Alex Hammond at home, while Kim was tasked with returning to the solicitors' office to collect DNA from the staff members who'd been absent on her previous visit.

Alex Hammond lived with his wife in a picturesque village three miles south of New Middridge. The short drive was pleasant on such an unusually bright day, with the hedges showing green and daffodils nodding in the breeze. As Samantha's sat nav announced they had reached their destination, she pulled up opposite the Hammond residence. They left the car to cross the road towards a five-bar gate set in a neat, thick privet hedge. The cottage stood twenty yards or so back from the road, and Jenny gave a low whistle when she glimpsed the whitewashed, double-fronted dwelling. A gravel drive crunched satisfyingly beneath their feet as they approached the front porch, which was flanked by two magnolia trees in full bloom. The porch itself was covered in a flowering clematis with cream bell-shaped flowers hiding rust-coloured speckles inside.

'Why don't I have flowering plants in my garden at this time of year?' Sam took in the beauty of the waxy magnolia blooms.

'It's all in the planning. Whoever planted these chose early flowering varieties. I love these star magnolias.' Jenny touched the delicate petals.

'I didn't know you were green-fingered. You don't even have a window box in your flat, do you?'

'It comes from spending a childhood with garden-mad grandparents. My knowledge of garden plants may be extensive but completely useless for a detective living in a first floor flat.' Jen grinned. 'I actually hate gardening.'

The door was answered by a tall, slim woman in designer jeans and a cream silk blouse. Her hair and make-up were impeccable for early on a Monday morning, and Sam guessed her to be in her late forties or maybe a well-preserved fifty.

'Mrs Hammond?' Jenny smiled and held out her warrant card. 'I'm DS Newcombe, and this is DI Freeman. Is your husband at home?'

Mrs Hammond raised a well-groomed eyebrow, grasped the collar of her blouse and rubbed it between her fingers. 'Is anything wrong?'

'We just have a few routine questions for him. May we come in?'

A frowning Elaine Hammond stood aside as the detectives entered. If the outside of the house was impressive, the inside was stunning. Decorated in modern, neutral tones, the hallway had rich wooden flooring, with a bright Moroccan rug adding a splash of colour. But what interested Sam most was what she saw leaning against the far corner of the hall.

Showing the detectives into a large lounge, Elaine Hammond waved her hand, inviting them to be seated on the large cream sofa. 'You're lucky to have caught us in. We're going out very soon.' After making her point, Elaine excused herself to go and find her husband. Taking in the spacious room, the detectives exchanged a look.

'You could fit the whole of my little flat in here,' Jenny chuckled. The furnishings were contemporary, clean lines, and nothing ostentatious. They sat to wait for Alex Hammond. It was a stunning room, although Sam wouldn't call it homely.

A relaxed and tanned Alex entered the room within a couple of minutes. 'Hello,' he smiled. 'What can I do for you?' Before they could answer, Elaine Hammond followed her husband into the room. 'Can I offer you coffee?' Her expression was stern, almost daring them to accept.

'No, thank you, Mrs Hammond, we won't keep your

husband any longer than necessary.' Sam smiled at the woman who understood the meaning and left the room.

'Elaine's rather tired after our holiday. It takes her a while to recover from jet lag.'

Sam nodded wondering why she didn't look so glamorous when tired. 'I wondered if Mr Birch or Mr Fox has consulted you regarding an audit of your accounts?'

'Ah, yes. James did ring after you visited the office. Is it really necessary? I rather think someone would have noticed if a significant sum was missing.'

'But wouldn't that someone have been Valerie Turner?' Samantha countered.

Alex stroked his chin thoughtfully. 'Yes, I see your point. Naturally, if you feel it's essential, I'll agree, but I'm assuming your investigations will remain confidential regarding the firm?'

'Yes, certainly.'

'Was there anything else?' Alex stood, as if he assumed the interview was over.

'Actually, yes. We've been gathering DNA samples from your colleagues at work and wondered if you would provide one, too. It will only take a minute. DS Newcombe can collect one now.'

Alex shrugged, resigned. 'Again, if you think it necessary.'

'Thank you, Mr Hammond, we do.' Jenny took out her kit and swabbed the inside of Alex Hammond's cheek.

Once outside, trudging back across the crunching gravel to the car, Jenny was the first to speak, 'Well, that went better than I thought, although Mrs Hammond was rather sour-faced, wasn't she?' She opened the door and strapped herself into the passenger seat of Sam's Mini Cooper.

'I'm sure you would be too if you'd just come home from two weeks in Mauritius.'

'Huh, chance would be welcome!'

'Did you notice the golf clubs at the end of the hall?' Sam paused for Jenny's reaction before starting the engine.

'Can't say I did. Why?'

'It's possible that our missing murder weapon may be a golf club.'

'So now we're suspecting anyone who plays golf?'

'Why not? Alex Hammond could be a suspect, but then he didn't protest when we asked for a DNA sample, did he?' Sam switched on the engine and they headed back to the station.

FIFTY-THREE

Back at New Middridge Police Station, Jenny asked Tom to take Hammond's DNA swab to the lab while she wrote up a report on their morning's visit.

'Two phone calls for you, boss.' Paul handed Sam a slip of paper. 'One from Simon Prentis and one from Steve Green. They both wanted to speak to you personally.'

'Thanks, Paul. Anything else?'

'Kim's back from the solicitor's office and has dropped the samples off. I can't remember ever taking so many samples in a case before.'

'No, and I'm beginning to think this isn't how we will solve this one. We need a break – finding the murder weapon would be great, or a gift-wrapped confession, perhaps?' Sam surprised herself at her attempt at humour, weak though it was, while Paul returned to his computer with a smile on his face.

Sam rang Simon Prentis first, assuming this would be the easier call. He'd been in her thoughts often since meeting him. This must have been a terrible shock for the young officer. 'Hi, Simon. How are you?'

'Okay, I suppose. Thanks for returning my call. I just wondered if there was any news?'

Sam sighed. 'I'm sorry, we're ploughing on without much success here, but I will let you know of any breakthroughs.'

'Thanks. I saw him on the television at the funeral, my brother, Ben. It was weird. Have you told him about me yet?'

'No, I've been waiting for the right moment. I'd hoped to solve this quickly and clear your brother. Then you could make contact if it's what you want.'

'It is. I have so many questions, and if Ben knew our mother, he might have the answers. And I'd like to meet my two half-sisters and grandparents. From being an only child, I appear to have quite a family; it's all rather crazy. I can't get my head around it at all.'

'I imagine it's strange for you, and I'm sorry we can't move things along any quicker. Are you back at work now?'

'Yes. My week off didn't go quite as planned, but it was good to have time with the family to talk things over.'

'Do you mind my asking if your adoptive parents knew you were a twin? It's irrelevant to the case but I've been wondering,' Sam asked tentatively.

'No, I don't mind. They hadn't a clue. We've gone over and over it again and still can't understand it. If they'd known, they would have offered to adopt us both; my mum, in particular, is horrified that we were separated.'

'It does seem odd. I'll certainly let you know of any developments and I'm sorry you must wait so long, Simon.'

'Thanks, I'll try to be patient.' Sam thought she heard a smile in his voice, and as she said goodbye, she had another reason to resolve this case.

Steve Green answered his phone on the first ring with no pleasantries or thanks for her call. 'What the hell do you think you're playing at? Asking questions at my place of work is uncalled for. It's harassment! I've got a mind to put in an official complaint!'

'My apologies if you're offended, Mr Green, but your lack of cooperation necessitated enquiries from other sources.'

'What d'you mean, *lack of co-operation*? I've answered all your questions!'

'Providing a DNA sample would be particularly helpful and enable us to rule you out of our enquiries.'

Sam could hear Green's raspy breathing as he considered her words. She allowed the silence to continue, waiting for his response.

'Okay. I'll give you your damn swab, but you can send someone round, I'm not coming to the station.'

'Thank you, Mr Green. And what about your wife? Do you think she'll be prepared to submit a sample?'

'Yes. We're in for the rest of the day, so if you want the samples, you'd better send someone soon!' The call ended abruptly before Sam could say more. A small smile played on her lips. It wasn't a huge victory, but anything positive was to be welcomed in this investigation. Samantha went in search of Tom Wilson, knowing he would be pleased with a mission to visit the Greens' home.

FIFTY-FOUR

Keeping the news about Simon Prentis from Geoff Turner bothered Samantha. Clearly, it would be another shock, another lie of omission from the wife he now felt he hadn't really known. Eventually Sam decided that concealing the information was serving no purpose, so she rang Geoff to fix a convenient time to see him. He had returned to work and was attempting to make up for the time he'd lost, but agreed to see her early, before his shift.

Juniper Grove was quiet as Sam pulled up at 7.30am. The peacefulness and signs of spring gave the street a different feel from the time it swarmed with the spectacle of a murder investigation, but was life returning to normal for the Turner family?

Sam rang the doorbell. It was opened by Geoff who put his finger to his lips. 'The girls are still in bed.'

'Sorry!' Sam followed him into the lounge.

'I've just made coffee. Would you like some?'

'Yes please, coffee would be very welcome.'

As Geoff went into the kitchen, Sam heard someone coming

downstairs, and Lizzie entered the room. 'Oh, hello,' the girl said, looking startled.

'I'm sorry, Lizzie, did I wake you?'

'S'alright, I have to get ready for school.' She scratched her head and yawned.

'How are you doing? Are things okay at school?'

'Yeah. The teachers have been cutting me some slack and my friends have been great. There are days I don't want to go, but when I'm there, it's okay, better than moping at home.'

'And is Anna doing well too?'

'Think so, pretty much the same, I suppose. Did you want to speak to me, or can I go and get a shower?'

'No, it's your dad I need to talk to, but it's good to see you, Lizzie.' Sam smiled as the girl turned and plodded back upstairs just as Geoff appeared with two mugs of coffee.

'Milk, no sugar, is that right?'

'Great, thank you.'

'So, any progress?' Geoff looked hopefully at Sam, who was pleased at how he'd recently appeared resigned to the investigation taking time and hadn't been harassing her for daily updates.

'There is something I need to tell you, although it's not necessarily progress in the case.' Sam sipped her coffee while Geoff frowned and tilted his head towards her. 'There was a familial DNA match on Val's clothing to someone on our system.'

'What's a familial match?'

'It's a match to a relative of the source of the sample, rather than the person themselves, and it can provide a lead. In this case, the relative was a police officer who we've been in contact with, but who I'm certain has nothing to do with Val's murder.'

'So, are you saying it's a relative of this police officer who killed her?'

Sam drew in a deep breath. 'It's not quite so simple. When we interviewed this officer, it was clear that he was the twin brother of Ben Chapman.'

'A twin! But Ben was Val's son...' Geoff put his coffee cup on the side table, his hand trembling. 'Bloody hell, Sam, are you telling me Val gave birth to twins?'

'Yes, it appears so. Neither of them was aware of this, and when I tell Ben, I'm sure it will be a shock to him too.'

'What's his name?'

'Simon. That's all I can tell you for now.'

'And you haven't told Ben yet?'

'No, so perhaps you can hold off from telling the girls until I have?'

'I'm getting confused here. If this Simon's DNA was a match to a sample on Val's clothing, does that mean Ben killed her?'

'Not necessarily. Ben willingly provided a sample, which matches Simon's but is only a familial match to the sample from Val's clothing, which clears both of them. It does, however, confirm they are brothers, therefore half-brothers to Anna and Lizzie.'

Geoff ran his fingers through his hair, shaking his head as he tried to comprehend Sam's words. 'I thought I knew everything about Val. Huh, it seems she's made a bloody fool of me – twin sons, a pile of money stashed away and dead parents who are very much alive – what does it all mean?'

'I take it you've not had any more thoughts about the money?'

'No. But I'm convinced she couldn't have saved it up. We struggled through lockdown and I'm pretty sure there was nothing spare to squirrel away. What do you think?'

'We're making enquiries, but nothing's come to light so far.' Sam finished her coffee. 'I'll leave you to get to work, Geoff.

Thanks for the coffee, and I'm sorry to bear more difficult news. As I say, it's better if you keep it to yourself for now until we can work out the relevance, if any.' Sam stood to leave and Geoff saw her to the door.

On arrival at the station, Sam met Tom Wilson in the corridor. 'I've dropped the Greens' samples off at the lab, boss.'

'Thanks, Tom. What sort of reception did you get from them?'

'Frosty – they clearly resented my presence and very little was said. Steve Green did ask if we'd caught the perp yet but I gave the stock answer of enquiries being ongoing.'

'Good work, Tom, thank you. Let's get in and see if anything's cropped up while we were out, shall we?'

The answer to Sam's question was no. An air of despondency hovered over the incident room. Evidence and statements were being checked and double-checked, a frustrating but necessary process in the hope of something new coming to light. Sam sighed as she sat at her computer to write yet another report.

FIFTY-FIVE

Alex Hammond sighed while driving home after a difficult week at work. The auditor had been with them most of the week, finding nothing amiss, as Alex knew he wouldn't. One thing you could say about Valerie Turner was that she was meticulous in her bookkeeping.

Rain was falling again, and as Alex nudged on the wipers, he hoped it wouldn't last and prevent his golf game on Saturday. He needed the exercise and fresh air after being stuck in the office all week and he could do with getting away from Elaine, too.

His wife had been a real pain to live with lately – even the holiday to Mauritius didn't appear to alter her mood, although it was her choice and had cost a fortune. Elaine had insisted on flying business class and on a five-star hotel, which he'd assumed would at least put a smile on her face. But no, nothing was up to her standards, least of all him. He'd hoped for harmony at home, especially as Alex's major problem at work had finally been sorted out.

Enough introspection – Alex pulled into the drive of the house he loved. The shrubbery was at its best, manicured to perfection by the wizard of a gardener they'd found and the borders were dug over and mulched in preparation for the bedding plants. Money certainly had its advantages and a comfortable home was one of them. Alex attempted to rally his mood. It was the weekend, the rain was easing off, and he could leave his work problems at the office and enjoy a couple of relaxing days.

As soon as he closed the door behind him, Alex knew something was wrong. Usually, his home was warm and welcoming, with lamps glowing and the aroma of a meal to greet him. Not so this evening. The house was gloomy, cold, and inhospitable, and Alex pulled the collar of his coat around his neck rather than discarding it in the hall.

'Elaine!' He called, but there was no reply. Heading for the lounge, Alex found no sign of his wife except for an empty wine bottle and a glass perched on the mantel shelf. The rest of the downstairs was unlit and clearly uninhabited, so he made his way up the stairs, calling his wife's name. Throwing open the master bedroom door, Alex was greeted by the sight of Elaine sprawled across the bed, another empty wine bottle cradled in her hand as she snored loudly, in an almost comatose state.

Alex had been aware that his wife was drinking more than was good for her. Their holiday had been marred by her excesses and he'd been embarrassed by her behaviour on more than one occasion. Moving to the bed, Alex shook her shoulder with no response. He shook her more firmly and she rolled over and muttered a couple of undistinguishable words. Alex was sickened by the sight of her. Elaine had always been one for appearances – immaculately turned out, even at home. Suddenly she lurched over the side of the bed and vomited, narrowly missing Alex's leather loafers.

'What the hell do you think you're playing at?' His stern voice brought her back to consciousness, bleary eyes trying to focus on him. Elaine laughed at her husband and rolled over so he was no longer in her line of sight. 'Leave me alone...' she muttered.

Alex did exactly that. He thought about covering her with a throw but decided she could stay cold for all he cared – and she could clean her mess up when she came round. Slamming the door, he ran downstairs, turned up the thermostat and wandered into the kitchen. The acrid smell of his wife's vomit turned his stomach – he would eat later, but he needed a glass of water.

Turning on the lights throughout the house, Alex put a Marvin Gaye CD in the player, hoping the music would relax him. When Elaine sobered up, they would talk seriously. He wanted to know what her behaviour was all about and how they could address their worsening relationship.

After an hour, Alex returned to the kitchen and made a sandwich with ham and cheese which looked past its best. Strong coffee helped to make it palatable and while waiting for Elaine to make an appearance, he took papers from his briefcase to do some work.

It was 9pm before Alex heard his wife stirring. The noise of the shower was a welcome indication that she was coming to her senses.

Half an hour later, a bedraggled Elaine entered the lounge, her hair wet, wearing a bathrobe and holding a mug of black coffee. 'Don't say anything!' she snarled.

Alex turned back to his papers, happy to oblige, but they both knew the silence was a precursor to a long overdue conversation.

'What's going on, Elaine?' Alex wanted to get the discussion out and over with.

'I think you should be telling me what's going on!' She almost spat the bitter words at her husband.

'Are you still drunk? I haven't a clue what you're referring to.' Alex's mouth twitched. He didn't sound confident, and his wife smiled slowly.

'You see, Alex. I know your dirty little secret. I know exactly what you've done!'

FIFTY-SIX

Sam took Friday off as a rest day, intending to enjoy a long weekend and some much-needed respite from the pressures of work. The working week had again proved fruitless, with much tedious checking and comparing of statements revealing nothing new, and on Thursday, just before Sam left the station, Alex Hammond rang to say the audit was complete and there was nothing untoward in the finances of Hammond Birch and Fox. Their auditor had double-checked Val's bookkeeping going back two years and everything was in order.

'Another question without an answer. When are we going to find something to break this case?' Jenny asked her boss as they left the office together. Sam's reply was little more than a shrug; she needed to distance herself from the Val Turner case and hoped a long weekend would help her do just that.

Waking on Friday morning, Sam experienced the delight of feeling her baby moving within her. There'd been movements before, fluttering sensations that she was unsure of and put down to wishful thinking, but this was a definite kick. Rubbing her hand over her bump, Sam smiled. 'Are you going to be a football player?' Her baby responded with another strong movement. It was a great way to commence her long weekend.

First on her list of plans was some indulgent shopping therapy for baby clothes and equipment, after which a quiet afternoon was in order. Over the weekend, Sam hoped to spend time with her parents and treat them to a nice meal out in thanks for their support. Another more challenging plan was to make the time to seriously consider her future. Ever since discovering she was pregnant with Ravi's child, her perspective on life had started to shift in gradual, almost imperceptive ways. Yes, she would always miss Ravi; his absence left a huge, sometimes overwhelming, void in her life, but their son was her future. Sam was making a conscious effort to maintain a positive outlook, and her baby was instrumental in this transformation.

After a light lunch, Sam sought out the journal she'd recently bought. Today was the perfect day to commence work on her book of memories. Settling by the fire with a fresh coffee beside her, Sam smoothed the first page, noted the date and began writing.

> Today, without a doubt, you made your presence felt. I already love you so much and can't wait to meet you! Will you look like your daddy? I hope so. Ravi was so handsome, but even if you don't, it'll be okay. And now I want to tell you about your daddy – how we met and how happy we were. I want you to know what a wonderful man he was – principled, kind, intelligent, funny – all of the things I wish for you...

Sam put down her pen and sipped the cooling coffee. Photographs would jog her memory and illustrate her book, so when she'd drained the last of her coffee, the search began in earnest. Most photographs of Ravi and herself were on her phone and a half hour passed quickly as she browsed through them, then printed off the ones she wanted to include. Her son would never meet his father in the flesh but Sam was determined he would know as much about him as possible. Perhaps she would invite Divya to contribute to the book, or better still, make one of her own from memories and photos of Ravi's childhood. It would be interesting to compare her son's childhood to his father's.

Sam halted her project after a couple of hours. This wasn't something to be completed in a day and would offer more enjoyment if stretched out over a longer period of time. So many memories were flooding back into her consciousness, happy times she'd remember forever, and which were crucial to record in her book.

As Sam settled down with a fresh coffee and a book she'd wanted to read for ages, her phone rang. Jenny's name flashed up and Sam knew it must be important for her sergeant to disturb her rest day.

'Hi, Jen, what's new?'

'The best news yet!' Jenny's voice was unusually high-pitched. 'Rick has sent over the DNA results on Alex Hammond and would you believe – he's Ben Chapman and Simon Prentis's birth father?'

'No!' Sam hadn't guessed this one. Having not considered Alex Hammond as a likely suspect, the news suddenly threw him right into the centre of their investigation. She looked at the clock, 4pm. 'I'll be there in half an hour. Get Paul onto the paperwork for a search warrant and Layla to do a background check and if the DCI's still there, can you update him? This could be the break we're looking for. We'll line everything up and then bring him in for an interview under caution.' Sam's switch to professional mode was instantaneous. Her mind raced as she dashed upstairs to change for work, then headed out less than five minutes after the call. So much for her long weekend and her plans; it could all wait as this interesting new development took priority.

FIFTY-SEVEN

'Why didn't we look more closely at Hammond before?' Jenny greeted her boss with frustration in her voice.

'Because he's a respected solicitor and, we erroneously assumed, one of the good guys, but we shouldn't jump to conclusions. Being Ben and Simon's biological father gives him one hell of a motive to silence Val Turner, but that doesn't make it a slam-dunk conclusion. This has to be done by the book – any slip-ups won't go unnoticed.' Sam headed for Layla's desk. 'How's the background looking?'

'As you'd assume from a solicitor, there's no criminal record, not even a hint of anything untoward. He appears to be an upright citizen, a member of the Rotary Club, sponsor of a couple of local charities – what you'd expect. He was born in Scotland and the family moved to Liverpool when he was a teenager. He attended university back in Edinburgh. His first job was at a firm in Liverpool, where he married Elaine, and they had two children, a boy and a girl, before moving to Carlisle in 1997. I'm just about to pull up his financials now.'

'Thanks, Layla. The Liverpool connection could be relevant. Print what you have so far for me, please. I'd like it to hand when we interview him.' Sam glanced around the office, grateful that most of her team was still there. Hurrying over to Paul's desk, she asked how he was progressing with the search warrant.

'I've completed the paperwork but there's no way we can get authorisation now. Friday evening and all the magistrates have left early, but I should be able to get one signed in the morning.'

'Thanks, Paul. Hammond's unlikely to be a flight risk. It does seem strange that he gave a DNA sample so readily.'

'Maybe he was confident there wasn't any DNA at the scene to connect him, or he didn't think we'd know about Ben Chapman's existence?'

'Hmm, possibly. Are you in tomorrow, Paul, to see the warrant through?'

'Yup. If tomorrow's the day we solve this one, then I'll be here.'

'Great. You can be at Hammond's house for the search, and the first thing I want is the man's golf clubs.' Sam smiled and left Paul to continue his work.

'Boss!' Layla called for Sam's attention. 'Hammond has access to a Peugeot 208 Coupe Cabriolet convertible. There's one registered in his wife's name.'

'Really?' Sam's pulse raced. 'That's interesting.' Finally, the breaks were coming in. Although waiting for a search warrant was frustrating, it gave the team time to plan and prepare the necessary documentation. A warrant could be obtained early the next morning, and the search could be conducted soon after.

'Do you think he's the one?' Jenny shoved a deli coffee in front of Sam.

'Thanks, you're a lifesaver. I'm leaning towards saying yes, although there are one or two things I'd like to know first.'

'Like?'

'Like his alibi for the day of the murder. And he may have got Val pregnant all those years ago, but why murder her now?'

'Do you think they've kept in touch?'

'I doubt it. Hammond's only been in New Middridge since last summer, so I guess they reconnected by coincidence. Hopefully, we'll learn the truth tomorrow when we bring him in.'

During the next couple of hours, everything was prepared to the nth degree to make the following day's events as smooth as possible. Paul was tasked with getting the warrant and executing the search of Hammond's house – Sam's only instruction was to get the golf clubs straight to forensics. Alex Hammond would be brought to the station for an interview under caution conducted by Sam and Jenny, and hopefully, the day would end with an arrest for murder.

Only when she was convinced there was nothing more to do in preparation did Sam head for home. She had set aside her former plans for the weekend. They could wait; now it was time to solve the Valerie Turner case.

FIFTY-EIGHT

Alex Hammond stared at his wife with contempt. She may have showered but she was still drunk.

Elaine staggered across the room towards him. 'Don't pretend you don't know what I'm talking about.' Her voice was slurred and spittle flew from her mouth as she spoke. 'Mr Perfect – always in the right, aren't you? Well, I know what you've done!'

'Elaine, if you have something to say, just say it. If not, I suggest black coffee and sleeping it off. We can talk in the morning,' Alex was about to turn his back on her when his wife suddenly lunged towards him, arms reaching up, fingers splayed as if to scratch his face. Swiftly, he grabbed her wrists and pushed her away.

'Ow! Get off, you're hurting me!' Elaine yelled. As soon as he let go, she sprang forward again, her right hand catching him below his left eye and drawing blood. As Alex turned away, instinctively raising his hand to his cheek, his elbow caught Elaine's face, and she screamed with pain and fell to the floor.

'Stop this!' he shouted. 'It's ridiculous – you're acting like a child!' His words appeared to anger her. Suddenly she was on her feet again, jumping on him like an animal. Alex attempted to defend himself without hurting his wife, but as she rained blows on him with her balled fists, he had no choice but to pull her off him, twisting her arm behind her back to keep her still.

Elaine writhed and kicked, determined to free herself from his hold, but Alex kept his arms firmly wrapped around her, preventing movement until she finally calmed and relaxed from her thrashing. Slowly, Alex released his hold and stepped back from a sobbing Elaine. They were both panting, Alex with blood trickling down his face and Elaine with the beginnings of a swollen eye.

'What the hell's brought this on?' Alex sat on the chair furthest from his wife and looked at her dishevelled figure. Elaine flopped on the sofa, dropped her head into her hands, and wept bitterly. Alex watched, unsure whether to attempt to comfort her or if physical contact would anger her again, so he waited.

It was ten minutes before Elaine pulled herself sufficiently together to talk. 'You've made a fool of me. All these years pretending to be the perfect husband and father, and you had a secret love child! How do you think that makes me feel? Bloody stupid, that's how!' Angry tears flowed again. Elaine turned away, biting her bottom lip.

Alex's heart sank. *How on earth did she find out?*

Elaine broke the silence. 'So, how much has this child cost us over the years – did you send him to private school with *my* money? And his mother. Has she been your bit on the side all these years?'

'No, Elaine, you've got it all wrong! I didn't know about the child until recently. Please believe me.'

'Why should I when you've lied about it all this time?'

'But I haven't. Listen, Val Turner was a mistake – a stupid affair that should never have happened, and I regretted it immediately. When she told me she was pregnant, I suggested an abortion, which is what I thought she wanted.' Alex held his hands up, palms outwards, 'She was just a kid herself and didn't want to be saddled with a baby. I thought she'd gone ahead with the abortion. I didn't see or hear from her again, and we moved away shortly afterwards...' Alex dabbed at his eye with his handkerchief; it stung and probably needed a stitch. Elaine had curled her knees onto the sofa and was hugging them close, her face an angry tear-streaked mask.

'When we moved to New Middridge, it was a shock to see Val again, and I didn't recognise her at first, it had been so long. Then one day she reminded me – said she'd not gone through with the abortion and had the boy adopted. He'd recently contacted her and they'd formed some sort of bond. I didn't believe her, it could have been all lies, but somehow Val managed to get a sample of my DNA, a coffee cup I should think, and the same from the boy. When the results proved she was telling the truth, Val started blackmailing me.'

It struck Alex then that his wife must have found the document confirming the DNA match. 'Have you been searching my papers?' His nostrils flared.

'Is that any more of a crime than having a secret child?' Elaine spat back at him.

Realising he in no way held the moral high ground, he lowered his eyes, thinking of what to say to sort this fiasco out. Alex wouldn't be devastated if this was the end of his marriage, but the last thing he wanted was for his children to find out what he'd done and that they had a half-brother. Life could become very messy – he'd lose their respect...

'I'm sorry, Elaine. I was young and stupid. I never meant to hurt you, and, honestly, I've never done anything like it again.'

'Am I supposed to believe you? I don't know you any more,

Alex.' She shook her head slowly, and seeing the disappointment in her eyes, Alex loathed himself.

'Please. We can sort this out. Val's the only one other than us who knew I was this boy's father. She's dead now...'

Elaine's face blanched, and her eyes grew wide as she appeared to sink into the fabric of the sofa. 'That's what really terrifies me, Alex. Who killed Valerie Turner?'

FIFTY-NINE

Samantha slept very little. Adrenalin coursed through her veins, and each time she closed her eyes, they popped open again at the thought of something else to consider for the following day. *Calm down; everything's prepared and will be checked and double-checked in the morning.*

Strangely, Sam welcomed the sleepless night. The focus of her restlessness was work, the climax of a case which had been bugging her for weeks, and she relished the excitement of a potential arrest the next morning. Eventually, sleep came, and on waking a few hours later, she was immediately alert and in the zone.

Forcing herself to eat breakfast and drink coffee, Sam left the house, jumped into her Mini Cooper, and drove to the station through the quiet early morning streets. Rain lashed down almost horizontally; the wipers laboured to clear the windscreen while the street lights dazzled Sam's view of the road. Slowing down prolonged her journey, but it was early, and driving conditions were bad; she wouldn't be taking risks today.

Paul and Layla were the only ones in her team at the station before her. Paul grinned as he flashed a search warrant in front of her face.

'Well done. Who did you bribe?' Sam returned his grin.

'I heard a whisper that a friendly magistrate was having an early breakfast meeting. Not strictly work but he was happy to sign this before his bacon and eggs cooled.'

Layla was at her computer. 'Nothing of note overnight, boss.' She confirmed just as Jenny walked through the door, shaking off raindrops and mumbling about the weather. When everyone was assembled and coffee cups filled, Sam briefed the team on roles and responsibilities for the morning, reviewing everything planned the evening before. Belts and braces – Sam was nothing if not thorough.

At 8.30am, Samantha was once again in her car, Jenny beside her, as part of a convoy heading off to search Alex Hammond's house and request his cooperation for an interview under caution. The rain had eased slightly, but the roads were hazardous, with surface water akin to a minor flood. 'At least we should find the Hammonds at home. I shouldn't think they'll be planning a trip out in this weather.' Jenny shuddered in her still-damp coat.

The house was in darkness, curtains closed with no sign of life. A uniformed officer hammered on the door, shouting their presence in a voice loud enough to wake the neighbours. Sam cringed, anticipating Hammond's bad mood at being woken so abruptly on a Saturday morning. When the door opened before the officer could bang on it again, a clothed but dishevelled Alex Hammond stood in the doorway, his mouth open in surprise. Samantha was close enough to see a small gash on his face, a fairly recent injury judging by the swelling surrounding it. She stepped forward, Jenny close behind.

'We have a warrant to search your home and vehicles, Mr Hammond. While the officers proceed, I'd like you to accompany me to the station to answer questions under caution.'

'Let me see that!' Hammond snatched the paper from Jenny's hand.

'It's all in order, sir. Perhaps your wife could remain here while you come with us?' Sam climbed the step. Alex Hammond stumbled backwards, reluctant to let her in.

'This must be a mistake! You can't seriously think I had anything to do with Valerie's death?'

'Please get your coat. We'll discuss it at the station.' As Sam spoke, Elaine Hammond appeared in the hall looking even worse than her husband. She sported a full-blown black eye and the side of her face was swollen. Jenny stepped forward, weaving around Sam and Alex to reach Elaine.

'Mrs Hammond, are you alright? Can you tell me what's happened?' Jenny ushered the woman into the lounge while Samantha took Hammond's arm and led him to the waiting police car. With instructions to take Alex Hammond to the station, she returned inside, instructed the officers to begin the search, and then joined Jenny in time to hear her ask, 'Do you want to press charges against your husband?'

'I don't know what to do.' Elaine rubbed her wrists where bruises circled them both. 'Maybe it's my fault for confronting him... What's going on? Why are there police in my house?'

'We have a search warrant, Mrs Hammond, and we need to speak to your husband. Do you want us to call for medical attention?'

'No, I'll be fine.' Elaine appeared anything but fine. Her pale features were drawn, emphasising the black eye, and her speech was slurred due to her swollen cheek. She was wearing clothes that looked as if they'd been slept in, barely resembling the smart, stylish woman they'd met previously.

'Perhaps we can take you to the station where you can see a

doctor and tell us what happened here. Would that be okay?' Jenny asked gently.

'Yes. I don't want to stay here with all this activity going on. Are you arresting Alex?'

'You don't seem surprised to find us here. Why would you think we were arresting him?' Sam asked.

'Because you have a search warrant, and you've taken him away in a police car.'

'We'll be interviewing your husband under caution, so no, he's not been arrested. We'd also appreciate it if you would answer some questions at the station. Do you need to change or anything?'

'Give me a couple of minutes.' Elaine headed into the downstairs cloakroom, returning a few minutes later after washing her face and brushing her hair. She threw a coat over her clothes, grabbed a handbag from the console table and followed Samantha and Jenny outside.

SIXTY

Alex Hammond was left in an interview room with only a lukewarm coffee for company while waiting for the detectives. When Sam and Jenny arrived at the station, they escorted Elaine into the family room and arranged for coffee and toast to be sent in.

Taking a pause to reset their plans in the incident room, Sam decided to interview Alex with Tom Wilson, tasking Jenny and Kim Thatcher to speak with Elaine. Curious to learn what the couple had argued about, they wasted no more time commencing the interviews.

Alex Hammond sat, elbows on the table and his head in his hands, the personification of a dejected man. Glancing up only briefly when Sam and Tom entered the room, he lowered his eyes again to stare at something in his lap.

Tom switched on the recorder and addressed Hammond. 'You do not have to say anything but it may harm your defence if you do not mention something when questioned that you later rely on in court.' Sitting back in his chair Tom waited for his boss to take the lead.

Sam clasped her hands together on the table and looked at

the unhappy man opposite. 'We wanted to speak more formally to you, Mr Hammond, regarding your relationship with Valerie Turner. Firstly, I want to make sure you understand that you have not been arrested, although you are under caution.'

Hammond gave a wry smile. 'Yes, I understand.'

'Good. And do you require the presence of a lawyer for this interview?'

'No. I may not practice criminal law, but I'm well versed in it.'

Samantha nodded and opened the file in front of her. 'We have the results of the DNA sample you provided for us. They are a match to two other samples on our system. One of which is Ben Chapman.' She watched Alex wince as he recognised the name. 'The other is Ben's twin brother, who is a serving police officer. We'll leave his name out of this for the moment.'

'Twin brother? Hell, are you telling me Val gave birth to twins?' Alex's jaw dropped. He looked deflated as if his breath had been punched from him. Having expected this revelation to come as a surprise, Sam was pleased to see from his reaction that she was right. Hopefully, the news would set him on the back foot for the remainder of the interview.

'That's correct, and it appears you are their biological father.'

Hammond nodded slowly, his face crumpling as if struggling to hold back tears. 'I'm sorry. I should have come clean about my past relationship with Val at the beginning of your investigation. I suppose I hoped, as it has nothing to do with her death, I'd be able to keep it a secret – Elaine and the children – you know?'

'With your understanding of criminal law, I'd have expected you to understand the relevance of such a past relationship. If we'd known about it, you would have been at the top of our list of suspects. Your secret history with Val is a strong motive.'

'You don't think I killed her, do you?' Alex grew more animated and Sam wondered if he hadn't realised this was why they were questioning him. Clenching his fists until his knuckles were white, his face reflected tension as he continued, 'I can see how it must look but I had nothing to do with her death!'

'Then perhaps you can tell me where you were six weeks ago today. I know you were at home in the afternoon as we spoke on the phone, but what about the rest of the day?'

Alex sank lower in the chair. 'I, er, I can't... yes, I remember being at home all day. There was some paperwork to catch up on, so I worked in my study.'

'And can your wife confirm this?'

'Hell, I don't know! She may have gone shopping or something, I really don't know.'

'I think perhaps the time has come when you should tell us everything, Mr Hammond.' Sam sat back in her chair and closed the file in front of her.

———

Alex Hammond inhaled deeply in an attempt to steady his trembling body. When the police turned up at his door with a search warrant, he stupidly thought they were still looking for evidence of the money Val had amassed.

His next erroneous assumption was that having seen the state of his wife, they decided to interview him under caution as an abusive husband. How stupid he felt now, knowing they'd worked out his relationship with Val and her son's parentage – of course, they were looking at him for murder – it was a convincing motive. It didn't take a solicitor to work out that he was in deep trouble.

'Look, I'm sorry I didn't come clean about knowing Val, but

it was so long ago, and we hadn't had contact until I moved to New Middridge.

'Val was eighteen when I met her, working in a pub in Liverpool where I occasionally went after work. It started with a mild flirtation. I know I should have known better – I was married with two children – she was just a kid herself and I suppose I was flattered by her interest in me. Val seemed to be waiting for me whenever I visited the pub and one thing led to another.' Alex gulped down some of the disgustingly cold coffee. Nothing else was on offer, and his mouth was dry; the words were difficult to form.

'Val lived in a bedsit near the pub and one night I told Elaine I was away for a meeting and went back to Val's. Hell, I've regretted it ever since and have never done anything like it again, honestly. It only lasted a few weeks – stolen lunch times, an hour after work when Val wasn't working – until she told me she was pregnant. At first, I didn't believe her. She'd been getting too clingy, talking about me leaving Elaine when we both knew it was just a bit of fun. I thought she was making the pregnancy up until she did a test while I was with her.

'Val insisted she wanted to keep the baby even though I tried to persuade her she was too young and we had no future together. She threatened to tell Elaine, and that's when I offered her money. Val promised she'd have an abortion and use the money to move away to start a new life. I stressed that it was over between us, and she agreed. I didn't see her again after I gave her the money and assumed she'd moved away and had an abortion. I regretted the whole affair. It was stupid and vain, and I vowed never to do such a thing again, which I haven't.

'You can imagine my horror when I started working in New Middridge and discovered Val was the office manager. I didn't recognise her at first; she was very young when we last met and had changed considerably. I wouldn't have taken the job if I'd known who she was, but she recognised me. Val initially kept her silence. Everything was very professional until she dropped the bombshell and told me who she was. I thought maybe I could persuade her to leave but then she came up with the story that she hadn't got rid of the baby and he'd recently been in contact with her. They were building a relationship, and Val threatened to expose me to Elaine.

'I didn't believe her and assumed she was trying it on for more money until she produced the DNA results. Somehow, she'd managed to get a sample from me, which proved she was telling the truth. I have a son who I knew nothing about, and now you're telling me he has a twin brother... Val threatened to go to my family unless I paid her.' Alex ran his fingers through his hair, then rested his head in his hands, elbows on the table.

Sam asked, 'Would you like a break, Mr Hammond? We could get some fresh coffee.'

'No thanks, I'd like to get this over with.' He took another minute to compose himself. 'You have to believe me – I didn't kill Val – I'm not a murderer! Okay, I've made mistakes, but I agreed to give her money, which I did. I wouldn't kill anyone.'

'How much money did you give her?' Sam asked.

'Five thousand, then she came back for another five. I gave it to her and said it would have to be the last. I'm comfortably off, but it couldn't go on forever without Elaine finding out.' Alex's head dropped again.

'And did Val come back for more?'

'No. Perhaps she would have done... Well, she didn't get the chance.' Alex's voice cracked. He knew how bad this looked, yet the facts couldn't be altered. He was now at the mercy of the justice system he'd put his faith in all his working life and he hadn't a clue what would happen next.

SIXTY-ONE

D S Jenny Newcombe studied the woman sitting on the sofa in the family room. Elaine Hammond was an attractive woman, tall and slim, possibly in her late forties, with fashionably cut honey-blond hair – expensively styled – Jenny thought. Her face appeared quite different from the last time the women had met as bruises marred the perfect skin, and swelling altered the contours of what Jen remembered as a flawless complexion. Elaine's body language lacked the confidence of their last meeting, too; the woman was shredding a tissue, her shoulders hunched as she stared into her lap.

Domestic violence was nothing new to Jenny, and the fact that Elaine was a solicitor's wife didn't surprise her either. As Elaine stuffed the tissue in her pocket and sipped her coffee, the two detectives allowed her time to collect her thoughts, hoping the distressed woman would open up, rendering it unnecessary for them to ask probing questions. On arriving at the station, Kim called for the duty doctor to see Elaine and he confirmed her injuries were superficial with no broken bones. After taking photographs of her injuries, they decided to proceed with the interview.

'Are you in pain, Elaine?' Jen asked.

'It's nothing, I've had worse.' She took another sip of coffee and Jenny raised an eyebrow. *Is violence a regular occurrence?* she wondered.

'Mrs Hammond, Elaine. Could you tell us how you sustained your injuries?' Jenny finally threw in an open-ended question, wanting to progress the interview.

'It was Alex. We had a row and he completely lost it.'

'You do know you can press charges against him, don't you?'

'No, I wouldn't do that. I probably provoked him.'

'And what was the argument about?' Jenny prompted.

'I found out he'd been giving money to that woman who was murdered. I knew something was wrong. When you've lived with a man for over thirty years, you know him pretty much inside out, and Alex had started behaving strangely.' Elaine finished the last of her coffee and raised her face to continue.

'Our move to New Middridge hadn't gone as well as we'd hoped. Alex was excited about being the senior partner at work, but I found it difficult to settle. We've always been able to talk our problems through, yet when I tried to speak to Alex about my feelings, he was short-tempered with me. His attitude changed soon after the move. It was obvious he was anxious. I asked if there was a problem at work, and he denied there was. Something was troubling him and as I wasn't happy, we began arguing over the slightest things.'

Elaine paused and looked from Jenny to Kim as if judging their mood before continuing. 'I'm ashamed to say I went snooping. At first, I thought maybe Alex had overstretched himself financially when buying into the firm. If that was the case, I could help him out, but I wasn't prepared for what I found. It was a letter from one of those DNA testing firms confirming a familial match between my husband and someone called Ben Chapman. I was stunned and didn't know what to think or do. My instinct was to confront him and ask him how long this affair had been going on. You see, I thought Ben was a child, the result of a more recent affair. Anyway, I did nothing. Perhaps it would have been better to confront him there and then but I took the coward's way out and waited – for what I don't know – perhaps I have too much to lose?

'I suggested a holiday, hoping Alex might relax and confide in me, which he didn't. The rift between us was widening and I hadn't a clue what to do about it. Before we went away, that woman from his office was murdered. I didn't connect the dots until we came home from Mauritius. Her name sounded familiar when Alex told me about her death, and I assumed he must have mentioned her from time to time, but then it clicked and I remembered. While I'd been snooping, I found a bank statement with details of two transactions to Valerie Turner, both for five thousand pounds.

'Last night, I decided it was time to confront my husband, but I needed a drink first, which turned into a few. Stupid, I know. By the time Alex came home, I was drunk. It was an impossible time to talk rationally, yet I was determined to know the truth. I threw out accusations, and Alex tossed back excuses and lame apologies. I can't remember when things became physical, but they did – we'd both lost it by then.

'The next thing I knew was waking up this morning with you banging on the door. I must have passed out; things are certainly hazy.' Elaine massaged her neck, easing the kinks as she finished her story.

'Elaine, does your husband ever drive your car?' Jenny asked. Elaine looked puzzled at the question but agreed that he did. 'He often takes it when he plays golf – doesn't want to risk his own getting damaged in the car park.'

Jenny nodded. 'And did you ever meet Valerie Turner?'

'No, I didn't. I would have met her at the firm's Christmas do, but I had a migraine and didn't attend.'

'Valerie Turner was killed on a Saturday, six weeks ago today. Can you remember where you were that day and if your husband was with you?'

'Yes, I remember. Alex was working at home. He locked himself away in his study and I knew he'd be there all day. I was furious. He barely spent his weekends with me any more so I decided to go to the outlet centre to do some shopping. Retail therapy, I suppose. I left early to avoid the traffic and didn't return until mid-afternoon.'

'Thank you, Elaine. Going back to your argument last night, did your husband say anything else about Valerie Turner?'

'Like whether or not he killed her? No, he didn't.' Elaine's eyes brimmed with tears.

Jenny leaned forward. 'Do you think Alex is capable of murder?'

Elaine's voice dropped to a whisper. 'Until recently, I'd have answered no, but with all that's happened lately, quite honestly, I don't know anymore.'

SIXTY-TWO

'Any news from the search team?' Samantha entered the incident room, addressing anyone who may have an answer.

'They're bringing in Hammond's personal papers and his computer and have already bagged his golf clubs as you asked. They should be with forensics as a priority.'

'Great, Layla. Can you ring them back and request they search his wife's car too?'

'Will do, boss.'

Samantha and Tom began discussing the interview with Alex Hammond while they waited for Jenny and Kim. As Hammond was there voluntarily, they had to let him go when he asked but made sure he knew there would be more questions.

'He's plausible,' Tom stated.

'He's a solicitor.' Sam responded. 'We'd better hope the search turns up something by way of solid evidence. We're out on a limb here without witnesses, CCTV footage or DNA.'

'He doesn't have an alibi.' Tom was grasping at straws.

'Neither do I. Let's hope Jenny and Kim have had more

success.' As if to order, the DC and DS entered the room. Sam and Tom looked expectantly at them.

'Elaine admits to getting into a drunken fight about Ben Chapman being her husband's son. She also discovered Valerie Turner was blackmailing Hammond. As for her injuries, she doesn't want to press charges and is a bit hazy about what happened.'

'Can she give Alex an alibi for the day of the murder?' Sam was eager to know.

'No. She went shopping, leaving her husband alone in his home office.' Jenny smiled. 'And the woman's a snooper. She'd discovered his secrets and kept quiet about them until the time was right, which apparently was after he took her to Mauritius on holiday.'

'You have to admire her pluck. So, what brought it to a head?' Sam smiled.

'Dutch courage, probably. She was biding her time before confronting him, giving him the opportunity to confess, she claims, which he didn't, so Elaine brought matters to a head. Oh, and she also said he often uses her car.'

The door to the incident room opened allowing Paul and two uniformed officers to enter, carrying large boxes. 'The first load from the search, ma'am.' The constable almost dropped the box on a table as Sam hurried over to inspect the potential evidence. 'You'll find his laptop in there.' The constable nodded to the box before leaving the room, closely followed by his colleague.

'The search is progressing well. I thought I'd be better off here to make a start on Hammond's laptop.' Paul had a satisfied smile on his face.

'Right! The laptop's all yours, and everyone else can divi up the paperwork.' Sam took her share first and disappeared into her office to commence the laborious task of searching for evidence.

The team endured three long hours without any developments before finally unearthing the paperwork Elaine referred to, confirming Alex Hammond as Ben Chapman's biological father. Furthermore, they discovered evidence of two transfers from Hammond's account to Val Turner's, each totalling five thousand pounds.

Breaking for coffee, Sam and Jenny speculated whether Val was pressuring for further transactions, which could provide a compelling motive. 'When you see how much money the Hammonds have, ten grand's just a drop in the ocean to him. Perhaps Val was trying to bleed him for more.' Jenny sighed.

'I think most of his money is Elaine's family money. She wouldn't take kindly to it paying off a blackmailer, and rightly so.'

'So do you think he'd try a more permanent solution to keeping his secrets?'

'Yes, it seems logical, but we need something more solid before we can charge him.'

Sam's phone rang and she was surprised to see it was Rick, the pathologist. 'Hi, Rick. Don't tell me you're working on a Saturday?'

'It so happens that I am. I thought you needed cheering up, and when I heard there was potential evidence coming in on the Turner case, I decided to do some unofficial overtime and rush it through for you.' Sam could imagine the smug smile on his face.

'I'm touched, Rick, but was it worth it?'

'Well, if you consider finding traces of Valerie Turner's blood on a steel golf wedge belonging to Alex Hammond, then yes, it's been worthwhile.'

'Rick, I could kiss you! Thank you so much. This is exactly what we needed. I owe you! Is it a hundred per cent?' Sam was beyond excited, and Jenny, who'd heard the conversation, punched the air with her fist.

'It is. Someone's cleaned it quite thoroughly so there are no prints on it, which in itself is suspicious, but traces of blood were still in the grooves; they hadn't been thorough enough. I'll send the report through as soon as I've finished.'

'Thanks, Rick. You're a star!' Sam was invigorated by the call, and sharing the news with the team caused great excitement.

'We can arrest the bastard now!' Paul stated the obvious.

'Kim?' Sam turned to her DC. 'Has Mrs Hammond gone home?'

'Yes, boss. When the search was finished, I asked a PC to drive her home as you said.'

'Great, thank you. And has Alex Hammond left, too?'

'He has, he left shortly after the interview.'

'Well, we're about to ruin the rest of his weekend. Come on, Jenny, let's go and arrest the man on suspicion of murder.'

The women commandeered a uniformed officer to accompany them to Hammond's home. They didn't expect him to resist arrest but were taking no chances. If anything, the rain was heavier, and a slate grey sky heralded even more. A low rumble of thunder made Samantha shudder as they made their way through the quiet streets of New Middridge. A wet March Saturday was sure to keep people indoors.

The last of the search team were leaving the property as they pulled up. Elaine Hammond watched their arrival from the large bay window in the lounge, her arms folded, expression inscrutable. Sam ducked under the porch to avoid another soaking and came face to face with Alex, who was asking an officer when he could have his laptop back. Their suspect turned, surprised to see the DI.

'Now what? When you said you'd have more questions, I

didn't expect another house call. Hey, I want a receipt for everything – itemised.' He shouted at the officer who was taking the last box to his car.

'You'll get your itemised receipt, Mr Hammond. Can we step inside, please?'

Alex led them into the lounge, where Elaine remained by the window, her eyes darting from her husband to the three officers. Samantha nodded at Jenny, who informed Hammond they were arresting him on suspicion of murder and proceeded to recite his rights.

Alex Hammond paled as he realised what was happening. As the uniformed officer took his arm to lead him to the car, Hammond turned and pleaded to his wife, 'Call Nigel for me!'

'This is your mess. Call him yourself,' she replied.

SIXTY-THREE

Alex Hammond would say nothing until his solicitor arrived, a man who was proving difficult to contact.

After booking their suspect, Samantha decided to utilise the time by paying Geoff Turner a visit to update him on the arrest.

Leaving instructions for Hammond to be allowed time alone with his solicitor, Nigel Porteous, when he arrived, she and Jenny braved the rain again to take the familiar road to Juniper Grove. On the way, they discussed the upcoming interview with Hammond, frustrated they couldn't immediately question him. They were both keen to hear his explanation of the blood on his golf club.

Geoff Turner was vacuuming the lounge when they arrived, a sight which elicited sympathy from Sam. 'Sorry to interrupt on a Saturday. May we come in?'

Geoff stood aside as they entered the lounge and settled themselves on the sofa with their host on the opposite armchair.

'Are the girls in?' Jenny asked.

'They're upstairs in their rooms. Shall I call them down?'

'Not yet, maybe in a while. We're here to tell you that we've arrested someone for Valerie's murder.' Sam went straight to the point. She wasn't a believer in dressing information up. Geoff's eyes widened as he sank lower into the chair.

'Who?' It seemed to be the only word he could manage.

'I'm sorry, we can't tell you yet.'

'Shall I make a pot of tea?' Jenny interjected and when her boss and Geoff both nodded, she headed for the kitchen.

'Are you sure you have the right man, or is it a woman?'

'Yes. We have evidence to prove this man had a past relationship with your wife. He's the biological father of Ben Chapman and his brother. We also have what we believe to be the murder weapon.'

'Has he admitted it?'

'No. Our suspect is at the station under arrest for suspicion of murder. We can't interview him until his solicitor arrives, so as yet, he hasn't responded to the charge. It's still early, but we're confident he's our man. It appears Val was blackmailing him, which is probably the motive...'

'So is that where the ten grand came from?' Geoff shook his head sadly.

'It appears to be, yes. I'm sorry, this must be hard for you to come to terms with.'

'Do you ever come to terms with such deception? I loved Val and thought I knew everything about her. All the lies she told me and the girls prove otherwise – I never really knew her, and now I don't think I even like her. Well, she's certainly beyond lies now.'

Empathy flooded Sam's consciousness. It was a relief when Jenny appeared with a tray of tea, and she had a moment to collect her thoughts. As Jenny handed around the tea, Sam asked if he'd like to tell the girls while they were still there to answer any questions they may have.

'No, if you don't mind, I'll wait a while to tell them. I need to get my head around it myself first.'

'That's fine. We'll leave you in peace now, Geoff. I'll be informing Ben Chapman of the arrest and it's probably time to let him know he has a brother, so maybe you'd like to consider telling the girls this, too?' Samantha and Jenny left a rather dejected Geoff and dashed back to the car through the rain.

———

'Was that the police?' Lizzie appeared in the lounge doorway.

'Yes, DI Freeman and DS Newcombe.'

'What did they want?'

'Perhaps you should call Anna down and I'll tell you.' Geoff sighed. 'I'm afraid there are a couple more surprises to take in.'

Lizzie called up the stairs to her sister. She'd have liked to see the police officers again. They'd been remarkably kind to her and Anna, even though the sisters hadn't been upfront with them. As Anna came thundering down the stairs, Lizzie raised her eyebrows, shrugged, and the girls filed into the lounge.

'I'd have made the tea for you, Dad.' Lizzie looked at the tray of empty mugs. She was trying to help in the house whenever she could. Doing something practical took her mind off their problems, and she was worried about her dad; he seemed depressed, but weren't they all?

'What's happened?' Anna wanted to know.

'There's a couple of things you need to know. Firstly, the police have arrested someone for your mum's murder.'

Lizzie shivered. How was she supposed to feel about this? Yes, she wanted justice for her mum, but was this good news? And who was it? If it was someone they knew, it was scary. She was almost afraid to hear her dad say the name.

Anna was first in again. 'Who is it?'

'They can't tell us yet. It's a man who had a relationship with your mum years ago... and he's Ben's biological father.'

'Bloody hell, she knew who it was all the time!' Anna's face contorted with anger.

'Anna, mind your language!' Geoff snapped.

'Does Ben know?' she asked.

'Not yet. I think Samantha's going to tell him soon. I promised we'd keep it to ourselves so we're not to talk about these developments. I'm trusting you both to remain quiet.'

Anna's nostrils flared. 'What else, Dad? You said there were a couple of things to tell us.'

'Yes. The police think they've found the murder weapon – they didn't give me any details so I can't tell you any more than that. They're waiting for this man's solicitor to arrive so they can interview him.'

'They must be sure it's him or they wouldn't have told you,' Lizzie added. 'And is that all, Dad?'

Geoff lowered his eyes. 'No love. It seems that your mum got the ten grand from this man.'

'I don't understand.' Lizzie struggled to hold back her tears. 'If he gave her money, were they friends? Had she been seeing him all this time?'

'Don't be naïve, Lizzie. Mum was blackmailing him, wasn't she, Dad?'

'Sadly, that's how it looks, although nothing's certain yet, let's not jump to conclusions.' Geoff again looked down into his lap.

'Is there more?' Anna snapped.

'Yes. Apparently, when Ben was born, there was another baby boy. Ben was a twin and the police have found his brother.'

It was all too much for Lizzie who suddenly burst into tears and ran upstairs to her room. Geoff rose to follow, but Anna stopped him, her tone softer this time. 'Give her a few minutes alone, Dad, then I'll talk to her.'

'Yes, you're right. I'm sorry about all this, love. It's been a bombshell for us all and I don't think I'm handling it well... Is there anything I can do to help you and Lizzie?'

Anna went to her father and threw her arms around him. 'It's not your fault, Dad. And you've been brilliant, honestly.' Father and daughter held each other while their tears fell. When they pulled apart, Anna sniffed and said, 'I'll go and talk to Lizzie now. Maybe a takeaway would be in order for tea tonight?' She grinned at her dad, who smiled and nodded.

SIXTY-FOUR

Lizzie lay sprawled on her bed, face down, sobbing into her pillow. Her face was wet, her nose and eyes sore, and she felt both angry and sad. 'Go away!' she shouted on hearing the knock on her bedroom door.

'It's me. Can we talk?'

Lizzie pulled herself up and blew her nose. 'If we must,' she replied, and Anna opened the door and hurried to sit next to her sister on the bed. Lizzie leaned her head on her sister's shoulder. 'I can't take it all in, Anna. I loved Mum, but she's done some horrible things. Did you mean what you said about her blackmailing that man? Would she really do something so bad?'

'Yes. If he was Ben's father, Mum would have something on him, and I don't think he'd have given her the money willingly and then killed her, do you?'

'I suppose not, unless it wasn't him who killed her and she was planning to run away with him?'

'No. Dad says the police are pretty certain he did it. They found the murder weapon so they'll have DNA and stuff. But what about Ben being a twin – that means we have another half-brother!'

Anna sounded excited, but Lizzie didn't want to think about it. All this new stuff was messing with her head.

'I wish Ben was here now.' Anna said. 'I wonder what he'll think when he knows he has a twin brother? I'd love to be a fly on the wall when DI Freeman tells him.'

'Don't, Anna!'

'Don't what?'

'Sound so pleased about it.'

'Hey, I'm sorry, don't cry again. I'm as confused about everything as you are but there are some positives coming out of it all – another brother and grandparents we knew nothing about.'

Lizzie nodded and sniffed. 'Yes, but I keep thinking about all the horrible things Mum's done. She left home when she was hardly more than your age without telling her parents anything – they must have been worried out of their minds. Then getting pregnant and giving her babies up for adoption – how could she do that? Just think, if they'd been together like brothers should be, their lives would have been so different. I'd hate it if you and I were separated. And then Mum's not only a big fat liar, she's a blackmailer! What was she going to do with the money? Leave us, I suppose. And when I think about it, she treated Dad badly this last year. I don't know how I feel about her any more. I loved Mum, and when she died I was devastated. I even felt terrible about lying to her, yet look at all the lies she's told us. Her whole life's been a lie and right now I feel more like hating her! I don't want to feel like this, Anna, but I don't know what to do.'

'You don't have to do anything. Try not to think too much; you'll only get confused.'

'Don't you have the same feelings?'

'Of course I do. I loved Mum too, yet I wasn't always nice to her either. We argued over stupid little things and I have regrets now. I'll never have the chance to say sorry or to say anything to her ever again! In a way I hate her for all she's put us through but I hope it's a feeling which will pass. It's probably better to think about the good times rather than the bad. They say time's a good healer, and I hope they're bloody right!'

'Anna, don't swear!' Lizzie sniffed and then grinned at her sister.

'Dad's getting takeaway for tea. I think we all deserve a treat. Come on, let's go down and see what he's ordering.' Anna pulled her sister from the bed, hugging her tightly, then led her downstairs to study the takeaway menu.

SIXTY-FIVE

The rain was finally easing as the detectives pulled into the station car park. Sam's phone rang and she eagerly stabbed the green button.

'Hi, boss. Hammond's solicitor arrived a few minutes ago and they're in conference now. Will you be back soon?'

'We're here, Paul, just parking up.' Sam glanced at her watch: 3.05pm. 'We'll grab some coffee from the deli and be with you shortly.' Sam ended the call.

'Good idea, boss. I'm starving.' Jenny grinned.

'You're always starving. We'll get coffee and doughnuts for the team and by the time we've eaten, Hammond and his solicitor will have had enough time to work out a story for us.'

Ten minutes later, they entered the incident room with a tray of coffee and a huge bag of doughnuts. A few cheers accompanied their entrance. Jenny played monitor and distributed the goodies while Sam checked her computer for any new developments.

'What's this Nigel Porteous like, Paul?'

'Expensive suit, handmade shoes, sniffy attitude.'

'Oh good, just how I like them.' Sam took a bite of doughnut and washed it down with coffee. 'Which interview room are they in?'

'Number three and they've had coffee – station special blend!' Paul smacked his lips as he sipped the good stuff.

'Good. I want you to search the ANPR for any movement of Hammond's car on the day of the murder. Look at every possible route from his house to Juniper Grove, and while you're on, search for his wife's car too. She said she went shopping, but maybe she used a taxi and left her car available at home – Hammond could have driven hers.

Twenty minutes later, Sam entered interview room number three and took a seat across from the two men. Jenny turned on the recording machine, sat next to her boss, and recited the names of their suspect, herself and Sam. Nigel Porteous introduced himself as Hammond's solicitor. Alex looked pale and tired. His usually immaculate appearance now reflected the image of a broken man as he looked directly at Samantha, with something resembling loathing in his stare, but his lips were pressed firmly together.

'I'd like to read a statement on behalf of my client,' Porteous said as he pushed his chair out, scraping the legs on the floor. 'Mr Hammond knows nothing about the death of Valerie Turner. On the day in question, he was at home working all day. Mrs Hammond can vouch for some of that time. If you have questions relating to any evidence you think you have, we'll listen to them and consider answering. Otherwise, I'd appreciate it if you would release my client on bail.'

'Thank you, Mr Porteous. We have arrested Mr Hammond on suspicion of murder based on evidence gathered during the search of his house.' Sam gave the solicitor her polite smile, then turned to look at Alex Hammond. 'Mr Hammond. Can you explain why Valerie Turner's blood was found on one of your golf clubs – a steel wedge, I believe?'

Alex looked at his solicitor, who shook his head. 'No comment,' he replied.

'And you have no one who can vouch for you being at home on the day of Valerie Turner's murder?'

'No comment.'

'But you do have a motive, don't you, Alex? You've already told us Val was blackmailing you, threatening to tell your family of the children you fathered with her?'

'No comment.'

Porteous interrupted. 'My client has told you everything about his past relationship with Mrs Turner.'

Sam ignored the solicitor, maintaining eye contact with Alex Hammond. 'Did you decide to stop the blackmail permanently by killing Val Turner?'

'No comment.'

'Come on, detective inspector,' said Porteous. 'Is this all you have? We both know this is circumstantial. You have no case here, and unless you intend to escalate the charge from suspicion of murder to murder, I'd like my client released on bail.'

Sam had known this would be a frustrating interview. Hammond was clearly obeying instructions from his solicitor to reply 'no comment' to all her questions. It was pointless to persist with such an interview. Sam reluctantly closed her file and stood. 'I'll begin the process for bail, Mr Porteous, but there'll be strict conditions for your client to adhere to. Please wait here; someone will come when everything's in order.'

Sam and Jenny left the room. 'Damn, damn, damn!' Sam said once they were out of earshot. 'We need more, Jen. Let's see if Paul's found anything else.'

'Hold on a minute. It's getting late and the team have all

been in since stupid o'clock this morning. Maybe calling it a day and getting some rest will be beneficial?'

'When did you become the sensible one?' Sam smiled. 'You're right. I'll get back to the incident room and send everyone home; you get the paperwork underway, please, Jen, and then we can both get home.'

SIXTY-SIX

A pleasant young constable drove Elaine home from the police station. He showed kindness and consideration in helping her out of the car and asking if he could do anything else before returning to the station. Elaine declined any further help, thanked him, and opened the front door to her home.

The house wasn't as pristine as Elaine usually kept it. A lingering smell of stale alcohol reminded her of the previous evening's confrontation with Alex, fetching a slow smile to her face. Hopefully, her husband would be suffering for his sins, and the humiliation of an arrest and consequent trial would embarrass him, giving him a taste of her feelings on learning about Valerie Turner and his illegitimate son.

Stepping into the kitchen, Elaine automatically picked up empty glasses and stacked them in the dishwasher. This house was her pride and joy and she had invested considerable time and money into making it the perfect home to reflect their standing in the community.

Apparently, it was all for nothing. Alex had ruined everything. Although she loved the house, New Middridge had been a disappointment in many ways, but being a woman with

275

drive and determination, she'd sought to make the most of a bad situation. Soon after they moved, Elaine volunteered for two local charities, rising to the position of chairman in one and secretary in the other. Her forte was entertaining, and nothing delighted her more than hosting a party or an intimate dinner for her new friends and acquaintances. Elaine shone as a hostess, accepting with grace the compliments she felt were deserved.

This was now behind her. Elaine's comfortable life was in shreds. Suffering the indignity of having her husband arrested, she'd been obliged to answer personal and somewhat embarrassing questions herself. She felt she had been a good wife to Alex and that he had let her down with his recent behaviour. It made the decision to leave easier – not only to leave Alex but New Middridge as well. Staying in New Middridge was no longer an option – life had become untenable – how could she ever face her new friends again?

With a glance around the bespoke kitchen which Elaine cherished, she made a coffee before moving into the lounge to refine her somewhat sketchy plans. She neither knew nor cared what would happen to Alex. Elaine had done her best to sort out his mess, but it was time to think of herself and her own happiness. At some point, their children would need to be informed, but not yet – Elaine needed facts before she notified them of their father's darker side. Telling them could wait; they were lax in keeping in touch anyway, even after all she'd done for them.

The sound of a car pulling up on the drive surprised Elaine. Looking from the window, the sight of her husband climbing from the rear seat of a taxi plummeted her mood. She'd hoped the police would at least keep him overnight.

When he entered the house, Elaine glared at him. 'Why the hell have they let you go?'

'I've been released on bail. We need to talk...'

Raising her hands, palms outwards, made it clear she wasn't going to cooperate. 'No, Alex, we don't. Sleep in the spare room again tonight.' With a dark scowl, leaving her husband in no doubt about her mood, she turned and climbed the stairs to her room, where she dragged a couple of suitcases from the top shelf of her walk-in wardrobe.

On Sunday morning, Elaine Hammond left her beautiful home before Alex was out of bed. While she'd been packing the night before, she heard him prowling downstairs. Whiskey would have been consumed and it seemed safe to presume her husband would be sleeping late. Not that she cared. Elaine simply wanted to leave the house and the town where everything had gone badly wrong for her.

With no fully formed plan and only the slightest regret, she set off towards Harrogate, where her sister, Frances, lived with her husband. The sisters hadn't been close since they hit puberty, and some of the jealousy that soured their adolescent relationship still lingered, but appearances were everything to both women, and she knew Frances wouldn't turn her down in her hour of need. Where she would go after that was yet to be decided. Perhaps when things settled down, abroad would be the better option. Her children no longer needed her and wouldn't miss her, and with Alex locked up, she would be a free woman.

The Duchy area of Harrogate is well known for its desirable residences, although it is located close to Harrogate Centre and Valley Gardens. As Elaine's satnav directed her to Cornwall Road, she felt a stab of envy at her sister's impressive period detached house. Frances had no children, and the five-bedroomed house was clearly a status symbol. As far as she knew, Frances and her husband, Brian, rarely had guests to stay. Elaine had visited only on three occasions and approached the stunning residence on this her fourth visit with mixed feelings.

'Elaine!' Frances' eyes widened, and her jaw dropped. 'What are you doing here?'

The sisters stared at each other, making rapid mental judgements of the other's physical appearance. *She's let herself go – that haircut is totally unflattering, and her roots need doing.*

But Elaine smiled and said, 'Surprise!'

Once inside, with the obligatory air kiss over, the sisters exchanged rather strained, polite conversation. Elaine asked about Brian – he was well apart from needing his cataracts removed – and Frances enquired about her nephew and niece. When she eventually asked about Alex, she was totally wrong-footed as her sister burst into tears.

SIXTY-SEVEN

Frances Meadows wasn't pleased to have her younger sister crying all over her new plush velvet sofa; indeed, she wasn't thrilled to have her in the house at all. Their relationship had never been close, even though there were barely two years separating them.

She was bewildered as to why Elaine should be in Harrogate at all. When her sister suddenly began to act hysterically, Frances was perplexed and unsure of the right reaction to such a rare occurrence. Frances didn't handle emotions well.

'There, there.' She patted her sister's shoulder, wondering how soon she could get rid of her. Brian was visiting his elderly mother and would be home soon. He'd be horrified to find his sister-in-law weeping all over the drawing room. 'Whatever's the matter?' Frances asked. She was more struck by how much she sounded like their late mother than by any desire for her sister to unburden herself of whatever petty problem was troubling her.

Frances assumed the histrionics must relate to Alex, as the mention of his name prompted the outburst. It was no surprise. She'd advised her younger sister against marrying him; the man wasn't good enough and would drag Elaine down – the proof that she was correct was sitting before her. Alex's good looks and easy-going manner had captured her vulnerable young sister, and no argument could change her mind. Frances considered Alex to be an airhead. He presented as an intelligent man, and she supposed he'd done reasonably well in his career, but he lacked common sense and was easily led. On one occasion, he'd confided in Brian that he'd made some bad investment decisions and lost a hefty chunk of Elaine's money. But she'd stood by him then. What could possibly have happened to drive her away from him now?

Frances' curiosity surpassed her desire to see the back of her sister, and she repeated her question, 'Whatever's the matter.'

'He's been arrested!' Elaine sobbed.

'Goodness me! What for?' Frances' mind was already considering fraud or embezzlement, so her sister's ensuing words came as a complete shock.

'For murder. At least suspicion of murder...' Elaine blew her nose on a crumpled tissue she'd dug out from the bottom of her bag. 'The police released him on bail last night and he came home. I was scared and didn't know where to go, so here I am. Can I stay here for a few days until I decide what to do?' Her watery eyes pleaded with her sister.

'Well, er... I don't think Brian would want the police sniffing around our home, and a murderer in the family won't look good...' Frances was uncharacteristically lost for words but those she did utter sent Elaine off in floods of tears again.

Frances did what her mother would have done. She pushed a box of tissues nearer to her sister and muttered something about making a cup of tea. Her absence gave them both time to order their thoughts. The idea of her brother-in-law being a murderer appalled Frances, yet, rather smugly, it was satisfying to be proved right about Alex. Perhaps she should support her sister and do the right thing – they didn't have to tell anyone why she was staying with them. Brian wouldn't be happy yet she could always talk him around.

'Here, drink this and tell me all about it. Who is Alex supposed to have killed?' Frances placed a delicate bone china cup and saucer on the coffee table near her sister and perched on the edge of the opposite sofa, keen to hear all the details.

'It goes back a long time... apparently, he met a girl when we were living in Liverpool. She was working in a pub where he occasionally went for a drink after work. A teenager, would you believe, and they began an affair. As if that wasn't bad enough, the slut became pregnant and had his child! I can't believe he's kept this a secret all these years. He claims not to have known about the child but this girl – woman – ended up working in his office and has been blackmailing him!'

Frances listened dumbfounded. 'I always knew he wasn't to be trusted. His eyes are set too close together. You should have listened to me...'

'Oh, don't start. I need help, not criticism!'

'Sorry, of course you do. Look, I'll make up the spare room for you, and you can stay for a few days while you make plans.' Frances forced a smile. Although she didn't relish her sister's company, the details of this murder were interesting – not that she was one to indulge in gossip, but Elaine needed someone to talk to and who better than her sister? She'd square it with Brian later. He'd not be inconvenienced as he'd be at work tomorrow. 'Finish your tea, then we'll take your case upstairs and make up the bed.'

Elaine thanked her sister, gulped down the now-cold tea and hurried out to the car to retrieve her case. She'd always envied her sister's house and couldn't deny it was superior to hers. A few days as a house guest might be quite enjoyable. Alex could face the music alone – he deserved everything coming to him.

As Brian Meadows pulled onto his drive, he frowned at the sight of a strange car badly parked in his usual spot. As far as he was aware, they were not expecting visitors.

'Brian!' Frances greeted her husband at the door, pulling his sleeve to steer him into the kitchen, where she whispered an explanation.

'What! That bloody fool's been arrested for murder, and you're welcoming his wife into our home?'

'Shh. Keep your voice down. Elaine's upstairs, unpacking.'

'Well, she can jolly well pack again. It's an imposition to expect us to give her sanctuary. Tell her she'll have to go.'

'Don't be so pompous, Brian. She's my sister. I can hardly turn her away in her time of need, can I?'

'Humph!' Brian was prevented from saying more as Elaine entered the room.

'I thought I heard voices. Hello, Brian. How are you?' Her smile was weak as she stepped forward to kiss her brother-in-law on his reddening cheek.

'Hello, Elaine. To what do we owe the pleasure of a visit?' He spoke through gritted teeth.

Elaine hung her head. 'I think I'd better leave you two alone for Frances to explain.' She turned and left the room.

'I'll put the kettle on.' Frances turned away from her husband. 'Or maybe you should have something stronger?'

SIXTY-EIGHT

Samantha had spent Sunday with her parents, enjoying being fussed over and eating one of her mother's excellent Sunday roast dinners. Keeping her mind away from work matters was difficult yet her body needed rest, so on her return home, a coffee and a nap on the sofa were welcome.

By late afternoon and feeling little benefit from her sleep, her thoughts raced, and she was tempted to call the station to ask if they'd made progress. While some of her team had taken the day off, others were still on duty, keeping the office ticking over and continuing the search for more evidence to consolidate their case against Alex Hammond. Reluctantly, she decided against ringing in, knowing they would have let her know if there was anything new to report.

The discovery of Valerie Turner's blood on Hammond's golf club had felt like a breakthrough, but without fingerprints, the solicitor was right; it was circumstantial. The Crown Prosecution Service would need something more solid before even considering proceeding with a charge – but what? Even though the man couldn't provide an alibi, they had no witnesses to place him near the Turners' house on the day in question.

The motive was good but again, a motive isn't evidence. Sam was now relying on the ANPR to place Hammond's car near the murder scene. It was currently their best shot.

Monday morning dawned with weak sunshine attempting to brighten the sky – it wasn't enough to brighten Sam's mood. The officer who had been trawling the ANPR footage had nothing to report, but due to the distance between Hammond's home and the Turners' and the number of possible routes, it would take time, so there was still hope of finding something.

When Jenny arrived, Sam left her DS in charge and set off to visit Ben Chapman, who had yet to be informed they'd made an arrest, albeit only on suspicion of murder. It was also time to tell the young man about his twin brother. It was to be hoped Geoff Turner and his daughters hadn't been in touch with Ben as they'd promised.

Before driving to Leeds, Samantha rang Ben to ensure he was available. He sounded upbeat and was keen for the update she promised to bring. The Monday morning traffic lengthened the journey, although at least it was dry. When she finally arrived, Sam was glad to get out of the car and stretch her legs. As her pregnancy progressed, she was troubled with cramps and promised herself she'd take more regular exercise. Surely the opportunity would present itself now this case was nearing its conclusion.

Ben greeted the detective eagerly and ushered her inside. 'I've just made coffee. Would you like some?'

'Yes, please.' Sam smiled, aware that this young man was about to have another major shock to contend with. Maybe in the long term, having a twin brother would prove a blessing. *What complicated lives some people lead,* she thought.

When the coffee was poured and they were sitting opposite each other in the tiny lounge, Sam launched into the recent developments, explaining how a man had been arrested on suspicion of murder and released on bail pending further inquiries.

'You mean you've caught the bastard and let him go again?' Ben's anger was evident.

'We haven't enough evidence to charge him with murder. The Crown Prosecution Service needs solid proof – DNA or a witness placing him at the scene. As yet, we don't have it. I can assure you that even now, there are officers working hard to find evidence, and I'm confident they will.'

'But what if he leaves the country – does a runner?'

'We've taken his passport as part of the bail conditions and he has to report to the station regularly. I don't see him as a flight risk.'

Ben rubbed his face with his palms and sighed. 'Who is this man? Are you going to tell me his name?'

'I'm sorry, Ben, I can't reveal his name at this point, but there are things about him you need to know.'

Eyebrows raised, he looked at Sam, eager to know what she meant.

'During our comparisons of DNA, we discovered a match to you and subsequently to our suspect. The man we're investigating is your biological father.' Pausing to give him time to process this information, Sam reached over and took Ben's mug, which was in danger of falling from his hand. His face crumpled, and silent tears coursed down his cheeks. After a few moments of silence, Ben sniffed and wiped his tears with his sleeve.

'Just my bloody luck. I found my birth mother, only for her to be murdered before we got to know each other, and it appears my biological father killed her! Whatever next?'

'Ben, the match we found to you is actually a policeman, a detective who lives in the Newcastle area. He's your brother – your twin brother.'

Shaking his head in disbelief, Ben covered his face with his hands and fell back in the seat. Sam remained silent. The emotions swirling in this young man's head must be so complex – he'd need more than a few minutes to grasp all the implications. Rummaging in her bag, Sam retrieved the photograph of Simon Prentis.

When Ben finally raised his head and looked at her, his expression was inscrutable.

'Ben, would you like to see a photograph of your brother?'

Ben nodded and took the proffered image. 'Well, I don't have to ask if you're sure, do I? It's not me, so there's no doubt he's my twin. Hell, Samantha, I don't know how I should be feeling about all this. I'd hoped to someday meet my birth father, yet now all I want to do is beat him to a pulp, and discovering I have a twin brother is mind-blowing. Can I meet him? What's his name, and does he have a family?'

'Slow down, Ben. I can only tell you he's called Simon, and yes, he is married with a family. It wouldn't be appropriate for the two of you to meet yet, but we'll arrange it as soon as we can. Simon knew he was adopted, but not that he was a twin, so it came as a huge shock to him, too. You're actually in the same position, and hopefully, when you do eventually meet, some good will have come from all this.'

'And what about my birth father? Does he have children?'

'Yes, but again I can't give any details. Believe me, we're doing all we can to tie up the ends of this case.'

A stunned Ben nodded at Sam. His questions were spent, and he needed time alone to process them.

'If you're okay, I'll go now. We'll keep you informed of any developments and all being well there'll be no more shocks.' Sam smiled as she left, wondering if Ben regretted his attempt to discover the identity of his birth parents.

SIXTY-NINE

'Hey, boss! Over here.' DS Paul Roper sounded excited. Jenny, Layla and Kim were gathered around his desk as his fingers danced over the keys.

'You're just in time. Look, Paul's found Hammond's car on the ANPR system. It leaves the house at the time Hammond said he was working.' Jenny's excitement matched Paul's.

'How many hits have you got on the vehicle?' Sam peered at the screen as she addressed Paul.

'I can trace him half a mile from his home at 9.15am heading in the direction of New Middridge. Then I picked him up on High Street, Prior Street, and Hillside Road, two blocks away from Juniper Grove. That's the closest camera we have and he passed it at 10.03am.' Paul pushed his chair away from the desk and turned to look at his boss, a huge grin giving him the appearance of a young boy.

'Brilliant, well done, Paul. I want printouts of all sightings and close-ups if you can get them. Finally, we have something solid to work with. Jen, when Paul has the printouts, you can add them to the murder book and copies for the Crown Prosecution Service file. I'll go upstairs and tell the DCI the good news. We can then arrest Hammond, this time for murder.'

Samantha, buoyed by this new development, almost ran up the stairs only to hear Jenny calling her name as she reached the top. The urgent note in her sergeant's voice wasn't a good sign. Sam retraced her steps and met Jenny halfway. 'You need to see this. Alex Hammond isn't the one driving the car!' Jen handed her a copy of the image from the ANPR, plummeting Sam's mood instantly. The image was grainy but clear enough to show the car's driver wasn't Alex.

'Damn it! I didn't expect this. I should not have jumped to conclusions.' As she entered the incident room, she saw the smiles of only a few minutes ago had vanished.

'That's the clearest image we have. The angles from the other cameras are all wrong to give us a view of the driver, but it's enough, isn't it?'

'Yes, Paul. It's enough.'

Ten minutes later, Samantha and Jenny were heading towards the Hammond's home, this time to arrest Elaine Hammond. Sam drove her Mini with two officers in a marked car following them.

'It's no wonder she hinted that her husband might be capable of murder. Being charged and found guilty would be the perfect punishment for his involvement with Valerie, and Elaine could pick herself up and build a new life.'

It was 2.50pm. when the little convoy arrived at Alex Hammond's home. Exiting the car, Sam noticed a curtain moving in one of the downstairs windows, so at least someone was home. Jen knocked loudly on the door, but it was a couple of minutes before Alex Hammond opened it. The man said nothing, just stood aside for them to enter. Sam wondered if he'd been sleeping; he looked dreadful, unshaven, with grey skin and bags under his eyes. He was clearly suffering, and a shudder of empathy took Sam by surprise – or was it guilt? She felt somewhat culpable; her mistake was responsible for the anguish Hammond was suffering, but then the man wasn't totally blameless.

They followed him through to the lounge, where he went over to a cabinet and poured himself a generous measure of whiskey. *Probably not his first of the day,* Sam thought.

'We'd like to speak to Elaine,' Jenny stated while looking around for signs of her in the house.

'She's not here.'

Sam sat up straight. 'Do you know where she is?'

Alex shrugged and took a drink from his tumbler. 'Why do you want to see Elaine?' His eyes narrowed as he appeared to be trying to connect the dots.

'I can't tell you at the moment, but it is urgent. Have you any idea where she is?'

'She left yesterday morning. Hardly spoke a word to me after we got home from the station on Saturday. I slept in the spare room, and when I woke, she'd packed a case and left.'

'Do you mind if we look around?' Sam asked.

'Be my guest.' Hammond waved his tumbler in the air, sloshing the amber liquid over his hand. Jenny and the uniformed officers went off to search the property. 'This is a bit heavy-handed just to speak to my wife, isn't it?'

'Mr Hammond, do you know where she might have gone – a friend or relative perhaps?'

'Elaine has a sister in Harrogate. Sour-faced bitch she is, and they rarely get together. I shouldn't think she'll have gone there.'

'Could you give me her name and address, please?'

Alex Hammond rose slowly from the chair. Opening a bureau, he pulled out a book, flicked through the pages and recited his sister-in-law's name and address as Sam wrote it down. Jenny and the officers returned to the lounge. Jenny shook her head.

'One more thing, Mr Hammond. Could you check to see if your wife has taken her passport?'

For an instant, Alex looked puzzled, then smiled. 'You're looking at Elaine as the murderer, aren't you? Is this a new way of investigating – arrest everyone who knew the victim until you get someone to confess? If it is, I think your tactics are stupid. Elaine's no more a murderer than I am.' Alex turned back to the bureau, opened the bottom drawer and began to rummage. 'It's not here.' He looked stunned. 'I don't understand…'

Samantha thought the whiskey must be dulling his brain.

'Thank you for your help, Mr Hammond. Don't attempt to contact your wife, and if you hear from her, please let us know. Goodbye, sir.' The officers trooped from the house, leaving Alex Hammond needing another drink.

'What now, boss?' Jenny glanced at Sam's face as they drove away from the Hammond's home.

'Do you want me to contact Harrogate police and ask them to see if Elaine's at her sister's?'

'What, when we can be there in less than an hour?' Sam had already stood the uniformed officers down; she and Jen could handle the trip to Harrogate.

'If I'm working late again, I need something to eat and a large coffee. You can decide where, as long as it's tasty and unhealthy.'

'There's a service station in a couple of miles. We'll stop there.'

'Do you think Elaine will be at her sister's? They don't appear to have been close.'

'It's as good a place as any to start. Ring Paul and get him to do the usual searches for her car; she's got a full day's head start; we'll be lucky if she's only gone as far as Harrogate.'

SEVENTY

'Is she still in bed?' Brian Meadows shuffled into the kitchen and scowled at his wife.

'Yes, it's been quite an ordeal for her, she probably didn't sleep well.'

'And will *Lady Elaine* be leaving today?'

'Don't be sarcastic. I can't put her out on the streets; she has nowhere to go.' Frances plonked a bacon sandwich in front of her husband.

'Well, you'll have to tell her she can't stay indefinitely. What will people think?'

'Nothing if we don't tell them her circumstances. Anyway, it won't affect you, you'll be at work during the day. I'm the one who has to put up with her.'

Brian took a bite from his sandwich with a harumph while Frances went back upstairs to finish getting ready.

'I'm off now!' Brian shouted up the stairs ten minutes later.

'Shh... you'll wake Elaine,' Frances whispered as the door banged louder than usual. Pausing outside the guest room door, she listened for any noise that might indicate her sister was awake. Nothing. Creeping downstairs, Frances busied herself in the kitchen, wondering how long Elaine would sleep for. There was a committee meeting that afternoon hosted by the Lady Mayor of Harrogate, which she didn't want to miss. Perhaps in an hour or so, she'd wake her sister up.

Fifty minutes later, there was still no sign of life in the guest bedroom, so Frances tapped lightly on the door. When there was no reply, she opened it and peered inside. A gentle sigh and a stretch signalled that Elaine was stirring.

'Good morning. I thought you'd like to be up and about. It's after 9.30am.'

Elaine poked her head from under the duvet. 'Any chance of a cup of tea?' She plumped up her pillow and settled back down.

'Oh, er yes, I suppose so.' Frances went back downstairs. *What a cheek. Who does she think she is?*

It crossed her mind to pop a slice of bread in the toaster for her sister, but that would be encouraging her, and Frances certainly didn't wish to do so. Carrying the tea upstairs, she found Elaine propped up in bed, waiting as if her sister was a maid.

'Thank you, Frances. Could you be an angel and run me a bath? I'm so stiff this morning; it must be all the stress I've been under lately.'

Frances bit her tongue to stop the sharp reply from being spoken aloud. Without comment, she marched into the en-suite and set the bath taps running. Returning to the bedroom, she saw Elaine had closed her eyes. 'Don't go back to sleep; the bath's running.' Leaving the room with a bang of the door, she hoped Elaine would get the hint that she wasn't going to wait on her.

Almost an hour later, Elaine appeared in the drawing room where Frances was flicking through the Lady magazine. 'A coffee would be wonderful, and perhaps a lightly poached egg?'

'Help yourself.' Frances didn't look at her sister.

'Oh. Actually, if you wouldn't mind doing it for me? I'm not feeling too well this morning.'

'Elaine, I am not going to wait on you. I have a meeting this afternoon and need to prepare.' Frances was pleased with herself for being firm. It was the same when they were children. If Elaine could get out of doing any chores, she would. She smiled as her sister stomped out of the room to make some breakfast.

Twenty minutes later, Elaine approached her sister. 'I thought we might go out for lunch to Betty's today. What do you think? My treat.'

'You must be feeling better then?'

'A little. A treat would do me good and we can have a good natter about old times.'

Frances couldn't imagine anything worse. 'Sorry, as I said, I have a meeting this afternoon.'

'Can't you cancel?'

'No, It's important.'

Elaine folded her arms, clearly unhappy, while Frances hid her smile, remembering the same stance from their childhood when her sister would sulk, her pet lip out and a scowl on her face. She'd taken control of the situation. Hopefully, if her sister accepted that Frances was in charge, the visit would be bearable.

Frances prepared for her meeting, ignoring the sighs of her sister, who clearly expected more attention from her hostess. When it was time to leave, she told Elaine to make herself a sandwich as she would be having afternoon tea with the committee.

'Can't I come with you? Some of my experience in charity work may be useful and I don't particularly want to be alone.'

'Sorry, that's not possible. We have some sensitive issues to discuss which wouldn't be appropriate with an outsider present.' Frances smiled as her sister flounced out of the room. Maybe which fillings to have in the summer garden party sandwiches wasn't a strictly sensitive topic, yet there was no way she was taking Elaine.

Returning home at 5pm, Frances found the house dark and quiet. Calling Elaine's name brought no response, so Frances went in search of her, beginning in the kitchen.

Dirty plates and cups littered the worktops. *Would it have been too much to stack them in the dishwasher?* she wondered. Tutting, she also noticed a couple of used wine glasses.

'Elaine!' She shouted, bounding up the stairs. Elaine was in her bedroom, snoring softly, another wine glass on the bedside table. Shaking her shoulder woke her up. 'Have you been drinking?' Frances demanded.

'What if I have? I'm grown up now and don't need my big sister's permission!' She turned over and then squealed as Frances pulled the duvet off the bed. Elaine was fully dressed. 'Get off, I'm tired!' Her gripe was ignored.

'If you want to stay here, you'll not drink during the day. Whatever Brian will say when he comes home, I dread to think!'

'You can tell stuffy Brian where to go!' Elaine attempted to grab the duvet again, but her sister pulled it away and disappeared downstairs. Elaine followed, shouting about being ill and needing to be cared for.

Frances ignored the complaints, regretting ever allowing her sister to stay. She put a prepared casserole in the oven, lit the gas and then pushed past Elaine to the drawing room.

'Don't ignore me! You always were an uncaring bitch.'

'How dare you!' Frances couldn't believe she was being

insulted in her own home. 'I offer you a bed for a few days and you haven't even the good grace to be grateful. Perhaps you should leave now before Brian gets home. He won't stand for such rudeness.'

'Oh, yes, Brian the perfect husband...'

'Well, he's turned out a damned sight better than yours!'

Instead of returning another insult, Elaine grabbed a cut-glass vase from the dresser and hurled it at her sister. Frances ducked, and the vase hit the wall, smashing into tiny sparkling shards all over the carpet.

'You're hysterical!' Frances slapped her sister across the face. Elaine gasped and then lurched towards Frances, her hands reaching for her throat. The sound of the front door opening caused the women to freeze.

'What the hell is going on here?' Brian exclaimed as he regarded the scene before him.

'She's drunk!' Frances offered the obvious as an excuse. Brian rushed angrily towards Elaine, who grabbed a bronze statue and raised it above her head as if in defence.

'Get away from me!' she screamed.

'Don't be so stupid, woman. Put it down...' He took two steps towards her and lifted his arm to grab the statue, but Elaine was already wielding it at his head. Frances heard her husband groan, followed by a thud as he fell to the floor. She ran to him, knocking into her sister, who was dashing from the room and knelt beside Brian's unconscious body.

SEVENTY-ONE

It was 5.35pm when Samantha and Jenny pulled up in front of the Meadows' home on Cornwall Road, and already dark and damp. Jenny had commented on nearly every house they'd passed, declaring them to be on Millionaire's Row. 'I thought the Hammonds were loaded but her sister's done even better for herself.' The house they were seeking was lit up by the blue flashing lights of an ambulance

Hurrying from the car, they were in time to see a man being loaded into the ambulance on a stretcher and a woman sobbing beside him. Sam pulled out her ID and approached the paramedic to ask what had happened.

'The wife called to say the poor devil had been attacked by his sister-in-law! I thought you lot would have been here sooner. We called it in on our way here.'

Sam was about to explain that they were from out of town when a marked car pulled onto the drive and parked up beside the ambulance. 'Is he going to be okay?' she asked.

'Nasty gash and concussion, although I've seen worse.' The paramedic jumped into the rear of the vehicle beside his patient while Sam greeted the police officers to explain her interest.

Jenny was talking to the man's wife, presumably Elaine's sister and trying to calm her down.

'Boss, she wants to go in the ambulance with her husband – says Elaine left about fifteen minutes ago in her car – drunk!'

'Okay. Let her go with him.' Sam turned to the uniformed officers, who intended to make a quick search of the property before going to the hospital to get a statement from the couple. Following them into the property, Sam witnessed the evidence of the fracas which littered the drawing room.

Shards of glass sparkled like diamonds from the deep pile of the carpet, and a coffee table was upturned. After another quick discussion with the officers, she took directions to their station while they headed off to the hospital.

'What now, boss?'

'We'll liaise with the local police and ask for their help in tracking down Elaine Hammond. If only we'd been twenty minutes earlier.'

As they pulled into the station car park at Beckwith Head Road several marked cars were leaving, sirens blaring as they sped off in the direction the New Middridge detectives had come from.

'At least there's plenty of parking.' Sam swung into a recently vacated space. Inside the modern building, they approached the desk and showed their ID.

'What can we do for you, ma'am?' the sergeant asked.

Sam explained their mission and asked for help tracing a Peugeot 208 Coupe Cabriolet belonging to Elaine Hammond. The sergeant smiled as she recited the registration, which she knew by heart.

'I can tell you exactly where that car is. We've had reports of a multi-car pile-up on the A59 Knaresborough Road, and your missing car is apparently at the centre. Give me a minute and I'll see if I can get you an update.' The helpful sergeant made a phone call and after a couple of minutes of listening rather than talking, he ended the call and turned back to Sam.

'Not as bad as it could have been. Four cars were involved; initial reports suggest the Peugeot was going the wrong way around a roundabout and caused the collision. No loss of life, but five people are waiting to go to hospital, the driver of the Peugeot among them.'

Sam thanked the man for his help and made a note of the address for Harrogate District Hospital – Lancaster Park Road – and they left to find their suspect.

The journey was less than three miles and Sam and Jenny arrived at the hospital before the ambulances which were bringing the casualties. Attempting to keep out of the way of the A&E staff preparing for the accident intake, Jenny suggested coffee and went in search of some while Sam tried to make herself as unobtrusive as possible.

Ten minutes later, the ambulances arrived. Three stretchers were prioritised, and two walking wounded were ushered into waiting cubicles. Elaine Hammond, wobbling unsteadily on her feet, was one of them.

'Leave me alone!' She shrugged the paramedic's hand off her arm. Then, catching sight of Samantha, she collapsed in the man's arms. A nurse hurried to assist, and they effortlessly lifted Elaine onto the trolley in the cubicle. A doctor followed them inside, swishing the curtain closed behind him.

'That was convenient.' Jen, arriving back with the coffee, shook her head.

'We'll have to get past the doctor before we can speak to her, let alone arrest her.' Sam's frustration showed in her face. A young police officer appeared in A&E, looking as if he didn't quite know what to do. Sam and Jenny approached him to introduce themselves and update him on their presence.

'I could smell drink on her breath, but it wasn't possible to breathalyse her; the priority was to get her to hospital.' He looked afraid he'd be in trouble.

Jenny reassured him. 'You did the right thing. We'll try and see the doctor soon to ascertain her condition. Perhaps they can take a blood test, but the more serious charge is clearly paramount.'

As Jenny spoke, the doctor exited the cubicle. Sam was beside him in a flash, determined not to let the man go until she'd stated her case. They talked for several minutes, Sam animated, stretching her tiny frame to her full height before the doctor shook his head, and Sam turned away.

'He wants to keep her overnight to do CT and MRI scans. He's worried about why she collapsed, although it's pretty obvious it's because she saw us.' Turning to the PC, she said, 'He's taking a blood test, so we'll learn what her blood-alcohol level is. I'm going to have to get in touch with your station again to ask for an overnight guard. The doctor won't let me see her to formally arrest her; we'll have to wait for his say-so first.'

'I'm here to try and take statements,' said the PC. 'And it'll probably take time. Will you go back to New Middridge and come again tomorrow?'

'Yes, there's no point in us hanging about. We'll go back to Beckwith Head Road and sort out the finer details, then call it a day.' The detectives turned and made their way through the bustling A&E department.

'Not the outcome I'd hoped for, but at least we know where Elaine is.' Sam sighed when they were back in the car. 'It'll be another early start tomorrow, Jen. Okay with you?'

'Fine. I'm just glad it's all coming together at last,' Jen replied before checking the sat nav to see where the nearest service station was.

SEVENTY-TWO

Samantha arranged to pick Jenny up from her flat the next morning rather than meet at the station. The plan was to drive straight to Harrogate, and if things went well, they would return later with Elaine Hammond under arrest.

On route, at Sam's request, Jenny called Paul Roper at the station and asked him to update DCI Aiden Kent. Jenny smiled as she finished the call. 'He's quite enjoying being in charge when we're out.'

'The experience is good for him. The time's coming when Paul should be looking to move on, gain skills in other areas of policing.' Sam knew this to be true but she'd miss Paul when he did move on. 'It'll be good for him not to be working with Layla.'

'Good for her, as well. She's too happy to stay in his shadow rather than carve out her own career.'

'Agreed, the time will come, Jen. But Kim and Tom fit in well. When one door closes, another opens.'

Soon after 9am, Samantha pulled her Mini Cooper into the hospital car park. The A&E department was almost as busy as it had been the previous evening. A rather frazzled receptionist said 'yes' without looking at them.

'We're here to see Elaine Hammond. She was brought in after the accident yesterday.'

The receptionist looked up and clicked her tongue. 'Ah, yes. The lady with the police guard. She's on ward 32. Go back to the entrance and take the lift to the third floor.' Her head dropped to the computer screen again.

Elaine was in a room at the end of the ward, easily identified by the police constable sitting outside the door. After a quick word with him, Sam established that their suspect had already seen the doctor that morning, the scans were satisfactory, and she was cleared for discharge. Jenny had a brief conversation with the ward sister, and they were given the all-clear to arrest Elaine Hammond.

The woman in question looked startled when Sam and Jenny entered the room. 'Good morning, Mrs Hammond. How are you feeling today?'

'What are you doing here?'

'Please, don't insult us by pretending you didn't see me yesterday?'

'I don't know what you're talking about! Why are you here? Has something happened to Alex?'

'We're here to arrest you for the murder of Valerie Turner. Jenny...' Sam turned to her sergeant, who stepped forward to read Val her rights.

'This is ridiculous! Alex killed her. You know he did. Has he been trying to blame me because it was him? I know it was!'

'Please get dressed, Mrs Hammond and we'll escort you to New Middridge Police Station.'

Elaine reluctantly dressed, and after receiving her discharge letter from the staff nurse, Samantha and Jenny escorted her from the hospital.

'You've got this all wrong. Alex told me he killed that woman – he begged me to lie for him and say he'd been with me all day... what's he been telling you?' Elaine sat in the back of Sam's car, quite indignant, her face flushed with anger.

'Mrs Hammond. If you intend to use the services of a lawyer, I would suggest you say very little until you've spoken with him. And we're not going to discuss the case until we're at the station.' Jenny's words had the desired effect, with Elaine remaining silent for the duration of the journey.

At New Middridge police station, Elaine was processed, allowed to call a solicitor, and locked in a cell until he arrived. Her silence ended as she objected strongly to being in a cell and demanded to see the chief constable. It was a relief for the detectives to get back to the interview room and prepare themselves for questioning Elaine Hammond when her solicitor arrived.

Samantha thought it was time to see the DCI. Paul had updated him on the new developments, but she knew he'd appreciate her perspective. The flight of stairs seemed steeper than usual, and Sam was quite out of breath when she knocked on Aiden Kent's door.

'Come in!'

Sam entered the room and smiled at her DCI. She'd always found him approachable, and since Ravi's death, he'd been very considerate, overly so Sam thought at times, almost fatherly.

'Ah, Sam. Have you made an arrest?'

'Yes, sir. Elaine Hammond is in custody, waiting for her solicitor. She's been denying her involvement and pointing the finger at her husband, but when they see the evidence, I'm hoping her solicitor will persuade her to confess.'

'Is the evidence sufficient to convince the Crown Prosecution Service to proceed?'

'Yes, sir, it is.'

'Well done, Samantha. Perhaps you can take a few days off when this one's wrapped up. You deserve it.'

SEVENTY-THREE

Elaine had been given coffee and a sandwich, which she threw at the door when the officer serving her left. Sam fleetingly wondered if it was ethical to interview a suspect when they were hungry. The solicitor, Kevin Dixon, took four hours to arrive, having been in court on another case. He was then allowed time alone with his client.

The detectives received word that Mr Dixon and his client were ready at 4.20pm, and they waited another ten minutes before entering the interview room. Jenny switched on the recorder and introduced everyone present. Elaine's red-rimmed, puffy eyes avoided contact with the detectives as she picked at her thumbnail with great concentration.

Samantha opened the interview. 'Mrs Hammond, you've been charged with the murder of Valerie Turner. Would you like to answer that charge?' Kevin Dixon coughed and sat up straighter in his chair.

'My client understands the charge but would like to explain what happened that morning. She accepts that Mrs Turner died from a blow she administered, but it was purely in self-defence.'

He looked at Elaine, who sniffed, lifted her chin and commenced her version of events.

'Soon after we arrived in New Middridge, I knew something wasn't right with Alex. Initially, I thought it was work – he'd taken over as senior partner in the firm, and there was pressure to live up to the role. I tried to be supportive, yet it was taking me time to settle in, too. When I found the documents from that ancestry place proving him to be the father of someone called Ben Chapman, it completely floored me.

'Alex had always been a good husband and father, so I assumed it was a mistake. Digging deeper, I discovered that my husband had been paying Valerie Turner to keep quiet! Yes, I was angry, but it was never my intention to hurt the woman.' Elaine looked from Samantha to Jenny as if expecting a reaction which wasn't forthcoming. She then looked at her solicitor who nodded for her to continue.

She sniffed and wiped her eyes with a scrunched-up tissue. 'When the anger died down, I was curious. Her address was on the letter, so I drove past a few times hoping to see her. There were girls living there but no signs of this Ben, which was puzzling, so I decided to visit Valerie – to confront her in the hope of stopping the blackmail. My reasoning was that if she thought I knew, she'd stop...

'Anyway, I went on that fateful Saturday. I knew her family usually went out then, so it seemed a good time to see her alone. My intention was to have a civilised conversation, but things got out of hand, and the woman went for me – she was wild, uncontrollable, and left me with no choice other than to defend myself.' Elaine finished her account abruptly; the details were sketchy, to say the least.

Sam wondered if she expected they'd accept her version, and leave it at that. She looked directly at Elaine and asked,

'Why didn't you ring the bell and introduce yourself if you only wanted to talk to her?'

'I did ring the bell. She didn't answer,' Elaine snapped.

Samantha tapped her pen on the table, 'So, you went around the back of the house?'

'Well, yes. I thought she might be in the garden.'

'On a freezing cold February morning?'

Elaine remained tight-lipped, so Sam continued. 'You went to the back of the house, not the front, didn't you? If you'd approached the front door, CCTV would have picked you up. You smashed the back door to get in, and when Valerie found you, you killed her, which was your intention from the start, wasn't it?' Samantha put her pen on the table, folded her arms and waited for Elaine's response.

Her eyes widened. 'No. Honestly, I only went to talk to her!'

'Then why did you take one of your husband's golf clubs with you?'

Elaine lowered her eyes. 'I, er... I wanted to scare her, let her know I meant business.'

'No, Elaine. I don't buy it. Taking a weapon with you suggests pre-meditation. I think you purposely went to Valerie Turner's home to kill her, not to talk to her. And when your DNA has been processed, I'm confident we'll find a match to as yet unidentified trace samples we found at the scene.'

'You're wrong! I tried to talk, but she laughed at me. She said some horrible things about me and my marriage and then attacked me! I pushed her away. She was crazy and kept coming at me until I had no choice but to defend myself.'

Jenny chipped in, 'You could have left.'

'She wouldn't let me near the door... I couldn't get past her.'

Samantha sat forward and spoke slowly, 'I think you took the golf club intending to kill Valerie Turner, and when we found the victim's blood on the club, you let your husband take the blame. You told me he'd admitted it to you. Why would you say that?'

'I panicked, didn't know what I was saying.' Elaine started to cry. Putting her head in her hands, she turned towards her solicitor, who asked, 'Could we have a break now, please? This is proving a very stressful experience for my client.'

Sam raised an eyebrow but stood to leave. Jenny verbalised what was happening and then switched the tape off. 'Would you like coffee?' The answer was yes, so she followed Sam from the room to organise some coffee for Elaine and her solicitor, as well as for Sam and herself.

In the incident room, Jenny placed a coffee on Sam's desk and asked, 'Got any biscuits?'

'Top drawer, help yourself,' Sam replied.

Jenny opened the drawer and pulled out a pack of chocolate digestives and a jar of pickled gherkins. She grinned and asked, 'What are these doing here? Cravings ruling your life?'

'Don't judge until you've been there, Jen. Sometimes, I can't settle until I've eaten at least two – they go down well with the chocolate digestives!' Sam replied, unscrewing the jar. 'Want one?'

As the detectives were about to leave to continue the interview, a police officer brought a message that Mr Dixon had requested a doctor for his client, who was feeling unwell. Jenny rolled her eyes, 'Bloody tactics!' Sam responded,

'It's okay. We'll give Elaine another night's accommodation in the guest suite, and we can head home. We'll resume in the morning.' Sam smiled as the police officer scurried off to make the arrangements.

SEVENTY-FOUR

E laine Hammond was afraid, or terrified, might best describe her feelings. Perhaps the reality of her situation affected her, as she truly felt ill. Yet the doctor summoned at her solicitor's request was brusque and unsympathetic, offering only paracetamol, which she took eagerly.

Kevin Dixon left as the doctor arrived, informing his client that the detectives did not wish to see her again until the following morning. She suddenly felt very much alone.

Elaine found a couple of blankets had been folded onto the plastic-covered mattress in her cell, and the sight of them made her burst into tears. Was she expected to sleep here? This was the lowest point in her life. Trembling, she flopped down on the bed before her legs gave way and, pulling the scratchy blankets up to her chin, closed her eyes.

Burying her face in the blankets, she let the tears stream down her cheeks. The image of Valerie Turner's body, motionless and bleeding on the kitchen floor, was a haunting imprint behind her closed eyelids – one which would stay with her for the remainder of her life.

The night was restless, filled with the sound of the metallic door hatch opening and closing as someone checked on her regularly. It seemed they were concerned about her well-being, perhaps thinking she was a suicide risk. In the quiet night hours, Elaine had plenty of time to consider her actions.

Elaine's mind drifted back to the day she killed Valerie Turner, and she felt the almost palpable weight of her guilt. She had extinguished another person's life. Was foolishness an excuse for such a terrible act, or had she suffered a psychotic episode? Perhaps it was the shock of discovering Alex's hidden truth or even the sting of jealousy. She loved Alex, and the idea of him being with someone else was unbearable. Whatever it was had driven her to act recklessly, and Elaine had completely abandoned her usual cautious nature, disregarding the potential consequences of her actions.

Elaine remembered fleeing from the Turners' home. It was surreal, a nightmare which she couldn't believe was happening. Her body shook violently and waves of panic made driving almost impossible. She barely remembered the journey.

When Elaine finally arrived home, all she craved was a large glass of wine – followed swiftly by another. But even the numbing warmth of alcohol couldn't erase the haunting image of Valerie Turner's body or the weight of the golf club in her hand as she swung it high, bringing it down onto the woman's head; or how the impact of metal on bone felt and sounded; or the look of pure terror on Valerie's face as she realised what was happening.

For the following few days, despite feeling guilty, Elaine continued to tell herself that Valerie was a bitch and a heartless blackmailer, attempting to justify her actions and convince herself she'd done the right thing. Her rationale was that Valerie was evil and deserved to die. In her heart, she knew her actions were wrong, but Elaine was in denial.

Difficulties at home were exacerbated. Alex was overwhelmed with the extra work resulting from the murder of their office manager, and Elaine struggled to act normally – drinking more and often moody. Alex was too preoccupied to notice. Elaine kept track of the case through the newspapers and gradually believed she had pulled off the perfect crime. After all, who would suspect her?

It took nearly five weeks for the police to make the connection and discover that Alex was the father of Valerie's son. By that time, Elaine was thinking more rationally. Having convinced herself she'd killed Valerie to save her marriage, five weeks down the line, she saw things more clearly. Her feelings for Alex would never be the same. She could barely look her husband in the eye and blamed him for her actions. If only he had never been embroiled with that woman... Yes, she decided Alex was to blame, so when the police arrested him, Elaine had no intention of confessing to save him.

But events had shifted. How the police connected her to the murder was a mystery. It had all gone so badly wrong, yet even to her muddled mind, it was clear that the truth was now out in the open. Alex had been released, and she was the one locked in the cells.

How the hell did things get this far? Was it my intention to take her life? It's a question I struggle to answer. Yes, I was armed, convincing myself that it was solely to intimidate her, to instil the same fear in her that she'd instilled in me, and not with the intent to cause any harm. Subconsciously, it's possible I wanted her dead; it had crossed my mind more than once, but intentional or not, I did it. I killed her.

The actual killing surprised me. I enjoyed her fear, the wide-eyed terror and the look of surprise on her face. She grovelled, pleading with me not to hurt her, offering me money. Even after all these weeks, I replay those words, that moment, with an almost frightening thrill. The sense of power, of being in control of another human being, was intoxicating. In some ways, I'm appalled at myself, yet in others, proud.

I refuse to accept the label of a bad person. My actions were motivated by self-preservation, a natural response to the circumstances. I don't feel remorse for what I did; she received the consequences of her actions. She was a liar who had crossed the line. Maybe I should be commended for eliminating such a malicious presence from the world.

Yet now, I must face the consequences.

I'm not the type to commit murder. I'm just an ordinary person trying to live a reasonably happy life. But perhaps we all have the aptitude to kill – when we feel threatened, trapped, or scared of what might occur. Yes, I believe that under certain circumstances, we all have the potential to be killers – the capacity to murder.

Elaine carefully contemplated her next steps and decided what she would do.

SEVENTY-FIVE

DI Samantha Freeman was determined to resolve the Turner case swiftly. Elaine Hammond's solicitor had been provided with copies of the evidence, which, to Sam, was irrefutable, and his client's guilt was plain to see. If Elaine Hammond continued to claim innocence and went before a jury, Samantha believed the woman would be viewed as an unreliable witness. The DI was as confident as she could be that Elaine would be found guilty.

At 9.30am on Wednesday, the same four people gathered in the same interview room as the previous evening.

Jenny switched on the tape and when the formalities were over, Kevin Dixon was the first to speak. 'My client wishes to change her plea to guilty,' he said, surprising everyone. Saying nothing more, he turned to Elaine to explain. Samantha saw a little of the composed woman she had first encountered and wondered if a night in a cell had brought her to her senses.

Elaine, with tears in her eyes, started to speak. 'I've been under considerable stress lately, which I know isn't an excuse, and now I've had time to think about my actions, I'm ashamed. I killed Valerie Turner. I don't think it was my intention to do so, but I did take the golf club with me and broke into her home when I knew she was alone. I can't offer excuses other than it was perhaps a moment of madness, and certainly, I'd been drinking too much. I deeply regret my actions, which I know can't be undone, so I'm willing to plead guilty, accepting this will result in a justified prison sentence.'

To say the detectives were surprised was an understatement. Judging from Elaine's belligerent attitude the previous day, they'd expected more excuses, but it seemed the woman had engaged in some serious thinking. Perhaps her solicitor had explained how a plea of guilty may possibly bring a more lenient sentence. They would never know, but it appeared the case was drawing to a close, with only the paperwork to complete before they passed it over to the Criminal Prosecution Service.

Sam hurried upstairs to update DCI Kent, accepting his congratulations – even though she felt they should have solved the case sooner. Jenny went to the deli for coffee and doughnuts, and the team enjoyed a cautious celebration in the incident room. As it was still early in the day, Samantha was able to tie up a few loose ends.

The first call she made was to Geoff Turner. Finally, she could give the man more details. Finding the culprit wouldn't bring his wife back but the family could support each other in moving on to build a new life together. Sam offered to visit them later in the evening, but Geoff declined; he'd tell the girls himself. There would be other times to meet; although the case was solved, the process was only just beginning.

Her second call was to Ben Chapman, who expressed surprise at the perpetrator being a woman but relief that she was behind bars. Ben asked if it was an appropriate time to meet his brother. The waiting had been tough.

'If you give me permission to pass your phone number on to

Simon, I'll do so immediately. And I'll be ringing your grandparents. Shall I give them your number, too?' Sam heard the excitement in his voice as he agreed. Although Ben had lost his mother, he'd discovered siblings and grandparents – the silver lining to the heavy cloud that had dogged his life recently.

Simon Prentis was the next to receive a call from Sam. His reaction was similar to his brother's, and he seemed equally excited to receive the phone number he was eager to dial. Sam wished him luck and offered to help in any way she could.

The following call was to Valerie's parents, Robert and Bella Edwards. Their existence had surprised them all. No one had doubted Valerie was telling the truth when she claimed they were dead.

Bella answered and broke down in tears when Sam explained her reason for calling. 'Such a shame!' She finally managed to speak. 'One thoughtless act of violence has caused so much suffering...'

Samantha informed Bella that Ben and Simon would be meeting soon and gave Bella Ben's phone number. As the call ended, it was unclear whether Bella's tears were of sadness or joy.

Joining the rest of the team for coffee, Sam skipped the doughnut and snuck a gherkin from her stash in the desk drawer. Updating Jenny on her phone calls, they spent a few minutes speculating on how these meetings would pan out before getting back to the serious business of preparing their case for the CPS.

SEVENTY-SIX

Simon Prentis trembled as he thumbed in the phone number for his twin brother. When DI Freeman rang him with Ben's phone number and news of their arrest, he felt relief. Relief because it appeared that the murderer wasn't his biological father as they'd initially suspected and also that events were coming to an end – or was it a beginning?

He'd had plenty of time to consider what he'd say to Ben Chapman, but now the opportunity was here everything he'd wanted to say and ask flew out of his mind. He hadn't rushed to make the call and first talked it through with Christine. His wife was almost as nervous as Simon but tactfully insisted he took the call on his own without her listening in or Noah distracting him.

'Er... hello? Is this Ben?' Simon felt like a shy child.

'Yes! Simon, is it? I've been waiting for your call!' Ben's voice was not very different from his.

'This is so odd, Ben. There's so much I want to talk to you about yet I don't know where to start.'

'I understand. I thought I was prepared for your call, but I'm not. You're married, aren't you, with a little boy?'

'Yes, Christine and our son's called Noah. How about you? I know from DI Freeman that you're not married, but do you have a partner?'

Ben chuckled. 'Not at the moment. Look, can we meet? Face to face will probably be easier. Would you like to come to me, or shall I visit you?'

'If you could come here, you can meet Christine and Noah, too. Could you make Monday?'

'Yeah, great. If you give me your address and postcode, I'll set off early and be with you late morning. Is that any good?'

'Brilliant, yes. We've got so much to talk about and you're right, it'll be easier face to face. Until Monday, then?' Simon finished the call and went to find Christine.

'That didn't take long. Is everything all right?' Having settled Noah down for a nap, she took her husband's hand and led him to the sofa.

'Yeah, it went okay, just a bit strange. Ben's coming here on Monday.' Simon smiled. Having not known what to expect, he felt slightly deflated, but Monday wasn't long to wait, and he was sure conversation would flow easier than on the phone.

Ben Chapman pushed his phone back into the pocket of his jeans. *'Well, Ben, you sounded like a proper airhead.'* He spoke aloud to the empty room. Since giving Sam Freeman his phone number to pass on to his brother, he'd been on edge, not knowing when the call might come or what they would say to each other.

The pressure of the extraordinary events of the last few weeks was catching up with him, making him restless and antsy. Finding his birth mother and building a relationship with her had eased the loss of his adoptive parents, yet Valerie was gone, taken in such a horrific way, and it appeared she was not the person he'd thought her to be.

Anna and Lizzie were certainly a positive in his life, the best thing to come from his newly found family, and Ben knew they'd always keep in touch. Would the same be true of Simon? Would his twin even want a relationship with him – he had a family and his adoptive parents. Would Ben be an intrusion into his orderly, comfortable life?

Monday dawned after a long weekend, and as Durham was an unfamiliar city to him, Ben set his satnav to the Belmont address his brother had given him.

My brother. He liked the sound of it and said a quick prayer for the morning's big meeting to go well.

After a journey of nearly a hundred miles, Ben arrived at Simon's home. It was almost 10am. The house was a fairly modern semi-detached on a neat, well-laid-out estate. A family home similar to the one Ben aspired to have in the future. A 2010 Nissan Micra was parked in the drive. He squeezed past to ring the doorbell. As Ben smoothed down his hair and stretched his neck to iron out the kinks from driving, he heard footsteps thundering down the stairs then a shadow filled the glass panel in the door.

The door flew open, and the brothers momentarily stared at each other. Simon stood aside and motioned for Ben to enter. Once inside the hall, they moved as one to embrace, both with tears welling in their eyes. Pulling away from Ben, Simon led the way into a large lounge furnished comfortably with two huge sofas and decorated in pastel colours with a grey carpet. The house was quiet, without the sound of a small child Ben had expected.

'Christine's taken Noah out to her parents. She'll be back at lunchtime so you'll meet them then. Can I get you a coffee?' Simon asked.

'Great, thanks.' Ben couldn't stop smiling. It was like seeing his reflection in a mirror. 'This is so peculiar, isn't it?'

Simon returned his grin and nodded, scrutinising his brother carefully. 'There's no doubting we're twins, is there? Same hair, eyes – hell, everything! Let me grab that coffee and then we can talk.'

Five minutes later the brothers sat opposite each other, cradling mugs of coffee and getting to know each other. Predictably their first topic of conversation was Valerie Turner. Ben showed Simon some photographs of Val, Anna and Lizzie on his phone. He admitted his disappointment at being deceived by Val. 'Wouldn't you think when I turned up, it would have been the opportune time to tell me about you? It appears our mother had a penchant for secrets and lies.'

'Yes, a pathological liar. And as for our biological father, have you met him?' Simon was keen to learn everything his brother knew.

'I saw him at the funeral but not to talk to. I had no idea he was our father then; he was pointed out to me as her boss.'

'And Val's parents?'

'Yes, I've met them briefly. They seem okay. I liked them, and apparently Val lied about them too...'

For the next hour, the brothers talked, asked questions, and learned of each other's lives. When Christine and Noah arrived home, a bond was evolving, and Simon and Ben felt at ease together. If Christine was surprised at the likeness, Noah was astonished, looking from his father to his uncle in disbelief.

Christine remarked that they were even dressed similarly, something the men hadn't noticed. They both wore blue button-down shirts with jeans, different shades but alike in style.

Ben remained with his newly discovered family until evening, enjoying being part of their routine and accepted as brother and uncle – a status that thrilled him. His reflections whilst driving home were all positive. Arrangements had been made to meet again and the brothers were keen to get together with Anna, Lizzie and their grandparents. It would take more than a few visits to catch up on years of separation. The day had given Ben hope and a warm, satisfying feeling, not readily identifiable, yet welcome and encouraging.

For the first time in months, he anticipated the future with optimism, looking forward to it rather than being fearful. Ben had a family; he was no longer alone. At least he could be grateful to Val for this.

SEVENTY-SEVEN

E laine Hammond's guilty plea spared Geoff Turner and his family from the ordeal of a trial. She was remanded for reports, and several weeks later, Geoff attended the sentencing hearing and listened as the judge imposed a life sentence with a recommendation of serving a minimum of fifteen years.

As Geoff left the court, he ran into Alex Hammond. The man's appearance took him aback. Alex, who used to be healthy, well-groomed, and full of vitality, now seemed to have withered into a mere shadow of his former self. The two men exchanged an awkward glance for a few seconds before Alex gave a quick nod, and they went their separate ways.

Anna and Lizzie asked their father what had happened at the hearing upon his return home. Geoff told them the salient facts, which they accepted without comment. Talk had been all they seemed to do these days, reaching no useful conclusions. Some of Valerie's personal effects still needed to be dealt with, and then finally, they could draw a line under the whole business and look to the future.

Anna and Lizzie had sorted their mother's clothes, most of

them going to local charity shops, and on the morning after the sentencing hearing, Geoff entered his wife's room to complete the task of erasing his wife from their lives. He'd tried hard to concentrate on the good things of their marriage but bitterness coloured every memory. Were they real or simply illusions? He didn't hate Val, yet felt uncomfortable about never having fully known her. The only good to come from their marriage was their daughters – at his lowest moments, Geoff reminded himself that if he'd never met Val, he wouldn't have them.

Val had kept her important papers inside a locked box with her and the girls' birth certificates, marriage certificate and other significant items. The box rested at the top of her wardrobe, but Geoff couldn't find the key. As the lock was flimsy, it seemed logical to break it, which he easily did with a pen. Tipping the contents onto the bed, he commenced sorting through them.

In addition to the expected documents, Geoff found a letter in a handwritten envelope addressed simply to *Valerie*. He slid the paper from the envelope and read the single-page letter.

> My darling Val.
> This waiting is driving me mad! Why can't we just disappear now? I know you're working on our nest egg and want to bleed the bastard for as much as you can get, which is exactly what he deserves, but this pretending is dire. It's no way to live!
> Hayley is getting more trying each day. When she discovered our affair, she supposedly forgave me, but hell, she's determined to make me pay! I'm not sure I can stomach much more – I only want to be with you – to take off into the night and forget our past lives.

Please, tell me you feel the same and we can go soon. I love you, and this pretence is making me crazy.

Think about it, my love, and let me know.

Steve xx

Geoff was unsure if his tears were of sadness or anger. He decided on the latter. Val had sworn her relationship with Steve was over, but here was the proof that it wasn't. So, she was planning to leave him and the girls, and the money Lizzie found was presumably her *little nest egg* to run away with Steve Green! Money extorted from Alex Hammond. More lies, even from the grave.

It crossed Geoff's mind that he could use the letter to exact revenge on Steve, but the thought didn't linger for long. He didn't want to be bitter. Negative feelings were destructive, and he wanted to create a better example for his daughters. Besides, he'd noticed a For Sale board outside the Green's house. Perhaps they were leaving together, or maybe Hayley had decided she'd had enough. Geoff didn't wish to know.

Tearing the letter into shreds felt cathartic. The future was what mattered now. Anna and Lizzie had recently met their other half-brother, Simon, and his family. Geoff had come to terms with their relationship – there'd been so much sadness and sorrow and if these new relationships were what his daughters needed, it was okay with him. The girls were enjoying getting to know their new grandparents, too, and Geoff had to admit they were lovely people. How Valerie could have treated them so badly was impossible to comprehend, but he wasn't going to let it trouble him. The events of recent months had taught him to choose his battles more carefully and try to accept what he couldn't change. His future was Anna and Lizzie. They were all that mattered now.

EPILOGUE

SIX MONTHS LATER

It was the beginning of September and the weather was finally cooling. Unprecedented high temperatures delighted most people, but not Samantha Freeman. With her huge baby bump, the heat had been unbearable, and her maternity leave was spent mostly avoiding the outdoors. And now, with only days before her due date, Sam was, as Jenny claimed, disgustingly organised.

After the Valerie Turner case, there were no more murders in New Middridge, a blessing to Sam and her team, who were kept busy catching up on ongoing cases and keeping on top of the new ones that crossed their desks daily. Jenny was delighted to be appointed acting DI for the duration of Sam's absence, her grin splitting her face each time she thought about it.

Sam finished work three weeks before her due date and left the station with arms full of gifts for the baby and for herself, promising a visit to show off the little one when he arrived. Jenny kept in touch daily, as did Sam's mother, Brenda and Ravi's mother, Divya – her three greatest supporters – she couldn't imagine coping with life without them.

It was during the early hours of the morning, three days before her due date when labour pains started. Awake early and listening to the music of the dawn chorus in the trees outside, Sam wriggled to get comfortable. Turning onto her side, a sharp pain shot through her back. Not taking too much notice, she closed her eyes and attempted to sleep again. The second pain left her in no doubt that her son was anxious to make an appearance in the world. Excitement and apprehension flooded her body. Deciding on a shower before alerting anyone to her predicament, she waddled to the bathroom but was halted by a rush of warm water soaking her pyjamas – it was time to get on the phone.

An excited Brenda promised to be with her in record time. Samantha managed a quick shower and dressed between contractions. Grabbing her overnight bag with everything she and the baby would need, she was ready and waiting when her mother arrived.

'Don't fuss, Mum.' Sam smiled at her mother's attentions. 'I'm not the first woman to have a baby!'

'But this is my first grandchild!' Brenda threw the bag in the boot and opened the passenger door of her car for Sam.

Fortunately, the roads were quiet. It was a lovely time to drive on a pleasant late summer morning – but labour pains were coming with alarming frequency.

'I thought first babies were supposed to be late and the delivery would be long. I want to push, Mum!' Sam wailed.

'Don't you dare! I've just had this car valeted.'

Parking was easy early in the morning, and Sam knew exactly where to go from her frequent antenatal visits. Brenda grabbed a wheelchair at the door and pushed her daughter into it.

'Mum, I can walk!'

'No, you waddle and I've always wanted to race a

wheelchair.' Brenda almost ran towards the lifts, pushed her daughter inside and pressed the button for the sixth floor.

They were met by a smiling, calm nurse who took charge of the wheelchair and soon had Samantha on a bed, ready for examination. Brenda stayed with her daughter, proud to be her birthing partner.

In less than two hours, Samantha's son made his entrance to the world. His forceful cry was an instant comfort; her baby was healthy. The emotions sweeping through Sam were indescribable. Naturally, her thoughts turned to Ravi, but with joy rather than sadness. This baby boy was a precious gift, and, yes, it would have been wonderful to have Ravi with her, but Sam was a realist and accepted the situation for what it was.

As the baby was placed in her arms, Sam's vision blurred with tears, and she fell instantly in love; the new baby scent, soft wispy hair and mewing cries, how could she not be? Tiny fists waved in the air as her beautiful dark-haired son cried.

Was it her imagination, or was he the image of Ravi? No doubt Divya would have something to say on the matter. His name was to be Rashmi. Sam wanted to acknowledge his father's heritage. The name Ravi means sun, and Rashmi means ray of sunshine – what could be more appropriate?

As Samantha pressed her lips against her son's forehead, a surge of love and strength filled her being. The uncertainty of the future didn't seem as daunting as before. In that moment, she realised there was still goodness to be found in life. Samantha found purpose and determination in her new role, giving her a powerful reason to embrace each day.

ALSO BY GILLIAN JACKSON

The Pharmacist

The Victim

The Deception

Abduction

Snatched

The Accident

The Shape of Truth

The Charcoal House

The Dead Husband

———

Remembering Ellie

Ask Laura

A Measure of Time

ACKNOWLEDGEMENTS

As always, I am grateful to my husband and family for their unwavering love and support during the countless hours I spend writing. And to the exceptional team at Bloodhound Books, your invaluable help in bringing this book to life is truly appreciated. Each book is a collaboration. I have the privilege of crafting characters and spinning plots, while you diligently work on the refining and presenting. Your dedication, professionalism, and guidance have been a great help throughout this process.

AUTHOR NOTES

Thank you for reading Little Black Lies, and I hope you enjoyed following the twists and turns of the Turner family, as well as catching up with DI Samantha Freeman and her colleagues. In my previous novel, The Dead Husband, Samantha's journey took a heartbreaking turn, sparking plenty of discussion about the ending! With this book, I wanted to give her a fresh and exciting new focus. I'd love to hear your thoughts. Did I redeem myself?

One of the greatest joys of writing is stepping into a character's mind and seeing the world through their eyes. Valerie Turner is a particularly fascinating character, her life woven from layers of deception. Unravelling her secrets, past and present, was an exciting challenge, and I hope you enjoyed uncovering them as much as I did.

Thank you again for reading. I appreciate your support more than I can say!

To read more of my work, please visit my Amazon author page, or find me on Facebook @gillianjacksonauthor Follow me on Twitter @GillianJackson7 or visit my website, www. gillianjackson.co.uk

A NOTE FROM THE PUBLISHER

Thank you for reading this book. If you enjoyed it please do consider leaving a review on Amazon to help others find it too.

We hate typos. All of our books have been rigorously edited and proofread, but sometimes mistakes do slip through. If you have spotted a typo, please do let us know and we can get it amended within hours.

info@bloodhoundbooks.com

Printed in Great Britain
by Amazon